LINE OF SUCCESSION

THE PRICE OF POWER

by Michael Vandor

Library of Congress Cataloging-in-Publication Data
Applied for.

ISBN-13: 978-1495918384 (CreateSpace-Assigned)
ISBN-10: 1495918386
BISAC: Fiction / Thrillers

<u>DEDICATION</u>

This book is dedicated to my loving wife, Lina, and my beautiful daughter Marie, whose inspiration and support fuel my dreams. It is also dedicated to the first female President of these United States, whomever that may be, and whenever such historic event shall occur in the future of our nation.

<u>PROLOGUE</u>

Arlington National Cemetery
February, 1997

"We love you and miss you, honey," Vice President Kathleen Canfield whispered softly, her voice trembling.

The nation's Second Family was together once again, if only for the moment. The six feet that separated the one from the rest seemed a short distance now. She stood beside the snow-topped grave, running her slender fingers over the marble slab etched with the name 'Canfield'. It was as cold and lifeless as the body lying beneath it. Still, she could feel his presence as though he were there. Yet it was not eerie; in fact, it felt rather comforting. God, how she loved him.

A hundred yards away, an uncomfortable Miles O'Keefe muttered under his frosty breath as he shifted his weight from one weary elbow to the other. "Damn it!" *Damn it!* The would-be assassin could hear his voice echo within the musty tomb he had hidden away in the night before. The head and shoulders of one of the Secret Service men assigned to protect his target was blocking his line of sight, and the tomb was freezing cold. Even his down parka was not keeping him from shaking. "Sonofabitch!" His breath had frosted over the telescopic lens. "Sonofabitch."

Jack Cutter scanned the perimeter through his Foster Grants. As head of the Vice President's Secret Service team, it was his responsibility to ensure her safety. He did not like it here, not one bit. *Too flat, too open,* he thought to himself. *And too many damned dead people around here!* "Western perimeter. Anything out there?" he said quietly into the microphone clipped to his lapel.

"Negative, chief." The agent stepped unknowingly closer to the assassin's nest. Before he could utter another word, a silenced bullet from O'Keefe's weapon struck him square in the forehead, dropping him like a deer. In that instant, he was dead. O'Keefe quietly drug the lifeless body into the dank tomb and laid it next to its original proprietor.

The voices in Cutter's earpiece told him he had no reason to be concerned. Still, he pawed nervously at the snow-covered ground with his freshly polished wingtips.

Kathy caressed the four-foot tall marble gravestone. "Our father who art in heaven..." she began. Her words carried in the cold morning air, nudged by the chilly, Arlington breeze until they reached the predator's ears.

O'Keefe brushed off the telescopic lens with the tip of the wool scarf clinging to the stubble of his unshaven neck, and re-sighted his target. Jack Cutter's head was no longer in the way.

"...hallowed be thy name."

2

The assassin flicked off the deadly rifle's safety. A tense thumb hugged the bolt-action weapon's trigger, preparing to squeeze it.

"Thy kingdom come, thy will be done..."

CRACK!

CHAPTER ONE

Washington D.C.
August, 1996

"Just a couple more votes," Kathy muttered to herself. With her beloved child care bill heading for a tight committee vote this afternoon, she needed all the reassurance she could get. After all, six years of hard work and her legislative credibility were on the line. Failure here would kill her efforts to be taken seriously in the male-dominated Congress. It was a 'must win' situation, and she knew it.

Gliding briskly down the Capitol Building's historic hallway, briefcase in hand, she found her own unique comfort. It came from the familiar sound and touch her two-inch heels made as they clicked against the hard marble flooring's smooth surface. The rigid material had become her only personal superstition, her Linus' blanket. But not even the soothing marble seemed to cure the nagging doubts. This time, she knew success would not come easily. Her whole

4

blessed life, opportunity had invited her in through its door, bowing, hat in hand. For the first time, she would have to knock on its door. Maybe even knock it down.

A disjointed chorus of 'good morning' broke her daydreaming as she passed through the dark wooden archway of her office suite in the old Senate Office Building. Introspection time would have to end. United States Senator Kathleen Canfield (R), California had a state to represent.

"Good morning, everybody," she chirped, as she made her way gracefully through the narrow corridor to the door bearing her name. As she passed the filing room, her fingers rubbed privately at the curvaceous muscles in her slim neck. They had tightened into knots.

Approaching her secretary, she exchanged 'hellos', and then asked what had become a standing joke between them. "Any calls from the President today? No? Well, maybe tomorrow..."

She paused at the water cooler to wash down two Tylenols, then continued toward her office. The child care issue had been her baby since joining Congress, and it was finally coming to a head. She was not about to let either negative thinking or a headache jeopardize its success.

"Good morning, Senator." Her Chief of Staff's welcome was, as always, businesslike.

"How's Abe doing, Mar?" Kathy replied, as though asking after the older woman's husband or child. In reality, the unattached Marva Franks' collie, named after a former President, *was* her family, just as her job *was* her whole life. A committed workaholic, the frumpy aide's work ethic and fierce loyalty had made her worth her weight in gold. She would take a bullet for her boss, if need be, and Kathy knew it.

5

"Abe? Crazy dog's pregnant. Gonna have to change her name," she replied, showing her annoyance at the inconvenience. "Maybe Abigail..."

As the Senator walked across the room to her desk, her aide marveled at the natural grace with which she moved. Although Kathy was in her late 40's, she was still strikingly beautiful, looking every inch the movie star she had been during her late teens and early twenties. Once one of 'America's Sweethearts', her shiny auburn hair now harbored subtle streaks of grey, and the lines around her eyes spoke honestly of middle-age. She reminded Marva of a post-Hollywood Grace Kelly, not just because of her elegant features, but because of the similarly regal way she carried herself. And it went deeper. In the admiring aide's opinion, Kathy presided over her staff like a benevolent princess, caring for and about her people, inspiring their loyalty in return. *Those qualities must not stand out much in Hollywood*, Marva thought, *or she would have risen to greater heights on the silver screen.* But in her eyes, Kathy was a glistening diamond, so bright it made her feel special just to be near her.

"Senator Markum phoned in his support. So did Senator Waters, but we're still short by one," Marva ticked off with her customary professionalism. "By the way, there're rumblings the Speaker'll oppose it if the Senate sends it to the House. The word 'revenge' came up in one of the conversations."

"Well that's a bridge we'll have to cross when we come to it," she said. "I just persuaded Senator Merriwhether to support us. With the others, that'll get it to the Senate floor."

After a colorless start to her political career, Kathy was finally picking up some momentum. She was starting to feel like more than just a pretty face elected because of her brief flirtation with celluloid fame. At this point in her life that was important to her, and those around her knew it.

"Congratulations!" Marva replied supportively. "Maybe the 'good old boys club' will have to stand up and take notice now." Privately, she was thinking, *half way home*. She had worked for others on 'The Hill' with more political clout, and she missed having influence, feeling like she could change the world. But she knew Kathy had it in her to succeed, if they would just give her the chance. Perhaps that was why she was so excited about the Senator's deft handling of the child care bill. She knew it could turn things around for them both.

"You want to call the majority leader to schedule the floor vote?" Kathy asked, jumping ahead.

"Not yet. Things've been pretty crazy up there since the Vice President's troubles. Everyone's focused on the issue of a successor. From what I hear, Burke's fraud indictment cost the President nine points in the polls." Marva brushed the ashes from her morning cigarette off her wrinkled jacket.

"Bad news," Kathy replied, realizing she had been so engrossed in pushing her bill that she had not thought about the bigger picture. In inside circles, Vice President Burke's guilt and eventual removal had been expected, and most in the party were glad it had happened sooner rather than later. Now the President could select a new running mate before the convention, diffusing the damage. Unfortunately, neither Kathy nor Marva had anticipated the resulting system wide slowdown in Congress.

"I guess we can wait a bit. So who're the current favorites, Mar? Last I heard Congressman Saunders and Senator Andonovich were neck and neck." Kathy's question carried an inflection of

7

curiosity - the curiosity of a little girl wanting to know what was in the neatly wrapped package with her name on it under the Christmas tree.

Marva winced. "Believe it or not, I'm hearing the Speaker's actually making a play for it. Everyone's pretty shocked. I guess he's counting on the President gettin' shot or something so he can move up to the Oval Office. Hell, with his reputation, he's probably already arranged the 'hit'!"

A slight smile forced its way onto Kathy's face, in spite of her efforts to hide it. Stewart Farley represented everything evil in American politics to her. And he was the only man she had ever grown to detest. He had muscled his way into the speakership through fear and intimidation rather than through respect and accomplishment, and that was not her style. He was brutal and arrogant behind closed doors, and not much better on the portal's public side. During her time in the House, the ruthless pol had not been the least bit subtle in his sexual advances, nor had he been ambivalent when she had spurned them. She could not recall his exact words, in fact he did not speak to her at all after that, including returning her phone calls on legitimate House business. The four years in that closet of an office he had kept her assigned to had spoken volumes, though. Largely because of him, her election to the Senate had seemed like an early parole for good behavior. And now the 'King of Payback' was threatening to kill her bill as though the knife needed one more twist.

"He'd better get a good one," the Senator told Marva. "The old cowboy probably packs a six-shooter under his coat."

Their light exchange was interrupted suddenly. The intercom's obnoxious buzz filled the room.

8

"Senator, the White House is on line two for you."

Kathy and Marva looked at each other, then at the audio speaker protruding through the sea of papers on the glossy mahogany desk - and then at each other again. The unison of their movements brought laughter to them both.

"Must be psychic over there," Marva quipped. "Who specifically from the White House, Ann?"

"He wouldn't identify himself. I could be wrong, but I swear it sounds like the President, accent and all."

A look of doubt came over Kathy's face as her smile melted away. "Is this your wicked sense of humor, Ann?"

"Not this time, Senator. I *really* think it's the President," came the secretary's serious reply.

Kathy had met Michael Burlington at various functions before, but her legislative work had never elicited a personal call from the leader of the free world. Somehow, he did not seem the type to waste time calling an undistinguished Senator on matters of state, and child care did not seem to be the elderly Texan's cup of tea.

Kathy's left hand drifted up to her head and her fingers began twirling aimlessly through the strands of hair dangling before her ear. It was the only telltale nervous habit the otherwise well-composed politician had as far as Marva could tell. Remarkably, the aide could detect no sign of nervousness in her voice when she spoke the words, *Ann, put the call through, please.* Her tone betrayed not a hint of anxiety, as though Michael Burlington were an old boyfriend or golfing buddy.

"Senator Canfield," she answered, as she had a thousand times before to lesser callers. The fingers on

9

her left hand stayed firmly entangled in the stray hairs, even as her right hand pressed the telephone receiver to the other side of her head.

Marva could feel her pulse quicken as soon as *Good morning, Mr. President,* made it from Kathy's lips to her ears. Being this close to power sent every political junkie's heart racing. Sometimes it was like an adrenalin shot, other times like an aphrodisiac. It always felt like a cross between a good drug and a top-of-the-line, Cosmopolitan-approved orgasm. This was a part of the psychic rewards she received as a legislative aide; God knows she wasn't doing it for the money.

Kathy's end of the conversation was anything but illuminating. "Yes Mr. President. Twelve-thirty will be fine," she indicated politely. "May I ask the subject matter for the meeting? That'll be fine, I look forward to it. I agree, it's been far too long. Goodbye, Mr. President."

Returning the phone softly to its cradle, Kathy turned from Marva and waltzed to the drapery-framed window joining her office to the outside world. Pulling on the frayed cord to open the blinds, she could see the White House's magnificent architecture peeking over the treetops.

After a moment of silence, Kathy could sense Marva's burning curiosity. She spoke without turning away from her view of the nearby executive mansion. "The President wants to see me tomorrow, Mar. He wouldn't tell me what he wants to talk about, but then I guess when you're the President of the United States you can keep those things to yourself. I have to admit, I'm dying to find out. This should be, well... interesting."

The surprise call from the nation's head of state left Marva struggling to collect herself. "I, uh, I mean, I'll rearrange your schedule, Senator. The revised one'll be on your desk before lunch."

"Thank you, Mar. Efficient as ever."

Kathy practically leapt back to her desk as soon as her aide departed, tripping over the cord to her reading lamp in the process. Undeterred, she made her way to the telephone and the auto-dial button to her husband's personal line.

While she waited for him to answer, she gazed at the brass-framed photo collection decorating the credenza behind her. The one to her left was so old the blacks and whites had faded to browns and grays. In it was a six-year-old girl, standing next to her father before a dilapidated old barn. Neither of them was smiling. Scribbled in the corner was the barely legible date: *1954*. The twinge of pain she felt told her those memories still hurt, even after all these years. Her eyes bolted away, to an old wedding photo of her and Mark Canfield standing arm-in-arm on the pale grey marble floor of St. Peters Cathedral. That picture, too, had faded. Like her husband's feelings for her.

After what seemed like an eternity, Mark Canfield's deep and sexy voice came on the line. "Hello, princess. How's politics?" A tone of polite indifference undermined the caring words.

Listening to the words coming from her own mouth, they sounded absurdly strange to her, not at all real. She felt like she was delivering a line from a bad 'B' movie script. "Honey, I have to break our lunch appointment tomorrow, something's come up." She paused for a breath. "No dear, no emergency. I just have to meet with the President of the United States."

<u>**CHAPTER TWO**</u>

When Marva arrived at the office the next morning the sun was just starting to rise over the Potomac. Funny how it looked like every other late summer day in D.C. she had experienced. Yet today felt different. As she turned her bleary morning vision towards the suite's kitchenette, she thought she heard the rustle of papers down the narrow hallway. The part of her that was awake was curious, but the part that needed that hot cup of coffee was calling the shots at this moment. Bumping her knee on the kitchenette doorway's pointed corner, a pained grimace flooded her face. The hurt quickly subsided as Marva noticed a three-quarter full pot of fresh coffee beckoning her, and her nostrils filled with the wonderful smell of Juan Valdez' best.

Now she *knew* today was different. Marva was always the first one in the door in the morning. Custom and necessity dictated responsibility for brewing that first pot of java fell to her. If she wanted any, that is. Wiping remnants of sleep from her eyes, she glanced at her watch. As best she could determine, it was just a blur past six o'clock in the morning. God, it was early even for her. *Did I forget daylight savings time again? Maybe the Democrats are pulling a Watergate and bugging the office...*

Slapping a palm across her cheek to pull herself closer to the waking world - cup of steaming coffee in hand - Marva followed the intermittent sounds of paper against paper down the hallway. The light at the narrowing corridor's end was coming from the Senator's office. Marva tread lightly as she peeked around the corner.

Kathy Canfield was not lazy, but she had become accustomed over the years to getting her beauty sleep. She definitely was not what you would consider a morning person, usually arriving at her Capitol office between nine and nine-thirty when she was in Washington. Her habits had their upside though, as she was almost always fresh and sparkling for those important state and political functions evening brought. Her early presence this morning was, indeed, unusual.

The Senator was sitting at her desk under an antique desk lamp's yellow light, staring intently at something in her hands. Marva thought she could see wrinkles around the beautiful green eyes peering through the glasses perched midway down her nose. Up until now, it had seemed to the aide time's harsher effects bowed to Kathy as though she were their mistress. As Marva drew closer, she could tell the Senator was wearing more makeup than usual in an effort to hide a sleepless night. Well, maybe her beloved boss was human after all. *Maybe, just maybe, having a luncheon appointment with the President has stolen some of her sleep*, Marva thought.

* * * * * * * * * *

Her father's picture she had taken from the credenza filled Kathy with memories. Unaware of Marva's presence, her mind was a thousand miles and forty years away, feeding chickens on a little farm in Argyle, Kansas. *My life has been a genuine fairy tale*, she thought to herself, *ever since I left that damned farm.* Opportunity had opened itself up to her as though it were a gift from God since then, requiring little effort or struggle on her part. *Ever since I left that farm...*

The gloomy memories of childhood in the tiny farming community still haunted her. She remembered it looking like a Norman Rockwell painting, but there had been the relentlessness and cruelty of the physical labor that had seemed endless. And...

She ran her fingers across the glass covering the farmer's picture, across the date in the corner. *1954. The year the farm failed. The year he brought us to California so he could find work.*

He had been angry and frustrated during that time, and for many years afterward. *"Damn it, Kathleen, can't you do anything right?"* she remembered him yelling, after she had tried to sweep up the chicken coup one time. *"You're just never gonna amount to anything, girl!"*

He had taken it out on her and her mother, and during that formative period of her development, it had seemed as if nothing she did was good enough for him. Things changed in later years, she recalled, after her mother's death. But that withheld approval when she needed it the most had left a hole in her she still felt. She wondered to herself: *Is that why I got into politics? To prove something to a dead man?* Were her adult ambitions a result of those years, an endless effort to reach the standards he had demanded, the unreachable expectations?

Marva's shadow crept over the room, finally catching Kathy's eye. Casually returning the picture to the credenza, and looking up from the eight-and-a-half by eleven-inch paper jungle before her, she smiled that perfect smile that caught Hollywood's eye all those years ago.

"Good morning, Mar. How'd I do on the coffee?"

Marva flashed the best return smile an average looking woman with teeth yellowed from years of smoking and coffee could muster. "It tastes great, but it must be decaf. I mean, it must not be waking me up...I actually believe it's six in the morning and you're already in."

"Just couldn't sleep, I guess. Kept waking Mark up with my tossing and turning. He has two operations scheduled for today and there's nothing more frightening than a groggy surgeon with a scalpel. Letting him sleep seemed like the humanitarian thing to do."

The all too visual picture of the esteemed Dr. Mark Canfield, plastic surgeon, snoring over a patient in the operating room, caused Marva pause. She nodded in agreement. "Well, like my mother used to say, 'Lose an hour in the morning, and you'll spend all day looking for it.' Nervous about your lunch with the President?" she asked.

"More curious than anything. On the outside chance the First Lady's gotten to him on my bill, I want to be sure I'm prepared to sell him on it. His support would make it tough for Farley to bury it when it reaches the House," Kathy replied. After a noticeable pause, she continued. "You've worked in this town a long time, Mar. What's your read on this?"

Marva pondered the question. *What was Burlington after?* He was generally viewed as sexist, so it was not likely he was seeking a congressional female's counsel on the pressing international or domestic matters before him. *Maybe he just wants to get to know Kathy better, do his own star watching*, she considered. After all, he was only human - a fact she had to constantly remind herself of when she met famous people through her work. *Maybe he's interested in her thoughts on selecting a running mate.* After all, Kathy's natural constituency represented most of Burlington's political weaknesses. She was popular among women and younger voters; she was from the west and was generally viewed as a moderate. It would not be out of the norm for an accomplished politician like Michael Burlington to seek knowledgeable input on who might best appeal to such a constituency.

"He might be interested in your thoughts on Burke's replacement. You represent a core group he needs to attract in November to win. I'll bet he wants to pick your brain on the frontrunners and which would best accomplish that for him."

Kathy had learned to trust her aide's judgment. More importantly, she had learned to have faith in her instincts where the often devious art of politics was concerned. Besides, Marva's analysis was as good as any that had crossed *her* mind while she had stared at the ceiling from bed earlier that morning.

"Possible. Well, whether it's about the bill or not it's still an opportunity to bend an ear while I'm there. Best I'm fully prepared."

"Good thing you're meeting Burlington over lunch. You might get a word in edgewise while his mouth is full. They say he's one of those guys who wraps up a two-minute idea in a two-hour vocabulary," the aide joked. Scarcely six-thirty and she was already rounding into form.

California's junior Senator pushed her glasses a bit further up the bridge of her nose and gave Marva that polite but unmistakable look that said clearly, 'play time's over'. Exiting just long enough for a trip to the kitchenette, the aide refilled Kathy's cup and returned to her own office. *The worker bees have a full day's work ahead in this beehive*, she mumbled to herself, as she headed off to the morning ritual of coordinating the day's labors.

The morning went swiftly as most mornings did in the political 'business'. Not surprisingly, before anyone knew it the old cuckoo clock on the wall in Senator Canfield's office was signaling twelve.

"Cuckoo, cuckoo..." It went on for ten more times.

"Can't think of anything more symbolically appropriate for this town," Kathy said under her breath. An old studio property piece from her first film, Mark had bought it for her at an auction as an anniversary present. It was one of the very few remnants of her film career gracing her Capitol office - a private reminder only she and Mark understood. The obvious photos and memorabilia were secreted away at home. *These walls will be filled with mementoes of a successful legislator's life*, she had promised herself. Thus far, a lot of wall space remained to work with, and only one bare spot had been promised. She already had picked out the spot for a framed copy of her child care bill once it was signed into law. "Visualize your goals," her father had told her, "and they will come." She had found his advice reliable over the years. *He would have liked that spot*, she thought, as she stared at the rich wood paneling across from her desk.

The walk to the executive mansion was a challenge in high heels, but traffic was worse and she needed the exercise. It had been a typically hot and muggy summer in Washington, and today was no different. She could feel the sweat dripping into her eyes beneath the $200 sunglasses she wore, and she could taste its saltiness as a drop crept into the corner of her mouth. No amount of fame, breeding or money could insulate her from the wilting heat.

Approaching the Marine guards at the pedestrian entrance to the grounds, her hands went into her bag, searching for her Senate credentials. Quickly producing them, it took but a minute for the guard to confirm her identity and her appointment.

With a loud buzz, the heavy wrought iron gate sprung open. With precision, the young soldier moved to hold it for her as she passed through.

"That's Mr. Mathers now, Senator."

Approaching from one side of the circular drive was a large black limousine, clean and shiny as any she had ever seen. As it neared, she could make out two small flags on the car's front fender; one was Old Glory. Only when it pulled to a stop before her could she make out the second. It was the same as the embossed symbol on the car's front doors. It was the insignia of the President of the United States.

Moving briskly to the limousine's right rear door, the corporal opened it with the crispness of a salute to an officer. Approaching the car's open doorway, she glanced politely at the soldier.

"Thank you, corporal."

For a brief second, the sentry's expressionless face betrayed a slight smile, and a glint of sunlight appeared in his eyes. In simpler times, she would have thought he was flirting. Today, that possibility did not cross her mind.

"Senator Canfield, it's been a long time."

The extended hand was a familiar one. Kathy had met Andrew Mathers on several occasions over the years, even sharing a dance with him at the Inaugural Ball one time. He was about forty-five years old, possessing an average height and build - and Kathy thought - a rather charming dance companion. A Texan like the President, Mathers represented the Lone Star state's 'new breed'. When he greeted her, he sounded much more like the Yale honors graduate he was, than a wealthy Texas oilman who never graduated high school's son, which he also was.

"Andy, yes it has been a long time."

"How are you and how's that child care bill doing?"

The all too proper choice of words becomes him, she thought. Knowing just the right topic of small talk for each individual he encountered made him almost legendary in ego-sensitive Washington. The polite query about her bill did nothing to detract from that reputation.

"I'm fine, and so far my bill is too. How are you holding up?"

She could not help but notice the eyes gazing out from his pale face. They had that Cheshire cat look in them, as though he knew a fantastic secret he could hardly wait to divulge. But the eyes were all that betrayed him. Everything else said 'business as usual'. A less observant person would not have even noticed.

"I've come to believe it's about as demanding a job as you can have, next to the President's, Senator. I earned the grey in this hair the hard way," he said with self-deprecating humor.

The limo's air conditioning system cooled her, and she could feel the nasty secretions on her face evaporating. The green beauty of the White House grounds added to the comfortable feeling that overcame her. Still, she would want to clean herself up before she greeted Michael Burlington. That made Mathers courteous anticipation all the more appreciated.

"I'm sure you'll want to freshen up once we're inside. I'll be happy to escort you to the nearest lounge," he offered graciously.

Slowing as the driveway's end neared, the presidential limousine stopped smoothly and another young Marine opened the door. He could have been the first's brother. Taking a hand for balance as she stepped out beneath the entry overhang, Kathy followed Mathers through the White House's arching entryway.

"It's beautiful!" she said to Mathers, who only nodded in response. Strange as it seemed, she had never been here before. Just as odd was her first thought as she stepped onto the ruby red carpet runner. The marble floors had been covered with it, leaving six inches on both sides of the runner and the rich marble walls exposed. *Now who would want to do that?* she wondered.

"Senator, you'll find the ladies' room right over there," Mathers indicated with a gesture of his manicured hand.

Restoring her sunglasses to their case in her purse, Kathy excused herself. Once inside the gold-fixtured ladies' lounge, she looked intently at the reflection in the gold-leafed mirror. The degree to which she monitored her appearance was a nagging byproduct of her acting career where the smallest blemish, expanded a hundred times over in a close up, could fill a theater screen. *Got off lucky*, she thought to herself. Fortunately, the heat had done only slight damage to her makeup which was quickly repaired. She could not allow excess time in the restroom making her late for lunch with the President. *Not if you want to be taken seriously*, she told herself.

Andrew Mathers stood patiently awaiting her return. A few turns to the east, and the doorway leading to the Oval Office stood before them. In front, several Secret Service agents stood near the President's secretary. The chief executive's gatekeeper picked up the phone on her desk to announce them to the tall statesman within.

"Mr. President, Senator Canfield and Mr. Mathers are here for your luncheon appointment... Yes, sir." Pausing only briefly, the secretary turned to them both. "You can go right in Senator, Mr. Mathers."

The final steps seemed familiar. She must have seen the office on CNN or other news programs a dozen times. Still, a sense of history overwhelmed her as she stepped into the historic Oval Office. With much to see in the large room, she stopped to absorb its full impact. Two things caught her eye immediately. First, the colorful and intricate presidential seal woven into the sky blue carpet, and mirrored above in low relief on the wooden ceiling. It seemed as though they took up the room's entire middle. Secondly, the large ornately carved desk sitting immediately before the presidential and American flags. *The same desk John F. Kennedy installed and used in 1960*, she thought in wonderment.

Her eyes soaked in the beauty, the ivory-colored walls with their intricate cornice moldings, the hand-carved doorway pediments. The royal blue and gold-trimmed draperies over the windows and French doors opening to the exquisite beauty of the Rose Garden took her breath away. And then under a painting of George Washington in full military dress, she noticed the fireplace's marble mantle. She could not resist running her fingers across its cool smoothness, before rejoining Mathers before the massive desk. The desk. She had read somewhere Burlington had returned it to circulation, much to the opposition party's surprise and dismay. *They say he did it out of spite for the Democrats*, she recalled. Like salt in a wound, it served as a symbolic reminder the Republicans now controlled both Congressional houses as well as the White House for the first time in half a century. She had heard some pretty vicious rumors about the President's ruthlessness over the years, but he had treated her kindly enough during their brief encounters in the past.

The sightseeing ended when two stewards entered, carrying silver trays with food and drink. Setting the light mid-day meal up on a small Hepplewhite table at the back, they moved with little clamor.

"Pretty quiet guys," she remarked to Mathers.

"They're trained to be, Senator. They serve dignitaries and Cabinet members during some pretty important meetings. An inconspicuous presence is considered essential."

"Makes sense."

"In fact, it's considered an honor amongst the White House stewards to be appointed to this team."

From the corner of her eye she noticed movement near the office's side door. Turning, she saw Michael Burlington's imposing figure stride into the room. Burlington looked presidential, a Mount Rushmore-like president straight from central casting.

He stood well over six feet, with a tan leathered skin that reflected a love of the outdoors. Straight, black hair heavily streaked in grays and whites, parted itself on his head. As he reached a hand out to shake hers, she noticed it looked large and strong, like a lumberjack's.

"Sen'tor Canfield, how're ya? Thank ya fer joinin' us today. Yer even more beautiful than the last time we met," the Texan drawled.

"Thank you Mr. President. You look wonderful yourself. And how is the First Lady these days?" Kathy replied.

"She's fine, visitin' family in Dallas this week. Andrew, why don't ya show the Sen'tor ta her seat. I need ta get somethin' from ma desk."

Within minutes she broke bread with two of the most powerful men in the world. She enjoyed their company, their conversation. Burlington seemed especially animated today, particularly 'on'. *Perhaps it's the Texas chili he's shoveling down...*

The President steered the conversation to Kathy's acting career, seeming more than a little interested in knowing the 'inside scoop' on a number of Hollywood celebrities. Over the years, she'd become accustomed to the natural human curiosity concerning Hollywood. It just seemed a bit strange coming from a man she knew had mingled with much bigger stars than she had ever been. But then some people just never got enough.

After about forty-five minutes, the jovial expression on the President's face melted into a serious one as he spoke. "Sen'tor...Kathleen. As ya know, Tom Burke's problems have become ma problems and our party's. The convention's scarcely spittin' distance away and the scandal he's caused has cost me ten points in the polls. Ten points this week alone!

23

Gov'nor Provelone's a cinch to clinch the Democratic nomination. This crap has pulled him ahead a me by five! We got ta' stop the bleedin'. Andy and I've bin meetin' all week with the campaign hacks and we've reached a conclusion. Sen'tor, we think you can help."

Well, it looks like Marva hit the nail on the head. The President does want my advice on Burke's replacement. Kathy favored Missouri's Senator, Bill Anders. *Bill would be a great Vice President,* she thought, *heck even a good President - but he won't solve Burlington's need to balance the ticket.* "I'm flattered you would seek my advice, Mr. President. Of course I'll be of service to you in any way I can."

The smile returned to the big man's face. "*Any* way, Sen'tor?" he asked coyly.

Inside Kathy cringed at the sexual innuendo the line carried. On the outside, she did not miss a graceful beat. "Of course, sir. I assume you've narrowed the field for your running mate to just a few. I'll be happy to share my views on the candidates. May I ask who you're considering?"

The President of the United States removed the bright red linen napkin from his lap, dropping it on the table. Leaning forward, he looked her straight in the eye. Exercising the command presence he possessed, he said, "To one, Sen'tor. Just one."

Suddenly, the waters seemed murky again. *If he's made up his mind, why am I here? Certainly he isn't seeking my approval. Certainly not!* She could not have been more wrong.

"Kathy, I din't ask ya here fer yer opinion on ma selection. I asked ya here fer yer consent," Burlington said as though reading her mind.

"Sir? I don't understand?" she stammered.

His next comment hit like a bombshell. It could not have been a greater shock if he had asked her to dance naked with him in the Rose Garden.

"Sen'tor Canfield, ah'm askin' ya ta *be* the selection. Ah'm asking ya ta consider servin' yer country as the first woman Vice President in United States history."

<u>CHAPTER THREE</u>

The rest of the day was nothing more than a haze to Kathy. She vaguely remembered agreeing to discuss the incredible proposition with her family that evening, and she recalled somehow getting back to her office and ending up at home before dusk. But she was not quite sure of much else. Other than having to peel Marva off the ceiling after she had told her about the astounding luncheon. The intensity of her assistant's squeal had embedded that in her memory.

Sitting alone on the patterned Victorian couch in her living room, she took another sip of brandy from the crystal glass that carried it to her parched lips. Her thoughts drifted aimlessly back to the childhood she had relived earlier in the day. *There was good that came out of the pain of '54. It was those years of unhappiness that led to my acting*, she reminded herself. She remembered her imagination blossoming in response to her dismay, carrying her away from her harsh reality. There had been the dreamy journeys to

Wonderland, Pooh Corner, and the Emerald City of Oz.

Oz. It seemed poetic justice to her that every so often, if one of her heels hit the beloved marble flooring of the Capitol Building, or her entryway, just right, it would produce a sound eerily like that of Dorothy clicking her heels together to return to Kansas.

I must have seen that picture a hundred times before we moved to California. She remembered well the sound of those glistening ruby slippers being tapped together; it was distinct. The only problem was, she had no desire to return to Kansas, either the cinematic or real version. *I liked it just fine in the land of Oz, thank you,* she recalled.

Then she remembered her country day school putting on that exact play, and her tenacious pursuit of the lead. She had finally won it with a dogged lobbying effort. It was her chance to bring the role to life, or more accurately from her child's perspective, to bring her life to the role.   *I   was   pretty convincing, wasn't I?* She recalled it not being so much because of an abundance of talent. It was more because she needed to believe it was real so badly, that she had actually convinced herself it was by the time she had stepped on the stage.

That applause at curtain call nearly lifted me to the rafters. She did not act again until many years later, but she never forgot the first time she had actually felt really good at something. Kathy smiled remembering the six-year old girl she used to be. Then she remembered how she felt when the play came to an end and the applause died, and reality called her home. The smile disappeared.

It was a long time from the close of that curtain to Hollywood, she mused. From that day in

Argyle forward, there was the recurring fear that her fairy tale would come to an abrupt end. One misstep, one involuntary bump of the ruby red slippers, and she would wake up back on that miserable farm. The fear was not with her often, but it seemed to keep calling on her when she least expected it, like a surprise visit from an in-law. Life had reinforced her child's fear. Her film career had ended suddenly enough when she outgrew her teen image, married Mark, and assumed the role of wife and mother. And just when it seemed she and her father were working through their problems together, he had died suddenly. *So young.* He went without warning from a heart attack, taking with him any chance she had of filling that nagging void inside her.

He would have turned forty if he had lived another three weeks, she thought sadly. *And if he had lived another year, he would have been able to see his little girl up on the silver screen.*

It was the waning days of the studio system. She remembered how the MGM family had taken care of her hair and makeup, taught her how to walk and how to talk. She had learned refinement, and class and dignity from the wealthy friends she had made in Hollywood. And she had never lost the drive to better herself. It was her film career that had afforded her a way to attend college at Stanford.

Just missed becoming valedictorian because of that damned publicity tour! She recalled that near-miss with regret.

Through all the glitz and glamour, she could not remember ever letting her feet leave the ground for long. *Must have been that old-fashioned, Midwestern upbringing.*

By the time she had met Mark, she knew that she wanted something more real and more meaningful from life. *Perhaps that's what led me into politics*, she considered, scratching her head.

The sound of the electric garage door opener being activated shook her back to the present. Opening the burgundy leather brief case lying on the leaded glass top of the coffee table, she withdrew the memo Burlington had handed her over lunch. It was addressed to the President's campaign chairman, and contained an analysis and recommendation from independent political wizard Rex Morgan. It read in part: *Polling indicates Senator Canfield to be the strongest candidate of the ten sampled capable of attracting the necessary votes to the ticket to offset the President's weaknesses. That being the key voter focus groups of 1) women, 2) men between the ages of 18-39, and 3) California and the western states. Not only did she test strongest amongst these constituencies, but the Senator's integrity rating polled off the scale, a result we believe, of residual public goodwill from her 'girl-next-door' film image. Given the damage done to the President by the Burke scandal, we can find no other candidate so uniquely qualified to meet the needs of the ticket.*

Kathy was not quite sure how she could have been so oblivious to the political winds blowing around her. After all, she certainly remembered George Bush's anointment of a young unknown Senator by the name of Dan Quayle. It was not that long ago that the Robert Redford lookalike had risen from obscurity to prominence. Like her, and like John Kennedy in 1960, he had brought a negligible legislative record to the race. His failing, she believed, was inadequate preparation.

A failing I can't afford to repeat, she told herself. *There will be nationally televised debates and the environment will be uncontrolled - it won't be*

*crafted from a carefully choreographed movie script.
In order to avoid the same pitfalls, the volumes of
information I'll have to absorb over the next few
months will be enormous. I won't be able to pick and
choose my targets the way I have in Congress. The
voters will want to hear from me on a lot more than
just child care.*

As she sat there playing recent political history
through her head, she heard the creak of the thick oak
entry door. Craning her neck to see who it was, Kathy
was thrilled to see the faces of those she loved most.

"We're home," they yelled to her playfully.

Mark stood straight as an arrow in the foyer
with one arm around their daughter and the other
around the shoulder of their son. It was evident
reaching the shoulders of young Billy had become a
stretch for Mark. It was simple physics. He now stood
some four inches taller than his physician father, and
the bright white uniform of the United States Navy
made him appear even larger. At the moment, his size
appeared a useful asset; it was enabling him to safely
carry a large package tucked under his arm. It was
festively wrapped in shiny blue and silver foil with a
plump bow, perfectly centered on the package.

"Mother, it's great to see you! Heck, it's great
to be home," Bill exclaimed with enthusiasm.

Setting the heavy box down against the wall,
the young officer strode briskly to the mother he had
not seen in six months. Swallowing up her 5'8" frame
in his lanky arms, he applied an embrace that squeezed
the breath from her, eliciting a groan as the tip of his
fighter pilot's wings poked into her flesh. If Kathy had
had any doubts before, they had just been swept away.
Her 'Billy' had developed into a full grown 'Bill'.

"Bill, honey, how are you? Let me see you,
Billy-Bear. My God, I can't believe how much you've

grown," she cooed. "Was your flight from Edwards alright?"

"Bumpy, but it landed in one piece," Bill said. "Feels strange flying in something so large after bopping around in an F-14 for months."

"How long are you home for?"

"Thirty days 'r and r'. Nothing but a nice quiet month in Georgetown."

"Fantastic," she replied before falling victim to her curiosity. "So, what's in the package? Present for a girlfriend?"

"Nope. It's a belated birthday present for you, mother. I was stuck on tour in the Mediterranean when your birthday came and went, so I wanted to make it up to you."

"You shouldn't have!" she said unconvincingly. Then, realizing she had not yet acknowledged her husband or teenage daughter, Kathy turned to them both for her usual hugs and kisses. The past few years, Mark seemed to be going through the motions when it came to demonstrating his affections. That pattern continued as he quickly released her after planting a peck on her cheek. Steeling herself to his continued indifference, she smoothly changed the subject back to Bill's package.

"Should I open it?" she asked.

"Of course! No reason to wait 'till your *next* birthday."

Kathy anxiously ran her perfectly manicured nail under a loose strip of tape, and began removing - not tearing - the pretty foil paper. In short order, her efforts revealed the gift's true packaging.

"A doll house kit?" Mark asked in surprise. "Isn't your mother a bit old for something like that, Bill?"

"You don't remember do you, Mark?" Kathy said to her mate with a touch of hurt in her voice. "Thank you Bill, you know I've wanted something like this for a long time. A very long time." The gift was now completely unwrapped, revealing a picture of a beautiful three-story Victorian mansion - a completed version of the kit inside the large box. It was painted nearly the same color yellow as their actual, albeit less grandiose, home.

"Dad, mother's talked about wanting one of these since she was a kid. I picked it up in New York on my way home. Pretty neat, actually. It's supposed to have working lights and everything!"

Kathy's face was glowing. It was a wholly impractical present, but it was the thought that counted. It was touching to know that her son had remembered the story she had told years ago about the doll house she had wanted as a child. The one her family had not been able to afford.

"So, when are you going to have time to put this together for me?"

Bill smiled sheepishly. "It'll take a while. It's a pretty big kit, plus you'll probably want to upgrade the windows and doors, pick out wallpaper." He laughed. He could see the joy in his mother's eyes. He could also see the impatience. "I thought I'd start on it tomorrow," he ad-libbed.

Mark was embarrassed that he had not remembered the conversation the way his son had. A change in subject seemed the best defense. "Well, how was your day, honey?" he asked her, obviously also forgetting about her scheduled luncheon with the President of the United States.

His oversight compounded her disappointment, but she pretended as though nothing special had happened. "Oh, you know, same ole, same ole."

Mark Canfield was a handsome, clean-cut man of nearly six feet, with the body of a tennis player. He was a disciplined human being who took pride in his appearance, frequently succumbing to his male vanity. He worked out daily at the medical center's gym, and seemed obsessed about maintaining his weight and making sure he got enough sun. He even colored his hair, much of which had grayed by the age of thirty, and which he always kept combed neatly into place.

Trying to show interest to lessen his guilt, Mark said to his son, "Why don't I give you a hand with that thing? I think I can make some time tomorrow."

The stresses of his medical career had taken a toll Mark fought hard to conceal. His family's move to Georgetown from California played a large part in the pressures he had endured. He was forced to sacrifice a thriving medical practice to keep the family together when Kathy had been elected to the Senate. Starting over was hell for him. It was tough enough for a man to be married to a beautiful woman these days - tougher still when she was a former starlet and current United States Senator. His California practice and the income it had produced had helped him to endure the challenges to his ego and maintain his self-esteem. Losing that had crushed him more than he had expected, certainly more than he would ever let on to his wife.

Looking at Mark, Kathy recalled, *He loved me dearly once, enough to face his own near self-destruction. What could have happened?*

He had responded to the difficulties by burying himself in his efforts to build up the small practice he had purchased here in Georgetown. After two-and-a-half hard years, the determined doctor had gone a long way toward accomplishing his goal. His income now came close to matching his California revenues before the move, and he had taken on two new partners to help manage the patient load. Unfortunately, those years had drawn the couple apart. His brief affair with a nurse eighteen months back had not helped.

As he backed away from her, there was none of the old passion in his lifeless azure eyes.

"Where should I put this junk, the dining room or the family room?" Christina asked her mother. Her hands were full with the evening's meal, courtesy of the nearby Kentucky Fried Chicken.

The Colonel may not be quite as good a cook as I am, Kathy thought, *but he has a heck of a lot more time to beat that bird into an edible condition than I do!*

"More cluck for the buck, they say," her daughter quipped as she set the plastic bags down on the $7,000 Chippendale dining table. Christina's irreverent sense of humor was a constant. Sometimes a *constant irritation*. It was her own way of exercising the age-old tradition of teenage rebellion. What made it so effective was its marked contrast with Kathy's refined demeanor. Her self-control and discipline were the envy of the family, but neither of her children had inherited whatever gene granted that gift to her.

"Bill, will you get the china? No reason we have to eat cheap food cheaply," Kathy said.

Christina had gotten worse over the past few years as she had grown tall enough to stand toe-to-toe with her mother. She now stood as tall as Kathy, but resembled her father more than the woman who had brought her into the world. Chrissie, as she preferred to be called, was pretty and had silky long light brown hair. But she was not blessed with that special beauty that could grab and hold an audience's attention upon entering a crowded room.

"My God, mother. It's just fast food!" Chrissie envied her mother, almost as much as she loved and admired her.

Like families everywhere, the Canfields settled down at the table to share dinner and conversation. For nearly thirty minutes, Kathy kept her day from the family as the conversation revolved around her newly returned son. Mark *still* had not remembered that his wife had shared lunch that day with the President of the United States. The anticipation was becoming painful. She was bursting to share the news, but she was also worried. *How will Mark take it? Chrissie?* As much as she wanted to accept the President's offer, she feared it would drive a final stake into her relationship with Mark and fuel Chrissie's adolescent rebellion.

Finally, a lull came to their discourse and Mark turned to his wife. "Did I ask you how your day was, baby?"

Her reply was succinct. It also carried a frostiness in its delivery. "Yes, you did, Mark. Remember, 'same ole, same ole'? Actually, it was really quite unique."

Her tease grabbed their attention, and Bill tried gamely to shed some light on the mystery. "Can you define 'unique' mother?"

"Have you been following the Thomas Burke story, Bill?" she asked.

"Sort of. He was indicted for some crime and resigned, right?" After a pause, the young man continued, "Geez mother, you're not in some sort of trouble are you?"

Mark remembered. "Damn, you were meeting with the President today, weren't you? God, I'm sorry, I plum forgot!"

"Good, Mark! A little cavalier about it aren't you? It's not like I have lunch with the man every day," she said.

"So what happened mother?"

"I don't know any way to tell you other than to just say it. President Burlington has asked me to join the ticket in Burke's place. He wants me to run as his Vice President."

The silence was deafening. The first reaction came from Bill in typical military fashion.

"Eeeeee hahhh," he screamed. "That's unreal, absolutely unreal!"

To her relief, Bill's euphoria was quickly followed by facades of support from the rest of the family. Even Chrissie *seemed* excited.

"My God, mother, if you win you'd be the first woman Vice President in history. That's so bitchin'!"

"Chrissie, watch your language," Mark warned. "Kath, that's absolutely amazing. Are you going to accept?"

"I told him I'd discuss it with you and the children this evening. He's asked me to let his Chief of Staff know later tonight. With the convention a little more than a week away, time is pretty tight."

Bill could not understand why such an opportunity required any consideration at all. He pledged his full support, and induced his sister to do likewise. "C'mon, sis. You're for mom, aren't you?"

"Sure." There was a twinge of reluctance in her voice.

Mark remained oddly noncommittal before decreeing the family hour over. "Kath, let me fill your glass and we can go in the study and talk."

She waited for him in the comfort of the wood paneled study they shared - his desk stood against one wall, hers against another - and she wondered what Mark's analysis of the situation would be. Her desire to accept had grown steadily stronger by the hour, but she wanted his support, sincere and complete.

No, I need it, she thought to herself. That thought repeated itself in her head as she settled into the blood red leather of the study's couch. *I need it... Or at least his absolution.*

Mark entered balancing two snifters of brandy in his hands. Handing Kathy hers, he sat next to her on the plush couch. "Honey, please don't take this the wrong way, but I've got two honest questions. First, why do they want you?" he asked with equanimity. "And secondly, and more importantly, why do you want them?"

Producing the consultant's memo for Mark, she paused while he read it carefully. After a few minutes, his eyes rose from the document to meet hers.

"I guess I can't argue with their logic. Right person, right place, right time. For their needs. Now, how about yours? Why do you want it?"

She paused to find the right words, admitting to herself that she hadn't had time to think about it. "Well," she began out loud, "I have to admit to the ego aspects of it. I'd be flattered under any circumstances, of course, but this isn't just a personal opportunity. It's an historical one for all women and for the party. Heck, for the country!"

"And?" he challenged.

"And I think I might be able to have more impact on the system, on our society, as a visible national symbol, a trail-blazer. That's mostly what the office is, you know. Symbolic. There's no real power. And you know the Senate's been frustrating for me, 'good old boys club' that it is. Plus I've been taking a lot of political heat since the family moved out here to be together. It'll solve that problem."

"Not entertaining thoughts about the number one job, are you?"

"Mark! You know I've always been ambitious, but not to that extent," she replied defensively. "Heck, the reason I didn't go further in pictures was I didn't have that driving need to be a number one box office draw. And the only reason I ran for the Senate was that the party back home lobbied me to death to do it. That, and to get out from under Stewart Farley."

Her answer reflected what she wanted to believe about herself. It was not necessarily the truth.

"Frankly, Mark, I can't think of a job I'd want less than the presidency. I don't have any interest in sacrificing my entire personal life, our entire lives together as a family. And I know that's what would happen. That glass ceiling'll have to be broken by some other woman."

A natural 'devil's advocate', Mark made sure she would consider the price she would pay. The price they'd all pay. He belted down the rest of his brandy before he spoke. "Have you thought about the level of scrutiny the press and the Democrats will submit you to over the course of the campaign? It'll be incredible. It'll be like doing a nude scene, seeing yourself sprawled naked across a screen for a million people you've never met to see. They'll dig up Chrissie's drug arrest back in Los Angeles, my indiscretions, and God knows what else! This isn't some Hollywood movie, babe. This is real life."

She did not appreciate his tone of voice, but she knew he was baiting her. "Mark, I honestly haven't had enough time or a clear enough head to consider every angle. You're right. It'll be tough. But Chrissie's arrest was in L.A. and she was released without charges being filed." She was rationalizing.

"Because of *who* you are, they'll say. If that comes out, they'll scream preferential treatment."

"They didn't have the evidence, Mark. The President asked me if we had any skeletons in our closet and I told him all of it. He's prepared to take the risk if we are. My God, Mark. Nobody's perfect enough for the standards the press and the public have been trying to exact from politicians. At some point, we all have to face that. It's not a perfect world. There are no perfect people."

Kathy's voice was filled with passion. She had just talked herself out of any doubts she might have had about how much she wanted to pursue this course, and Mark knew it. And the opportunity *was* too historic not to accept. They really had no choice, and he hated that. Still, he took one last futile stab.

"What would your father have thought? You know how he hated unfinished business. You'll be abandoning your commitment to California mid-term."

"Mark, Daddy would have been proud. His little girl, the Vice President? I'd like to think he would have seen the value of my opening up possibilities for little girls for generations to come," she said as a tear welled up in her eye. "Besides, the party's got the governorship so we won't lose the seat. It'll be filled by appointment."

He resigned himself to the inevitable. "I assume there'll be no free time between now and November. There must be a ton of preparation to attend to. I imagine there'll be televised debates, a hundred talk shows and speeches..."

Kathy could hear the mix of fatalism and concern in his voice, but she still wanted his approval. "Mark, I need to know you're behind me 100%. I can't do it without you." For an instant she could see a flicker of warmth in his softening eyes as he shook his head and silently mouthed *okay*. It was enough that she could believe him. So she did.

Kathy struggled to find the hand-scratched telephone number Andrew Mathers had given her. Punching in the numbers to his private office line, she waited anxiously. The old grandfather clock in the corner read five minutes to eight, well within working hours for the President's dedicated Chief of Staff. The phone barely had the opportunity to complete the first ring when Mathers' weary voice came over the line.

"Andrew Mathers."

"Hello, Andy, this is Kathy Canfield."

"Reached a favorable decision, I hope."

"We're in," Kathy replied.

Mark Canfield bit his lower lip and poured himself another drink.

CHAPTER FOUR

The term 'we' did mean something to Mark. He could not deny to himself that he felt overwhelmed and threatened by the whole thing, but he was going to do his best to overcome it, damn it. *This is big, and I'm going to be supportive, proud, and caring*, he demanded of himself. Her choice of words made it easier, made him feel a part of it all.

* * * * * * * * * *

Andrew Mathers had been direct after getting Kathy's commitment. "You'll need to be at the press briefing room of the White House at one o'clock p.m. tomorrow for the announcement," he had said to her. "The next several weeks will be spent studying with the campaign staff, preparing for the schedule ahead. The convention will be a formality, a rubber stamp. A draft of your announcement speech is already being written and will be faxed to you in the morning. You'll be fine," he had reassured her as they concluded their talk.

At bedtime, the sleeping pills Kathy had taken did their job. She awoke to a new day with the breaking sunlight, feeling refreshed and ready. This would be *her* day.

The statuesque brunette applied her makeup differently this morning - thicker than usual. After all, the former actress knew how the camera worked. She had always loved it and it had always returned the favor. She hoped today would be no different.

The drive to her office seemed to take forever. Once there, she barricaded herself inside with Marva. God bless the slightly overweight aide; she had already begun clearing her Senator's calendar and had spoken with Andy Mathers about the press conference.

"Senator, Andy gave me an outline of the agenda for the briefing. The President'll make the announcement, then introduce you. The White House's draft of your statement should be here shortly, and there won't be any questions taken. They're going to plead scheduling problems."

"You're telling me they've scripted the whole event?" Kathy asked incredulously.

"That's about it," Marva confirmed. She was wearing a new tan jacket she had bought for the occasion. The string from the price tag still hung from one sleeve.

Kathy did not know whether to be relieved or insulted. After a moment's consideration, her reaction was the former. "I know I'm not prepared to take the press on yet, and I certainly once built a career on speaking the words of others as if they were my own. But, Mar, I'm not a mindless face. I'm a competent, intelligent woman capable of thinking on my feet."

Marva tried to soothe her. "Senator, it's better this way. It's standard operating procedure until you've had a chance to get up to speed on the issues and campaign strategy. What's the old saying, 'better safe than sorry'?"

The knock on the door and the entrance of one of the secretaries interrupted them. In her hand was the speech Kathy was to deliver, fresh off the fax. It filled all of a singular page - double spaced. Reviewing it thoroughly, with Marva looking over the padded shoulders of her crimson cotton jacket, she concluded her 'lines' were safe and deliverable. "They'll get me through the first ordeal of the campaign. At this stage, I guess that should be enough."

When the time came, Marva joined her for the lengthy walk to the White House, up 'B' Street from the Senate Office Building to the gradual right on Pennsylvania Avenue. The oppressive weather seemed to be more forgiving today; they could only hope that the press would be as well. The walk and check-in procedure went as it had the day before with one exception; Kathy thought that the Marine sentries had been changed. Although she had some difficulty telling one from the other in those handsome blue uniforms, there was no glint coming from any eye beneath the neat white dress caps. The limousine arrived on schedule, but this time, the comforting face of Andrew Mathers was not inside. In his place were two of the senior members of the President's campaign team, Malcolm Tolliver and Bobby Joe Richards. Bobby Joe - like the President - was from the Lone Star State. It was his name, and his slight almost untraceable accent, that gave him away. Not his physical being. Even sitting, it was obvious Bobby Joe was shorter than the Senator.

Perhaps that's a blessing, Marva thought. *He has a face like a ferret anyway, so better his height makes him less conspicuous.* There was one thing big about him though, and that was his attitude. Within thirty seconds it was readily apparent to both Kathy and Marva alike that Bobby Joe was high on Bobby Joe.

"You may have read about me in *Time*. The media boys refer to me as 'the Sultan of Spin'."

They had heard about him alright. In cocktail party conversation Kathy had overheard someone say he had threatened the reporter that wrote the story if he did not use the term. He was a promoter alright. A self-promoter. From the moment they entered the limo, to the time they reached the ready area behind the White House press room, the good ole' boy dominated the conversation with a flurry of first person talk. The two women were not even sure if Malcolm Tolliver could speak.

"Blah, blah, blah." That was all they heard after the first two minutes. "Blah, blah, blah," and, "Y'all."

The long and 'short' of Bobby Joe's diatribe was simple enough. "Read the teleprompter, appear strong and confident, but warm." The rest of his ramblings went in one ear and out the other. Complicating matters, the vertically challenged cowboy's nervous hyperactivity was becoming a growing distraction to Kathy's efforts to prepare herself for the moment at hand.

Needing to marshal her composure, Kathy politely asked for time alone. "Would you mind giving me a moment alone, please? I need to go over my remarks. Don't want to make you gentlemen look bad, do I?"

Reluctantly acquiescing, the tightly wound pols cleared the room. Malcolm paused briefly at the doorway as if to prove nothing more than that he too could speak. All the tall consultant offered, however, was the wink of his middle-aged eye and a thumbs up gesture.

My kind of guy, she thought, *the strong, silent, Gary Cooper type.*

By the third read, she was sure she knew every word and the placement of every bit of inflection and emotion in the speech. Just as she began to wonder when the show would get going, Michael Burlington strode into the room.

"Ready fer hist'ry, Sen'tor? It's waitin' on ya," he chuckled.

"Ready or not is the phrase that comes to mind, Mr. President," she replied.

"Nuthin' to worry 'bout, not yet anyway. Those press vultures won't get a shot at ya jest yet. Bobby Joe tells me he and Malcolm got ya scheduled for a week's retreat at Camp David ta brief ya on the issues and strategies. They won't be able ta get at ya 'till after that. Jest look at it like political boot camp!"

Either the Mutt and Jeff of the campaign set had neglected to mention the planned summer camp to her, or it was a part of Bobby Joe's gibberish that she had failed to absorb. The news hit her hard given her last talk with Mark. She had not expected to be pulled away from her family so soon and so completely.

"Sir, can't we accomplish my briefings here in D.C.?" she asked pleadingly.

"Nah, the boys want ta make sure that them media types can't sneak up on ya. Plus they feel there'll be no distractions this way. Kathy, hon, we got precious little time ta git ya up ta speed here. Ah need yer full commitment and cooperation ta pull this thing off. Remember, you're now playin' for all the marbles. This is the big time!"

With that, the President put his hand on her shoulders and lead her to the threshold of the 'lion's den'. The next words she heard came over the press room microphone in an unfamiliar but rich voice.

"Ladies and gentlemen, the President of the United States..."

Kathy walked respectfully behind Burlington, taking great care to match him stride for stride. As she stepped up to the platform, she recognized the owner of the voice as Malcolm Tolliver. *Well, he does talk after all*, she thought to herself. Tolliver stepped discreetly away from the wooden podium embossed with the Presidential seal, as Michael Burlington stepped firmly behind it. He did so as though he had belonged there always.

As instructed, Kathy stood slightly behind and to the right of the President, taking care not to smile too much nor to frown. Looking through the piercing lights, she guessed there must have been a hundred people milling around in the cramped press room. *Not a particularly ruly bunch*, she thought, as the incessant chatter began to die down. Then she noticed the familiar figure sitting in the front row - ABC's Sam Donaldson, looking as intimidating as ever. Only the heat of the lights slowed the chill she felt trying to work its way down her spine.

Turning on all his Texas charm, the President took command of the press conference. "Settle down, boys 'n girls, settle down. I have a few brief remarks ta be followed by Sen'tor Canfield who'll also have a brief statement. There'll be no takin' of questions this mornin', folks. Sorry ta disappoint y'all in that regard."

The moans and groans that followed were widespread and audible even over the air. If this group had any sense of courtesy at all, it was certainly their own distorted brand. The President continued, "With the recent resignation of Vice President Burke, ah and ma party have found ourselves in the difficult position of havin' ta find a capable successor in time fer the convention which is but a week away. When ah asked ma staff to develop a short list of candidates, ah made it very clear that personal integrity would be the primary litmus test ah would apply ta each person on that list. The American people must have no doubts that their President will not tolerate, fer one minute or even second, dishonesty in this 'ministration. When that list reached ma desk in the Oval Office, one name stood out 'mongst all the rest as a beacon of honesty and integrity. That person stands beside me - the esteemed junior Sen'tor from California, Ms. Kathleen Canfield. Some of ya'll may best remember her from some of her films, like 'Ticket to Paradise'. Well yesterday, ah met with the Sen'tor to ask her to join our party's 'ticket ta paradise' as ma runnin' mate. Ah'm proud to say that she's agreed to this historic challenge and consented to join me in ma battle ta continue ta downsize government, reduce taxes, and revitalize this great nation. It is indeed ma pleasure ta present ta ya the fine lady I'll be askin' the convention ta support as my runnin' mate next week, Sen'tor Kathleen Canfield!"

The applause was surprising to Marva, given the generally accepted liberal leanings of the media. *It seems genuine and warm,* she thought as she stood at the rear of the press room. *I'm not sure if they're just surprised at a woman being nominated by the old redneck, or if the boss is gettin' to 'em in some way. Maybe it's just the historic nature of the moment.* Regardless of the reason, the warmth Marva felt seemed to turn to heat as Kathy stepped up to the podium to address the room and the nation. She liked the way she looked standing so straight and graceful behind the winged eagle of the presidential seal. She too, like Burlington before her, seemed like she belonged. Unlike the Texan, however, she looked almost regal standing there.

The room came to a quiet as the Senator adjusted the microphone, and prepared to speak. Connie Martin, CNN's Washington correspondent, was happy as a reconstruction contractor after a monsoon. *It's about time we got a woman in there!* she thought. When Kathy smiled and said, "Thank you for coming," it seemed to the newshound as though the room itself got just a bit brighter. *Even the toughest male scribe in the room'll have to admit there's something spellbinding about this one. Something special. Truly special.*

"I am flattered and humbled to stand before you today as the President's nominee to the Republican Convention for the Vice Presidency of the United States. The fact that I will become the first woman in the history of our party to be so nominated, if confirmed by the delegates next week, is an immense privilege. It is, however, a privilege that carries with it great burdens of responsibility. I pledge to President Burlington, to my party, and to all Americans to commit all that I am to bearing that burden with dignity, with sound judgment, and with the integrity the American people have a right to expect of our leaders in government. The sacrifices ahead will be substantial, but I and my family make them gladly with the hopes that by so doing we can create a better America for us all. We look forward to the convention, to a spirited debate of the issues, and to a decisive victory in November. Thank you all very much and God bless."

With that, she flashed the smile that imparted to all who watched that she meant every word, that by God she could make this a better nation. She had scarcely changed a word, hardly a preposition, yet she had made these words her own - her very own. The President quickly took her arm and guided her towards the door, away from the journalists now clamoring for answers to their questions. Not one of them had expected Kathleen Canfield as the President's selection. If nothing else, the choice had caught them off guard; they would be scurrying about for the next week trying to discover all they could about the political unknown that had been thrust into the spotlight. The White House staff would breathe a sigh of relief as the reporters diverted their time and efforts away from other events to concentrate on the beautiful and compelling newcomer.

Back in the ready room away from the throng, Burlington excused himself with a polite drawl, leaving his nominee in the hands of his campaign gurus.

"Damn fine job, Senator," Bobby Joe exhorted.

Malcolm's grin covered his face, silently communicating his pleasure. A swirl of behind the scenes handshaking overwhelmed them as a number of Cabinet members who had made their way into the ready room surrounded the woman of the hour. There was the familiar and rotund face of Secretary of State Edward Blankett and the ever scowling countenance of Secretary of Defense Paul Atkinson. Just as quickly as they had smothered her, they were gone, leaving her and Marva alone with the two consultants.

"Senator, you need to be at Dulles by 6:30 a.m. tomorrow morning. The campaign has a private jet on lease that'll fly us to Camp David for our retreat.

You're welcome to bring a member or two of your staff along if you wish. Here's a copy of the itinerary we've planned. You'll find it an aggressive schedule, but we only have a week to prepare you for the convention, the media...for the world. Please come prepared to put in some long hours," Bobby Joe said.

Shaking hands in agreement, the women began the trek back to the Senator's office. This time, the limo took them right to the entry to shield Kathy from any premature press attacks. In spite of the precaution, Kathy had repeated the words "no comment" a dozen times before they reached the inner sanctum of her office suite.

"This is gonna be a wild ride if ever there was one," Marva exclaimed. "Do you want me to join you for the retreat, or stay here and hold down the fort?"

"I'd rather you join me, Mar, if you don't mind. I'm not so sure I can spend a week alone with those gentlemen. Besides, two heads are better than one. Why don't you plan on picking me up at six-thirty sharp?"

"Six-thirty it is!"

There was much to do to get ready, making her early departure from the office necessary. Arriving home around three-thirty, Kathy was greeted at the marbled entryway by the furry face of Casper, the family's oversized, leg rubbing Himalayan cat.

"Meow, meow."

Casper had long, sandy-colored fur, punctuated by the most gorgeous light blue eyes. His mild, high pitched voice seemed borrowed, not at all fitting for his masculine frame. Dropping her briefcase and swooping him up in her arms, he responded as always.

"Purrrrr." It was smooth, and instantaneous. 'Old Faithful', Mark had jokingly nicknamed him.

Funny - no *wonderful* she thought - the way Casper seemed so unfazed by the head-spinning events. Kathy had to admire anything so well grounded in the middle of all this - even if it was just a cat.

"How are you, you little furball?" she said as she stroked his arching back.

"Meow." His soft reply came without so much as a hitch in the steady rumblings emanating from his throat.

Out of nowhere, Mark's drunken voice cut through the sunlit room like a dark cloud. "He's fine, but I'm not so sure about us," he mumbled as he stumbled into the room. The most recent of a long line of vodka and tonics was clutched firmly in his right hand. "Marva called and I understand you're leaving in the morning for a week at Camp David. Damned quick, aren't they? Oh, and she wants you to call Andy Mathers when you get in. Is that pretty boy gonna be there too?"

He was drunk. And as always when he drank, he was a different person. His grudging understanding from the previous evening had suddenly dissolved into a mix of booze, self-pity, and resentment. This she did not need. Not now, not already.

"Let me return the call first Mark, and then we can talk. And I'll ask Maria to get you some coffee," she answered, a furrow creeping into her brow.

Before he could say another word, she had set the hefty feline down and left the room. For the next thirty minutes, he shared his self-pity with the sympathetic Casper and the strongest cup of coffee he had ever tasted.

"You feel better after this, Doctor Mark," Maria promised him. After three years as the Canfield family maid and housekeeper, Maria knew her employers well. Blessedly for all concerned, she was an absolute Picasso when it came to the fine art of muting the effects of alcohol with her family's generations-old remedy of tabasco sauce and God knows what. Best of all, she was in the United States legally, and properly accounted for. That alone made her the envy of every respectable politician in Washington. The Canfields were lucky to have her.

By the time his wife had returned to the spacious living room, Mark Canfield's mood had swung to guilt mode. Kathy's refusal to get angry with him only compounded his self-condemnations.

"I'm sorry, Kath. It's just that it caught me by surprise, I didn't have time to prepare for it. You know how much I'll miss you," he apologized.

"It's okay, honey, I know this is going to be tough on you. It's going to be difficult on all of us. It caught me by surprise, too, and I'm not any crazier about it than you are. I just don't have any choice. Andy and I spoke about the time commitments involved in this thing, and he assures me that once the election's over, we'll be able to maintain a livable schedule. Just bear with me for awhile, dear. There's such a bigger picture involved than just us and our problems."

"I know. I'll get through it. It's just sometimes I feel I can't live up to your example. It's so God-awful tough," he confided.

"Mark, honey, don't do this to yourself. You are everything I've ever wanted in a man. At one time, I didn't think any normal guy could put up with all the garbage that went along with being married to a 'movie star.' But you proved me wrong. Then I drug you right back through it when I went into politics. Bumps in the road aside, you've stuck it out. We've been through so much, Mark, don't give up on me now," she implored.

Running his fingers through his hair, Mark tried to explain his inner demons to the woman who loved him. "I'm not, honey, I'm not. It just seems there's more I can be doing with *my* life. More I *should* be doing. I just need to figure out *what*."

Maria's interruption was a timely one. Kathy did not know what to say to her husband and the feeling of helplessness ate through her stomach like battery acid.

"A Mr. Tolliver ees on the phone for you, senora," the maid said in her natural Guadalajaran accent. "He says eet ees important."

Picking up the cordless phone from its carved teak cabinet on the coffee table, Kathy took the call. "Hello Malcolm, how are you? Is the schedule still set?" she asked.

Tolliver's mellifluous voice was as calm as he could make it considering the first words out of his mouth. "We have an unanticipated problem," he began. They were the first words he had ever spoken to her.

"What is it?" she asked.

The disclosure that followed was unexpected. "I'm afraid Speaker Farley has refused to accept the President's decision regarding your selection, Senator."

Bobby Joe Richards interrupted his soft-spoken partner. His anger rang like thunder. "The bastard's gonna take his own candidacy directly to the delegates at the convention! Apparently, the sonofabitch believes he needs the Vice Presidency to stake his claim ta the next presidential nomination." He paused to catch his breath. "Senator, the President'll give ya his full support, but the Speaker's a horny-toad of an adversary."

Mustering her strength, Kathy asked them to 'bottom line' things for her. "How bad is this?" she asked.

Kathy could hear the sound of a Breathalyzer working on the other end of the line. Apparently, Bobby Joe Richards was an asthmatic. It was Malcolm Tolliver who responded over the smaller man's wheezing. "The bottom line, Senator, is that we have a major battle on our hands. The nomination isn't going to be the 'given' we expected. You're going to have to fight for it! Fight *hard* for it, I'm afraid."

Kathy was stunned. This was not the cruise she had signed on for. It was starting to sound more like a trip on the Titanic than the Love Boat run she had been promised.

"I'm sorry," Malcolm concluded, "but we'll just have to work a bit harder to get you ready for the convention in San Diego."

Kathy hung up the phone and gazed at her stricken husband. *My God, what have I gotten myself into?* she wondered.

CHAPTER FIVE

The cool ocean breeze blowing across San Diego's Mission Bay rejuvenated the weary Senator. The break from the debilitating east coast summer was a godsend, and it felt good to be back in California. The week at Camp David had been a long and exhausting one, but she'd developed a sincere respect for her new 'guidance counselors', Tolliver and 'Tex' - her rather unimaginative nickname for Bobby Joe Richards. They'd been well prepared and had done yeoman's' jobs in educating her on issues ranging from tax reductions to the protracted conflict in the Balkans. She'd found the foreign policy briefings particularly interesting, since she'd had only limited exposure to such matters during her time in Congress. There'd been a few surprises during the week, such as her discovery that Michael Burlington was leaning in opposition toward her child care bill. Hopefully, her new relationship with the President would provide her with the opportunity to change his mind, she'd reasoned. Kathy had made several promises to herself before she'd agreed to be nominated for the Vice Presidency. One of them was that she would see her bill signed into law. With Stewart Farley's already declared opposition steeled by his battle for the nomination, the President's support would be vital to sway the necessary votes in the House. That battle would have to be fought soon after the election.

But right now Kathy was enjoying reacquainting herself with the warm California sun, sitting on the sand in a beach chair dressed in a white one-piece that accentuated her two-day tan. She was in heaven, if only for an hour or two. Regretfully, her relaxation was broken all too soon by the touch of Tolliver's long, slender fingers on her shoulder.

"We really need to be heading back to the hotel now, Senator. Bobby Joe'll have the afternoon's telephone calls to the first round of delegates ready to go in a few minutes." Over the past week, she'd grown accustomed to Tolliver's easy speech. He had a mellifluous voice that she found relaxing to listen to, and he was a very nice man, the perfect counterbalance to his abrasive partner.

Removing her designer sunglasses, she slowly turned toward her advisor with a wistful look in her green eyes. "Your wish is my command, oh master. Until November, anyway!" She knew that if she was going to succeed at the convention and still maintain her sanity, she'd need her sense of humor.

They walked briskly to the black Lincoln Continental that Bobby Joe had rented, and headed back to the Marriott in the big town car at the only speed Tolliver knew - light speed. Kathy lowered the electric window next to her in a desperate effort to quench her thirst for the sense of freedom she drew from the invigorating sea breeze. As it caressed her face and tousled her hair, she knew it was a feeling she'd feel precious little of in the months ahead.

The sleek Lincoln reached its destination all too quickly, and in a moment she was being whisked to her suite one floor below the penthouse. The spacious living area had been set up as the campaign's command center, populated by seldom fewer than five or six campaign aides at a time, and more phones than she could count. By the time they'd stepped through the door, the number of people had grown to more than a dozen.

Michael Burlington's nomination for re-election was a foregone conclusion. Accordingly, 'all the President's men' had been assigned to ensure Kathy's nomination. Not only did the Burlington team believe Farley's placement on the ticket would hurt their candidate at the polls, but if the President failed to secure the nomination for his publicly declared personal choice, it could yield a crippling public humiliation. Unfortunately, no one had been able to convince the self-serving Farley of that.

Pulling the telephonic headset from his thinning head, Tex motioned for them to join him in the next room. Rudely evicting a pair of coffee chugging aides from inside the room's doorway, Bobby Joe thrust a stack of papers into Kathy's hands.

"That's your phone list...and those are just the delegates that our people tell us have committed to, or are leaning toward Farley," Tex told her matter-of-factly. "Malcolm and I'll work the rest."

The task ahead carried all the charm of spring cleaning. Kathy knew she had to do it, but her mind was coming up with a thousand creative reasons why she could wait until later. It reminded her of another of her less favorite political activities, fundraising; the deceptively dignified name politicians applied to the process of begging for money. Malcolm sensed her hesitation. He himself had numbed to this portion of the political game a long time ago, but it helped that he knew a number of the people he'd be calling. He doubted she'd have that same advantage.

"Senator, for the next two days its good old-fashioned salesmanship. You've got to convince every delegate you talk to that you're the strongest candidate to boost the President's chances in November and that Farley'll be a disaster. Since we all truly believe that, it should be an easy sell," Malcolm advised.

Kathy's eyes narrowed as she looked at the aide with all the determination of a pit bull bitch protecting its young. In that moment, they realized for the first time that their charge would be capable of meeting any challenge the campaign might present.

"I understand, Malcolm. May I assume that if we're close when we complete our tallies, that the President's available and willing to make a few calls?" she asked.

The question produced a small smirk from the 'Sultan of Spin'. "Of course, Sen'tor. President Burlington's made it clear to the whole country he wants ya at his side for the next four years, not that bastard Farley. He's got as much on the line in this thing as ya'll do. Hell, more!"

Tex's accent seemed to get noticeably thicker when he got excited. Like most political junkies, he was a workaholic at election time. He ate, slept, and breathed 'the game'. Rumpled and abrasive as she found him, he was perfect for this job, and she knew it. And that made him tolerable.

The converted bedroom had been furnished with three small folding tables equipped with well used telephones. In her moment's hesitation, Kathy thought she could almost hear her late father speak to her the way he used to those many years ago. "When you've got something unpleasant to do, just do it," he used to say to his little girl. As though still the ever obedient child, she pulled one of the folding chairs toward her, sat, and wiggled a telephone headset into place on her auburn head. Within seconds, her perfectly manicured nails were scurrying across the numeric pad of the telephone.

For the next eight hours her corner of the room echoed with the salutary refrain "Hello, this is Kathleen Canfield..." Both Malcolm and Bobby Joe kept pace with her call for call. At five after ten p.m., Tex rose wearily from his seat, ripping his headset off and tossing it amongst the half empty pizza boxes on the cluttered tabletop. Catching the attention of the others, he made a motion across his throat with his right hand, as a director might signal 'cut' on a Hollywood sound stage. It took no additional persuasion. Both Kathy and Malcolm completed their calls and promptly tossed their headsets aside. The time for tallying their results into a preliminary count had come. Excusing herself, Kathy headed for the suite's restroom to freshen up. Her bleary-eyed team stayed behind to crunch the vital numbers that would determine their candidate's strength.

"Have fun with the totals, guys," she said as she closed the bathroom door.

Tally sheet in hand, Malcolm just grunted in response. "Yea, uh huh." He was past exhaustion. Bobby Joe, calculator at the ready, had already begun the tally.

Nearly thirty minutes had passed by the time Kathy had washed her face, attended to her other 'personal' needs, and called her family in Georgetown. Returning to the phone room, she stopped sharply when met by the downcast faces of her two 'chaperons'. Their silence was a disheartening sign until the moment was finally broken by the slight smile that crept onto Malcolm's lips, betraying the truth hidden behind their pranksters' masks.

With an unleashed enthusiasm, Tex gave her the rundown. "The numbers look good, real good. We're runnin' way ahead of our first projections. Malcolm 'n I have pulled together a short list of southern state delegation heads for the big guy ta call in the mornin' and a list of about two dozen for you ta meet with personally tomor..."

Interrupting him, Malcolm added, "By tomorrow night, it should be locked so tight even Farley'll have to accept it!"

"You're acceptance speech should be in from the writers by noon. That'll give us plenty of time to rehearse," his partner finished.

Fatigued, but excited, Kathy thanked her associates for all of their hard work and made her way to the nearby bedroom. She felt as though she'd just put in a long day on the farm. She was so tired she could hardly move, but she also had that warm feeling of accomplishment in her gut that made it all worthwhile. By the time she'd crawled into the inviting comfort of the suite's king-sized bed, she was sure the day's labors would reward her with a sound and rejuvenating night's sleep.

Kathy slept like a baby. Until, that is, her sweet slumber was shattered by the sound of bony flesh rapping at her door. Sliding across the comfortable cotton sheets to the nightstand, she groped in the dark for the suite's alarm clock. As her eyes slowly came into focus, so too did the luminescent red numbers. It was five minutes before six in the morning, an hour before the alarm had been set to go off. Rolling out of bed and slipping on her bathrobe, the ruffled beauty went to the door, stubbing her toe silently in the process. Cracking it open, she met the sunken eyes of the sleepless Malcolm Tolliver.

"What is it, Malcolm?"

"Bad news, I'm afraid. One of our guys just phoned from the coffee shop downstairs. He overheard a couple of Farley's people talking," he replied.

"Yes?"

The tone of his voice reflected anguish and worry. "Kathy, we'd hoped this wouldn't happen, but Farley's somehow gotten hold of the information on your daughter's L.A. arrest. From what our guy could tell, they plan on blowing it up and leaking it to the press this morning. You know, bad parent, bad politician and all that garbage."

The news jolted Kathy awake. The lump swelling up in her throat seemed to be working in tandem with the sickness in her stomach. It appeared the prior evening's elation had been naively placed.

"Are you alright?" the tall man asked as he brushed the door open wider to touch her shoulder. The lighting was poor, but it seemed to him that her face had suddenly become ashen.

"I'm fine. I'll *be* fine," was her brave reply. "I need to call my husband. He's got to know before he reads it in the paper. Could you..."

"Good as done. I'll get him on the line," he interrupted. The last word of his sentence trailed off, as he was already two steps toward the phone by then.

* * * * * * * * * *

Mark Canfield was pulling into the parking lot of his office building when the cellular telephone in his gold Mercedes SL convertible rang. Nudging into the space with his name stenciled on it, he hit the 'on' button with one hand while trying to finger comb his windblown hair with the other. The voice that came through the phone's speaker was an unfamiliar one.

"Dr. Canfield?"

"Speaking," he replied.

"This is Malcolm Tolliver calling from San Diego. I'm a member of your wife's campaign team. Can you hold for her?"

"Sure," Mark answered. He immediately knew something was wrong, not so much by instinct as by logic. He'd spoken to Kathy late the very evening before, and it was only around six in the morning San Diego time according to his quick calculations. What was wrong, he wondered.

"Mark?" he heard in his wife's distressed voice.

"Yes, hon. Is anything wrong?"

The disclosure that followed angered him. "It's Farley, Mark. He's gotten the dirt on Chrissie and he's going to release it to the press this morning."

"Sonofabitch," he muttered as he ripped at the handset of the cellular to prevent the woman in the Buick next to him from hearing the call. "You've only been a candidate for a little more than a week. How'd he get it so quickly?"

"I don't know, Mark, I don't know. We knew it was possible that it would come out, but I guess I really didn't believe it would. Our people on this end are meeting now to figure out how to respond," she stammered.

It took but a minute before Mark's structured mind began focusing on the problem at hand. He didn't know what the political solution was, but he did know what he had to do.

"Kath, I'm going to have Marcus take my appointments, and I'm gonna grab the kids. We'll be there on the next flight." His protective reaction was immediate and instinctive.

* * * * * * * * * *

There was a slight break in her voice as she thanked him and said goodbye. As frightened inside as she was over the development, it felt good to hear her husband's reassuring voice and to know her family would soon be with her in her hour of need. It felt good enough to enable her to restore her composure as she dressed to meet with her aides.

When she opened the door to her room, her ears filled with the lively debate that was going on between Malcolm, Bobby Joe, and two of their staff. A third aide, a young girl whose hair was still wet from her morning shower, was on the phone with Marva back in Washington. She was cautioning her in no uncertain terms to refer all inquiries to the campaign staff in San Diego. Kathy had complete faith that Marva could handle the damage control back at the Capitol. Although she'd had second thoughts on her decision to leave her behind, she was glad now that she had.

"That's it, then. We're decided," Bobby Joe decreed.

"We're decided," Malcolm agreed, sounding like the high priest Caiaphas in 'Jesus Christ Superstar'. Appropriate she thought. "There's a crucifixion in the making, and I'm the one being fitted for the lumber."

It was Malcolm that spoke for the assembled brain trust. "Senator, it's our best judgment that our only chance to beat this is to have you address the convention as soon as possible. You're going to have to face the delegates personally to explain what happened and to put a human face on the events. It's old news, she was a rebellious teenager experimenting like all other normal teenagers, you got it under control, etcetera, etcetera," he told her. "There's scarcely a parent, working or not, that won't empathize with you."

"My family's on their way out as soon as they can get a flight. Let's go with your plan, but I want them with me on the podium. How soon can you get us on?" she asked.

The actress turned politician was once again calm, cool, and collected. Her display of strength under fire inspired them, enabling the men to recover some of the confidence that'd been stolen away by Farley's ambush.

"Ah'll call the party chairman right away," volunteered the Texan. "We'll try and get a prime time slot tonight."

"I've got two dozen delegates to see today plus interviews with Diane Sawyer and Tom Brokaw. I think it'd be best if I sidestepped the tough questions and instead deferred to my convention address."

Tolliver's expression reflected the growing respect he had for his candidate. There was a lot more substance to this woman than he'd anticipated when he'd signed on. Burlington had led them to believe she was just a pretty face. He had been dead wrong. Her anticipation and instincts were right on target and she seemed to be rising to the crisis.

Looking at Tex for reassurance, and getting his nod, Malcolm sanctioned her suggestion. The plan was set and the wheels were in motion. The remainder of his day would be spent with the speechwriters preparing the words that would determine Kathleen Canfield's fate.

* * * * * * * * * *

By noon the networks were reporting the breaking story and every delegate she met with was opening with the same question. She could hear the whispers as she passed people in the halls between appointments. In spite of it all, she looked each of them straight in the eye when she said 'hello' or began to explain why she was withholding comment until her address. Even the usually intrepid reporters seemed to press more lightly than normal when they pursued the matter with her in the interviews. It seemed most everyone wanted her to succeed, wanted her to break the political glass ceiling that'd held women back for generations, wanted her to kick Stewart Farley's sizeable butt. As her family's flight touched down at Lindbergh Field that evening, Kathy and her aides were splitting their attention between watching the six o'clock news and putting the finishing touches on her speech which had been set for eight that evening. With four twenty-seven-inch color television sets receiving each of the networks and CNN, there was much to take in. By the time Mark and the kids had reached the hotel, the perspiration flooding the brows of each person inside the Canfield suite had started to dry. The news accounts had been blessedly mild, although CNN had referred to her impending speech as the first true test as to whether or not she had 'the right stuff' for national politics. No one could argue with that assessment.

Kathy had tweaked the egos of the speechwriters by drastically reworking the speech they'd prepared for her, and both Malcolm and Tex were 'scared to death' when she returned the chicken scratched copy to them.

"Here you go, gentlemen. I'd appreciate it if you'd check these changes for me to see if you have any problems with them. I felt it had to be more direct and concise," she said as she handed over the reworked copy.

Eyeing the mutilated speech, Malcolm reacted in horror. "Geez Kathy, you've gutted it! At least half the thing's been cut."

"Malcolm, they had stage directions in there for Pete's sake! I'm not an actress anymore, I'm a candidate for national office. I want the thing to be honest, I want it to represent what I truly believe. I don't want to feel like I'm just acting out a role!"

After reading the changes, the consultants relaxed. Her revisions were bolder and more honest than what they'd approved and, in many ways they felt the new text was riskier. But looking at her as she stood there serenely, like the calm at the eye of a storm, they believed she could make it work. They had begun to believe in *her*.

When Mark, Bill and Chrissie arrived, Kathy was barricaded in her bedroom in solitude, rehearsing the freshly retyped speech. Throughout the introductions around the room, the embattled nominee's daughter kept her eyes on the floor. There was a time that hurting her mother in this way would've brought some twisted joy to her, but this time it did not. Nevertheless, she was publicly humiliated by having her life dissected on national television because of her mother's candidacy, and this was the last place she wanted to be. It was one more reason to resent her.

The familiar voices of her family quickly pierced the door separating them. Laying the crisp pages of the speech on the table, Kathy opened it to greet Mark and their children. She found her way to

Chrissie first, taking great care to hold her as reassuringly as she could, knowing how important it would be to her. No one else could hear the words they shared, but all could see Chrissie's cold, stiff reaction to her mother's overture. Moving to embrace her husband, it seemed as though his hug carried a strength and a caring she'd not felt from him in a long time. He'd slowly slipped away from her these past few years, but this felt like a step back in the right direction.

The family followed Kathy into the privacy of the suite's master bedroom. The drawn blinds in the room created panels of alternating shade and light that gave it an oddly surreal look, like something from a 1940's detective novel. Mark had assessed his wife's state of mind in the fleeting moment of their embrace, so he cut right to the chase when he spoke.

"So what's the plan?" he asked. He spoke with an almost defiant confidence, like a warrior girding for battle.

"We have to make our way down to the floor in one hour. We'll all take the stage and I'd like you to stand behind me during my speech," she replied. Her voice, too, rang of determination.

Turning to face the uniformed Bill and misty-eyed Chrissie, Mark did his best to take charge of his family. "Kids, whatever you do, stand tall and stand proud. We may not be perfect, I know each of us has made their share of mistakes, but we're a family and your mother needs us now. She needs us at our strongest."

"Nothing less," Bill said.

"Sure, Dad," Chrissie conceded without conviction.

* * * * * * * * * *

67

In the anteroom, time seemed to go by slowly for Malcolm Tolliver. While there was optimism, none of the pairs of eyes present could quite seem to keep them from the ticking clock on the wall. It seemed like an execution watch to him. It was with relief that the hour finally passed, and Malcolm knocked on Kathy's door to let her know her time had come.

"It's time, Senator. Do you feel ready?" he asked, searching for an affirmative response.

"When the curtain goes up, you don't really have much choice, do you?" she answered with a nervous grin. "Let's break a leg, gang!"

The walk to the convention floor was a long one, and Tolliver began to feel like a trainer escorting his prize fighter to the ring for the big fight. With all the obligatory hand shaking along the way, it seemed to take forever. As his mind wandered, he looked ahead at the back of her head, and it struck him full force for the first time. He was watching history in the making. Hell, he was helping *make* history.

Malcolm, Tex and the others did their best to guard her from the throngs on the convention floor. As the entourage made its way with difficulty toward the stage, convention chairwoman Maggie King began to gavel the cavernous room to order. As they passed the Ohio delegation, speckled with hastily printed 'Farley' signs, the heckling began. This was the portly Speaker's home crowd, and the toughest part of the audience she would face.

"CAN FIELD but Can't Hit," read one of the more creative placards. The bright gold letters leapt out at them over the backdrop of a blue feather, a not too subtle swipe at the Senator as a political lightweight.

"Gotta appreciate a good line," Kathy gamely yelled back to Tolliver, making light of the criticism.

Malcolm strained to hear what she'd said but couldn't over the chaotic noise of a thousand different voices. What he heard all too explicitly were the crude insults being hurled by an obviously drunken delegate wearing a straw 'Farley' skimmer. Before he even knew what he'd done, the aide pushed aside the person or two that stood between him and the inebriated critic. The towering Tolliver reached out and yanked the straw hat down over the drunk's eyes, tearing the brim from the crown in the process.

"Stuff that, bozo," Malcolm challenged.

By the time the Ohioan could remove the tattered remnants of his head piece restoring his blurry vision, Tolliver was a distant twenty feet away and back in step with his colleagues, amazed at what he'd done.

"Damn, Malcolm, I think a little bit of my Southern manners are rubbing off on you! That was downright chivalrous. Stupid, but chivalrous," Bobby Joe screamed into his ear. "Good thing this is about over, or I'd be havin' to bail you out of jail."

It wouldn't be until later that evening that they'd discover his little escapade had been caught by a camera crew for NBC. The replays would provide a national audience with a bit of levity on the network's eleven o'clock news that night. It would be Malcolm Tolliver's reluctant fifteen minutes of fame.

When they reached the stairs to the stage and began the climb, one person was conspicuously absent from the support group that surrounded Kathleen Canfield. Nowhere to be seen was her benefactor, Michael Burlington. He'd helicoptered to the convention hours earlier from his Air Force One landing at Miramar, and Bobby Joe had spoken with him over the phone while he was in transit. Malcolm could tell his partner was keeping something from him when he asked him if the President would stand by her on the podium. Tex's answer was conspicuously evasive, leading him to believe that Burlington was keeping his distance until he could see if the pretty Californian succeeded or not. He wasn't taking any more chances than he had to.

"If the delegates would please come to order, if the delegates would please come to order," the flustered Chairwoman pleaded as she gaveled her heart out.

The tumult caused by the incited Farley supporters was threatening her control of the convention and her temper, all for the viewing entertainment of a prime time national television audience. Young Bill Canfield thought he saw sparks fly during her last spirited gavel slam on the podium. After a few minutes, the revolt subsided just enough for her to make the introduction.

"Ladies and gentlemen. Early this morning we received a request to address the convention from Vice Presidential nominee Senator Kathleen Canfield of California. Given the stir that's been caused by today's rumors, the Steering Committee has graciously acceded to the request. I will remind you that a nation is watching us to see how this party conducts its business. I ask you to maintain the highest levels of decorum and courtesy during the Senator's address."

Most of the delegates responded but some did not, and their shrill voices seemed to carry in the huge facility. After a few more largely futile efforts, the chairwoman finally conceded to the unruly and handed over the podium in frustration.

"Ladies and gentlemen, the distinguished Senator from California, Kathleen Canfield."

The drama on the television monitors was compelling, as was the graceful figure of the woman that bravely approached the microphone to address the millions of critics and doubting Thomases in the hall and in living rooms across America. Standing at the foot of the stage's stairs, Malcolm could see one of the immense projection screens that'd been installed by the convention organizers so all could see the stage. It seemed uncanny, nearly supernatural to him. As she stood behind the tempered glass of the podium, it actually looked as though the lighting was embracing the statuesque brunette, conforming to the contours of her face as though if by command. She seemed even more beautiful, more graceful, and more entrancing on camera than she did in person. Her whole faced beamed, her teeth seemed whiter, her eyes greener. As she spoke, the strength and natural magnetism of her voice coupled with the motioning of her arms, quieted the crowd. At this moment, it looked to Malcolm as though this woman could part the Red Sea.

"Ladies and gentlemen, fellow Republicans, Americans throughout this great country. Thank you for the opportunity to address you this evening. It is indeed a pleasure to be with you, regardless of the circumstances," she began. Only a few loudmouths continued across the room, and they were being elbowed into silence by people next to them.

"One week ago the President of the United States honored me by asking me to stand as a candidate for this party's nomination for the Vice Presidency. My family and I jointly agreed I should accept the President's invitation to seek what very clearly would be an historic moment for our party, for our country, and for women everywhere. I am humbled to stand here before you to ask for your support," she continued.

Chrissie Canfield had to fight hard to keep from dropping her head and shuffling her feet, knowing that soon the spotlight would turn unavoidably to her and the mistake she'd made when she was only thirteen. The room had turned so quiet you could hear a pin drop, and that made her feel even more conspicuous as her mother continued.

"There are those among us that in their competitive zeal have sought to hurt me and my family, all for their own personal political gain. Well, I stand before you this evening humbled, but not humiliated. Proud and unashamed, not beaten or embarrassed. I stand here as a woman who knows she's been blessed, not cursed."

There was a strength and defiance in her voice but no arrogance. As she continued, you could feel the momentum building.

"You see before you first a mother and wife, secondly a Senator and candidate for the Vice Presidency. The Canfield family has had its problems just as each family in America has had theirs. We do not deny it nor do we ask you to accept us as free of human flaws. For neither a genuine leader nor follower can offer perfection to his fellow man. That blessing awaits us in another time and place of God's choosing."

Motioning with her hands at every appropriate point, Kathy went on to explain with passion the teenage problems Chrissie had as the child of working parents, and how the family had pulled together to get her away from the negative influences in her life. She credited their success to a strong and loving family environment, God, and raw determination. By the time she'd finished, there wasn't a mother or father in the room that couldn't relate to what she'd said and the values she had represented. As Kathy paused to move to the close of her speech, the sound of a person clapping, barely audible to those on the stage, could be heard. One by one, the network cameras focused on a middle-aged woman standing alone in the middle of the Iowa delegation, applauding. One mother to another. And then there were two, and then three. Soon every woman in the room had joined in. As the men followed suit, the room erupted into a standing ovation that was both spontaneous and powerful.

And it was televised. Around the country parents were cheering tearfully in private. From the privacy of his carefully guarded hotel suite, the President of the United States was applauding too as he watched. After all, she'd just pried him out of the political coffin Farley'd tried to put him in. As the pandemonium carried into its fifth minute and beyond, and the cameras focused on the fuming Speaker as he stormed from the convention floor, the President's mood began to erode. The longer the applause lasted the dourer he got. Finally, the big Texan grabbed for the remote control, slamming off the television set. As he turned away, the Secret Service men with him heard him mutter something to himself.

"Ah've created a damned monster," he said jealously under his breath. "A damned Joan of Arc!"

* * * * * * * * * *

Back on the floor of the convention, the Canfield pack was slowly making its way out of the hall through the approving crowd of delegates. Their exit was interrupted repeatedly by impromptu interviews from a barrage of hungry television reporters. The bright lights of the cameras engulfed the reborn candidate on the long trek back to the hotel room, but eventually they made it to the sanctuary of the suite and the campaign's own small but intense celebration. Tex ordered up champagne for all, while

Malcolm tried to make sure no one had too much. By midnight the party had ended, leaving the Canfield family alone to set up the hastily provided cots for Bill's and Chrissie's use. The day ended with their feet planted back firmly on the ground. Twenty-five floors up.

As Malcolm left Tex at the door to his room, he asked his partner a parting question. The answer was expected, but still disappointing. There'd been no congratulatory call placed by the President to his shining new running mate-to-be. In thirty years of national politics, he'd never seen anything like the electricity Kathleen Canfield had brought to the stage this evening. He'd also never seen a more glaring political snub than Burlington's act of omission.

Each of the Canfields went to bed that night happy as could be. Kathy's nomination by the convention tomorrow seemed unstoppable. Bill was dizzy with pride that his mother could soon be just one step away from the Commander in Chief of the very military he served. Chrissie was relieved beyond description that her mother had turned her L.A. disaster into a badge of courage, muting her embarrassment in the process. Ironically, in some karmic way, she'd been the catalyst that'd set the stage for her mother's shining moment. And Mark was so filled with pride, so very proud to be married to her, that not a single thought of insecurity could pry its way into his mind. He held Kathy in his arms all night, stroking her hair and nuzzling her cheek until the wee hours of the morning.

As they drifted into slumber that night, they remained oblivious to the goings on in suite 2601 a floor above. Inside, Michael Burlington sat awake in bed, clothed in a dark blue pair of pajamas bearing the presidential seal and holding a pad and pen. The note he addressed to his Chief of Staff forecast the unpleasant realities of any Burlington-Canfield administration to come. It read simply, "isolate Canfield after election". And it was written in ink as black as the coarse Texan's heart.

CHAPTER SIX

The final day of the convention affirmed what had now become inevitable. The Burlington-Canfield ticket was nominated on the first ballot following Stewart Farley's abrupt withdrawal and contrived endorsement speech for the Senator. Trapped in a bog of his own making, the conniving Farley had correctly calculated that this hypocritical course would be less damaging to his political power than a humiliating defeat by a first term woman Senator. Ever the survivor, and a chillingly talented liar, Farley brought the delegates to their feet by giving them what they wanted - praise for the charming Senator from California. The forced withdrawal was so disgusting to the arrogant pol, that he vowed then and there that he'd even the slate with her, no matter what it took. On the 'Hill', Stewart Farley was known as a ruthless man who never let a score go unsettled. And he did not count patience among his limited virtues when it came to dealing with his enemies.

Michael Burlington bit his tongue that day too,

appearing on stage with a smile that went from ear to ear, his party's new shining star and Vice Presidential nominee by his side. In his acceptance speech, he trumpeted a new era for the Republican Party, an era where women and minorities were welcomed as equal partners in the political process, an era of inclusion of constituencies traditionally drawn to the Democratic Party. The speech was received with a grain of salt by a cynical and famously liberal press, but the nomination of the first woman Vice Presidential candidate in the party's history made it difficult to attack the now tefloned Burlington.

As the central players returned to Washington, Time and Newsweek magazines were hitting every grocery store, mailbox and newsstand with glossy cover photos of the Senator and headlines that ushered in the country's brightest political comer in over thirty years. "The Female JFK?," and "The GOP's Evita," they read. Neither chose to use photos that included Burlington, an intentional act against the unpopular southern conservative and one that dug Kathy's hole even deeper with the President. Late the dark evening after the magazines reached the Oval Office, White House janitors chuckled to themselves as they emptied the President's shiny trash can for the mandated and customary shredding process. Inside they found the already hand-torn issues that told a story even they could figure out. Burlington couldn't stand his pretty new running mate.

By late September, Kathy was feeling the chill from the White House as if she were an Eskimo. The campaign had kept her buried in small western town after small western town while Burlington and his wife Edith campaigned in the major metropolitan areas of the South and Northeast respectively. She hadn't seen the President since leaving sunny and temperate San

Diego, and her efforts to discuss her child care bill with him had been artfully rebuffed a dozen different times in a dozen different ways. Even the usually helpful Andy Mathers had been useless to her in her efforts on the bill.

During one of her daily check-in calls to the ever knowledgeable Marva, she'd learned that rumors were circulating cattily around Washington that Burlington resented her popularity and had given the word to the campaign to keep her buried unless absolutely necessary. She didn't take the news well.

"So *that's* what this is all about?" Kathy said angrily. "Petty male jealousy?"

On the other end of the telephone line in the Capitol, Marva was shrugging. "I'm afraid so, Senator. He's a good ole boy and behind the public face he wears, I don't think he has much use for women. Outside of the kitchen or bedroom, that is.

"So he sends me out on this backwater circuit of dusty western towns?"

"Afraid so," Marva replied.

"That pompous..." Kathy caught herself. "He's holding all the cards right now, so I guess I don't have much choice. But wait 'till he comes calling again, and he will. Sooner or later."   "Well, it's going to take a drop in the polls to force his hand," Marva judged astutely enough. "Since the convention, the ticket's been steadily pulling away. You've gained ten points in the last month."

And so it stayed as September came to a close. The Democratic candidates, New York Governor Anthony Provolone and his running mate, Senator Pat Farmer of Louisiana, began issuing public challenges for a series of debates. With the momentum the ticket was enjoying, the President and his aides had concluded the debates would only hurt them, so the challenge went unaccepted. That would change shortly as a result of a White House leak relating to the ongoing conflict in the Balkans. On October 2nd, the Washington Post's bold headlines reported to the country that the Burlington administration had silently approved an escalation of U.N. and NATO involvement against the Bosnian Serbs in the protracted bloody conflict. It further disclosed that substantial commitments of U.S. troops had been made by the hawkish Texan. While the White House issued first its categorical denials, then its qualified confirmations, the ticket started sinking in the polls leaving both sides nearly even before the disastrous week was out. On the following Sunday afternoon, after returning from a sweltering campaign rally on the outskirts of Phoenix, a dusty and exhausted Kathy was handed a small pink phone message slip by a disheveled desk clerk as she returned to the air conditioned relief of her hotel. 'Andy Mathers in D.C.' was scribbled on it as though it'd been written with a pen that was about out of ink. By the time she'd reached her room, she'd had enough of the cold shoulder treatment from the White House. The peeling wallpaper and the cobwebs in the corner of her 'luxury' accommodations only added to her frustration as she called Mathers back.

"Vanessa, this is Kathy Canfield returning Andy's call," she told his secretary politely while running a damp washcloth across her face.

After several minutes the formal voice of Andrew Mathers came over the phone. "Senator, thank you for returning my call. How's Arizona?"

"Hot as hell! And still here, and still as safe in the Republican column as ever. For God sakes, it's Goldwater's state," she replied, her voice rising. "Andy, we need to talk."

If the unflappable Chief of Staff was taken aback by her uncharacteristic display of temper, he didn't let it show.

"Sure, just let me fill you in on a few things first," he said.

"Andy, 'filling me in' would *be* a first." Her temper was as hot as the Arizona sun.

"Senator, I just met with the President and Rex Morgan. The Bosnia thing's killing us in the polls. A number of decisions were reached this morning which'll affect you," he told her. "First, the President has asked me to take a leave of absence to head up the remainder of the campaign. Second, the drop in the polls has forced us to negotiate for two debates, one presidential and one vice presidential."

Kathy's response was forceful. "Fine, I have no problem with that. But Andy, since you're now this campaign's operating head, let's get a few things straight. Number one, I want a straight answer on why I've been swept under the rug. I've been buried on 'the 20 Mule Team' route, ignored by the White House concerning my bill, and kept totally uninformed on just about everything starting with the Bosnia deal."

She continued without so much as pausing to take a breath. "Number two, I'm hearing disturbing rumors that the President has some kind of a problem with me. Of course, I wouldn't know from firsthand experience, since I haven't talked to him in over a month!"

Noticeably off balance, Mathers did his best to cover for his boss. "Senator, I... I assure you everything's fine, the President's just been extremely busy with priority matters. There's also a bit of a legal problem sharing classified intelligence information with you since you're not yet a member of the administration and won't be 'till after the election."

The excuse didn't wash with her. "Andy, let me bottom line this for you. I'm tired of being unable to respond intelligently to questions from the press because I'm being kept in the dark. If you want my full cooperation, then you're going to have to give me some. I want daily briefings, starting on Bosnia. And I want the President's support for my bill. It's scheduled for a floor vote in the Senate next week and you and I both know it'll die in Farley's House unless the President pushes for it."

Her position didn't sound negotiable to the Yale educated Mathers. "I'll talk to him. We need you to come back anyway to prep for the debate with Farmer. I'll set up a meeting with someone at the National Security Council to fill you in on Bosnia while you're here. We'll work it out," he promised.

"I hope so Andy. I didn't agree to risk giving up my Senate seat to become a White House ornament. I expect to be included."

Hanging up the phone, a bruised Mathers cleared the line, then punched the intercom button to the Oval Office. When Michael Burlington answered, the Chief of Staff's comment to his superior was direct.

"Mr. President, I just got off the line with Kathy Canfield. We've got a problem..."

* * * * * * * * * *

Back in Georgetown, the weather was grey and overcast but the humidity had subsided as Mark Canfield prepared to tee off on the doglegged 17th hole of his country club golf course. Today's foursome was a medical quartet that included his screwball partner, Max Gaugin, an old podiatrist friend that couldn't putt his way around a miniature golf course, and a nasal sounding anesthesiologist that was said to put his patients to sleep through the sheer monotony of his voice. Carefully gauging the mischievous autumn breeze, Mark pulled back the graphite driver and smoothly snapped it forward into his Titleist 3 with a sharp "crack". In a sight even a non-golfer could appreciate, the traitorous ball hooked wildly into the leafy trees sending a frightened bird scurrying for a safe haven.

"Damn!" Mark yelled in frustration.

Snickering at his partner's stroke of bad luck, the curly haired Max slapped him on the back and taunted him. "No respect for the endangered species act, eh buddy?"

The others jumped in with the poorest imitations of bird calls Mark had ever heard. But it was all in good fun, even the small side bets along the way, so he took the needling in good humor.

"What do you want, I'm a Republican, not a bleeding heart liberal. I was aiming for that damned bird," he joked.

"Don't let the press getta hold of that," Max laughed, as he yanked the golf cap from his head and kneeled as though he were trying to hide. It was a comical gesture given that he was six feet six inches in height and weighed about three hundred pounds. The huge black man was a former professional football player who'd been well schooled in the art of locker room levity and had become quite the accomplished physical comedian.

"You play like a friggin' Democrat, Canfield."

"Shhhh," Mark whispered.

The foursome eventually bogeyed its way through the last two frustrating holes and adjourned to the comfort of the club's bar for a thirst quencher. It was somewhere during the second round of cool Amstel Lights that the droll anesthesiologist, Jerry

Lake, began talking to his increasingly disinterested audience about his vacation plans. As he told it, for the past several years he'd been volunteering two weeks of his time to an overseas mission program that sent several teams a year to various parts of the globe to help those "less fortunate". This year, he'd gone to the Honduras. The year before, he'd traveled to the battle scarred but beautiful Croatian port city of Dubrovnik, and this coming March he was planning to participate in a special Red Cross sponsored journey to inner Bosnia.

The story piqued Mark's interest. After all, with Kathy tied up in the campaign he had time on his hands, and he did originally go into medicine to help people. Or at least that was his recollection. And something about the danger and excitement of going to the war-torn region on a mission of mercy made his pulse race.

Taking the frosty glass from his lips, he began to listen intently to Jerry, raising his opinion of him just a bit as he continued.

"Tell me more about it, Jer," he encouraged.

"Well, we're supposed to try and get a medical team into Sarajevo, but the military situation changes about every day. So does access to the city and the level of risk," he told him. "If the danger's too high, we'll probably be diverted somewhere else."

Mark was growing increasingly excited. It sounded like something only a nut or a man of courage would do, leave the safety and comfort of an American doctor's life to dodge shells and bullets in the dreary Balkans. It was also noble and crazy, and both aspects strangely appealed to him. It didn't cross his mind, at least not the conscious part of it, that he might just be trying to compete with his exceptional spouse.

"You know, Jerry, I might enjoy something like that. Got a need for a plastic surgeon?" Mark asked.

Max's intercession was brutally direct. "Are you out of your mind? You guys'll get your fool selves killed," Coming from a three hundred pound former defensive lineman, the words of fear he used were an effective attention grabber.

The much smaller Jerry just looked the big man off the way a quarterback would look off a defensive back, and continued his story. "I believe we've already filled the team, but I don't think we have a plastic surgeon. We can always use one of you guys. How about I check it out in the morning and give you a call?"

Max sat up straight looking like a grizzly bear and continuing to growl like one. "Mark, get real. Do you really think the State Department's gonna let the Vice President's husband go traipsing off to an unsecured war zone? Not likely!"

The hair on the back of Mark's neck began to bristle. Like most men, he didn't like being told what he could and could not do. The more he thought about it, the more he wanted to go. As the friends split up to go their separate ways, Mark Canfield made a mental note to himself to check out his ability to travel there. His mind had been all but made up. As he counted out the twenty simoleans he'd lost to Max on the treacherous golf course, he resolved to make the trip. It would be, well, heroic. And right now Mark needed to feel like a hero.

* * * * * * * * * *

Two hundred miles off the eastern seaboard, the U.S.S. Kitty Hawk was completing routine maneuvers. As young Bill Canfield ignored the frantic

Landing Signal Officer's wave-off in favor of his own judgment, he had no doubt that he'd catch the arrestor wire dead on. Determination had always been a Canfield trait. Or was it stubbornness?

Coming in 'hot', his F-14 slammed onto the deck of the bobbing carrier, scaring the daylights out of his frightened communications officer. The sudden and violent stop of the heavy fighter threw him headfirst into his instrument panel. Only the shoulder harness kept him from more painful damage than the lump on his forehead he felt swelling up. As the deck crews worked feverishly to clear the grounded plane from the deck before the next fighter came in, Bill could see the LSO animatedly waving at him with his square jaw working overtime and blood vessels popping out in his leather skinned neck. Bill smiled and waved back, but he was truly glad he couldn't hear him over the roaring din of the jet's turbines.

He could hear his communications officer just fine, though. The back seater wasn't at all pleased when his voice came crackling over the intercom.

"Damn Shadow, you trying to ditch us or just get us busted?" Bill had picked up his code name in flight school when the instructors had difficulty shaking the young flyer from their tails during mock dogfights. Like a shadow, he was always there, a part of the wild blue yonder they couldn't escape. Because he was so good, he flew on the edge. It wasn't really that he was a hot dog like many of the other flyers thought, it was simply that he had a more acute sense of what he and the plane could and could not do. His thresholds were not the same as the ones taught by the plane's owners, the United States Navy. Unfortunately for Bill, this minor discrepancy kept him in hot water with some of his more rigid superiors.

Squeezing out of the tight cockpit and sliding down the side of the jet's hot metal, the handsome blond lieutenant pulled off his helmet and shook his sweaty, closely cropped hair in the winds blowing across the carrier deck from the Atlantic. As his partner joined him, he just smiled with a quiet confidence and widened his blue eyes.

"Made in the shade. Had it all the way," he said to Lieutenant J.G. Tommy Brunarski, aka 'Scarecrow'. "All the way."

Tommy wasn't the gutsiest flyer in the world as his code name hinted. Neither of them were quite sure why they'd been paired together given their differences. They had two theories. The first, that Scarecrow had been assigned to Bill as his conscience or 'mother hen' to slow him down. Second, that the young Pollack must've really pissed off an Admiral or Admiral's daughter and that his assignment to daredevil Billy Canfield was his penance. Either way, it really didn't matter. They were a combat team and the life-and-death bond forged in the skies above had developed into a solid friendship on the ground.

"Canfield, Brunarski get your butts in here," yelled Lt. Commander Butch Norton. "You know better than to ignore a wave off!"

The squadron commander could be a truly hard case. At forty-five he still looked as if he could kick the tails of just about anyone in his command. Tommy thought he looked a little like Robert Conrad in 'Baa Baa Black Sheep', and teasingly called him 'Pappy' behind his back. Lucky for Bill he prized ability over conformity, otherwise he'd have spent the last tour peeling potatoes in the carrier's hell-hole of a galley. The pair snapped to attention as sharply as their spines would allow.

"I'm sorry, sir. The sun blinded me for an instant, by the time I saw the signal, I'd already committed," Bill explained creatively but firmly.

"Save it for somebody who'll buy what you're selling, mister," grunted the chiseled older flyer, "and that ain't me!"

"Yes sir," came their replies in unison.

"Get yourselves cleaned up. We've got a briefing in the flight room at fourteen hundred. Dismissed!"

The Lt. Commander had a knack for letting you know he understood while all the while yelling at you. Butch Norton was a crack pilot himself, he knew what it was like to have 'the edge' and to live precariously close to it.

Most of the pilots thought maneuvers in the Atlantic weren't all that bad, but they all knew they weren't the real thing. The word swirling around the ship was that the Kitty Hawk might get the call to go to the Adriatic as part of the UN/NATO buildup. The ethnic war in Bosnia was largely a ground war, but there were a few older Russian manufactured MIG's that occasionally showed up in the mix. Bill drooled over the thought of getting a crack at one. The Canfield offspring's need for challenge and the opportunity to distinguish himself was stronger than his sense of self-preservation. With four more months remaining on this tour of duty, anything was possible. His only concern was that his mother's prospective election might cause the Navy to keep him back. He could picture the diplomatic debacle that the capture of a Vice President's son by a foreign warring faction might create, but he didn't want special treatment, at least not working against him he didn't. As he bathed in the intermittent flow of one of the showerheads in the officers' bath, he wondered how his mother's campaign was going back home, how his father was holding up, and whether or not his sister had a boyfriend yet. Mostly he wondered how long it would be before they were all together again.

Returning to the tight confines of his steel-walled cabin, Bill picked out a fresh set of khakis, taking care to make sure his lieutenant's bars, pilot's wings, and multi-colored combat ribbons were all straight as an arrow. He not only flew with great precision, he also tried to dress the same way. Parting his damp yellow hair with a new black plastic comb and brushing his teeth, he got quickly dressed returning to the mirror for a moment to straighten the gig line from his freshly pressed shirt to his sharply creased slacks. Taking a step back, he surveyed the results.

"Not bad," he said under his breath. And then he was on his way to the briefing.

Tommy Brunarski caught him from behind in the narrow passageway and joined him as he entered the crowded and stuffy briefing room. Butch Norton was only two footsteps behind and they'd scarcely reached their seats when they had to pop back up to snap to attention.

"At ease, ladies and gentlemen," Norton ordered. Signaling to a young female lieutenant, she strained to her tip-toes and pulled down a yellowed roll up map attached to the wall. Bill and Tommy had difficulty seeing from the back of the room, but it looked like a map of Europe to them. Taking a laser light pin from the podium, Norton pointed its red beam at the discolored old chart. "That's the military for you." he mumbled under his breath. "A five dollar, thirty year old wall map and a $200 high tech pointer the government probably paid triple the price for."

"I'll make this brief," he said as he pointed in a circular motion to the Adriatic Sea. "We're being dispatched to the Adriatic coast as a part of a combined UN/NATO military mission. The mission's been code named 'Back Breaker'. We'll be posted on standby in the Adriatic as part of a multi-national force, awaiting further orders. If called upon to help break the Bosnian Serbs' stronghold around Sarajevo, our F-14s'll be flying air to ground sorties against military targets in order to force a withdrawal from the perimeter of Sarajevo. If that happens, we'll be facing a variety of ground-to-air defenses which we'll brief you on later. We will be operating on very tight rules of engagement. We do not expect to be challenged in the air."

As he gazed out on the sea of youthful faces, he saw both looks of excitement as well as looks of fear. "Are there any questions?" he asked.

"How soon and how long?" came the first reply from a skinny bespectacled Georgian in the front row.

Norton answered as honestly as he could given the sparse information his tight-lipped superiors had provided him. "We expect to arrive there in twenty days. How long we stay will depend on the Serbs, the UN/NATO leadership, and our Commander in Chief."

A few innocuous queries later and the squadron commander was gone, leaving the flight crews to shoot the bull amongst themselves concerning the call to duty. The reactions varied from the sanely scared who said little, to the John Waynes of the Kitty Hawk's Winged Liberty Squadron who salivated over the chance to wreak death and destruction on an enemy, any enemy. It didn't much matter to these guys even who that enemy was. The high tech equipped F-14 Tomcats had desensitized the horrors of war so effectively that combat sorties seemed like some sort of high flying Nintendo game dominated by laser guided smart bombs and video monitors. From the air, war was clean and sanitary. Only the risk of a flyer's own death from any one of a number of his opponents' weapons reminded him it was all real. But there was an odd self-centeredness about it. The older pilots with combat experience had said a pilot's mind could focus on his own potential destruction or the loss of a friend, because that was personal and up close. The loss of life and the horror resulting from a reign of terror by a squadron of F-14's was not.

Perhaps it was those forces that worked on Bill that evening as he turned down a big time poker game to instead curl up on his bunk and write an overdue letter home. It began "Dear Family, Life as I've known it is about to end..."

* * * * * * * * * *

Back in the safety of suburban Georgetown, the lonely Chrissie was thinking the same thing about her life as dusk settled in to the east coast suburb. Sitting under the shade of the old oak tree in front of her family's canary yellow Victorian house, it seemed to her that everything was changing. The brother she fought with constantly but loved was gone. She hadn't seen her famous mother in a month and she wasn't sure if that was a good or a bad thing. Instinctively, she wanted her mother's love, attention, and approval like any child. She always had, but her mother's frequent absences over the years had left her yearning and resentful. Still, it seemed as though things were a little easier sometimes when she and her mother were apart. There wasn't this constant reminder of how comparatively imperfect she was staring her in the face on a daily basis. Leaning back against the tree, she stared wistfully into the star-specked sky until a bright orange and black butterfly fluttered through her line of sight. As it neared, Chrissie reached out and caught it carefully between her two hands. Opening them ever so slightly until she could see the gorgeous creature, she marveled at how naturally beautiful to the eye it was. How she wished she could be so attractive. Letting go of the butterfly, she held on tightly to the dream. Even butterflies started out as caterpillars she reminded herself, and at sixteen there was still plenty of time to blossom. Jumping up from her resting place, Chrissie trotted up the wooden stairs to the yellow house's porch and through the screen door.   It was Saturday night, and she'd told her friend Cindy she'd join her for an evening of club crashing. There was just enough time to clean up, get dressed, and grab a bite to eat - say two or three hours.

Cindy Shanahan was a tall, pretty redhead with porcelain skin and just enough freckles to make her look wild and sexy to the boys. She lived down the street and attended the local public school, unlike the upper-class Chrissie who'd been sent to a private Catholic girls' school here in Georgetown.   Cindy looked a good several years older than her sixteen years, smoked and drank, and occasionally did coke or whatever else was available. She was a certifiable rebel and that attracted Chrissie to her. Cindy's world was sensual, brash, and in Chrissie's opinion more honest. Nobody asked who your parents were, what you wanted to be when you grew up, and what kind of car you drove. That circle only cared about you for what you were then and there, here and now. Immediate gratification. When you were hurting, it seemed the best medicine.

Chrissie was certainly no angel. Her drug arrest in L.A. had been a solid one and the only reason she and the others had gotten off was that the evidence had disappeared mysteriously from the police car before reaching the L.A.P.D. property room. Nobody knew if it was incompetence, theft, or personal consumption that was at fault. She'd sometimes wondered if her mother had used her connections to resolve the mess, or if someone in the department where her mother had a number of supporters had silently helped her out.

She'd promised her parents after she was released that she'd go straight, and they'd helped ensure that by moving the entire family east after her mother's election to the Senate. Then, as added insurance, they'd sentenced her to that Catholic girl's school. She knew her mother's campaign made it absolutely necessary she stay out of trouble, but there was trouble and there was trouble. She wouldn't do drugs, but she wasn't going to give up boys, or dancing, or what other bits of fun she could carve out for herself.

By seven o'clock, Chrissie had reached her father at the country club and obtained his permission to spend the night at Annie Johnson's, her goody-good classmate from St. Joseph's Academy for Girls. Putting on the finishing touches, she zipped up her black leather mini skirt and tugged upward on the charcoal lace thigh highs she'd kept hidden under her dresser. Settling into the wicker chair in front of her makeup table, she examined herself in the mirror to consider what efforts she could make short of plastic surgery to get 'the look'. She decided she needed something more to make her seem older, so she frantically pulled up her hair, taking great care to leave a few wild tufts hanging in front of each ear. She then added a second layer of makeup. For a final coup de gras, she pulled a pair of lace gloves from the adjacent chest of drawers and squeezed into them. With the cleavage from the low cut black top, she thought the reflection in the mirror staring back at her looked pretty *and* sexy. Maybe tonight she'd meet a gorgeous guy who wasn't a total ass. One quick spray of *Passion*, and she was out the door until she remembered the forgotten and illegally procured fake i.d. she'd gotten through the well-connected Cindy. One u-turn and a lifted mattress later, and she was back on track headed clickety-clack down the poorly lit street toward her girlfriend's.

The drive to the avant-garde Zebra Club was an adventure in itself. The wild Cindy loved to push her 1980 candy apple red Porsche to its limits with her Blaupunkt blaring away. With the sports car's top off as usual, the winds whipping through the compartment made her short gelled hair look even wilder. Unfortunately for Chrissie, her hairstyle wasn't faring as well, and she could hardly wait to arrive so she could fix herself up in the cracked plastic mirror clipped to the passenger side visor.

"Cindy, pull over before we get to the valet so I can fix my hair," she begged.

Laughing, her insensitive friend made sure she drove the last block even faster before screeching to a halt in front of an annoyed parking attendant in a bow tie and black and white zebra-like vest.

"Hey, slow it... well, Cindy, I shoulda known it was you," the startled young man yelled. "Trying to kill me?"

"Nah, just tryin' to scare the crap outa ya. How ya been, handsome?" she replied.

Talking and flirting all the while, the good looking valet opened first Cindy's door then Chrissie's.

He wasn't very tall and his skin was scarred from acne, but he had a 'rad' haircut Chrissie thought, long on top and chopped short on the sides. He had mischievous green eyes like a cat's and an open and fun personality to match. She believed tonight was starting out pretty well.

After ten minutes in line, the two girls reached the doorman, a muscular hulk of about five feet ten inches in height garbed in a white tuxedo, accessorized with the same zebra-like vest that the parking attendant had on. Cindy introduced her to Jamahl as though he were her long lost brother. He was as black as the bow tie he wore with teeth as white as ivory, and he looked like a cover model for a bodybuilder magazine. Were it not for the breadth of his smile and his effusive charm, Chrissie would have been scared to death of him.

"Baby, howya been? Ain't seen you in a loooong time, not since, oh let's see... last night?" he teased.

"How's it goin' big, black, and beautiful?" she replied as she nuzzled a kiss onto the big man's cheek.

"It is perfection my Lucy Ricardo, perfection. Who's your accomplice here?"

"Jamahl, this is my friend Chrissie. Her mom's..."

The sharp pain from Chrissie's pointed shoe striking her ankle stopped her from revealing that which Chrissie preferred to keep to herself. Wincing, she backtracked.

"Her mom's a friend of my mom's. Chrissie this is Jamahl, the baddest bouncer this side of the Potomac."

The muscular man gently took her hand and lifted it to his lips, kissing it affectionately.

"Any friend of Cin's is a friend of mine. I take it you lady's have the legally required i.d.?"

Chrissie had used the newly acquired forgery only once at another bar, so she hadn't developed much confidence in its passability yet. Nervously, she pulled it from her small purse, handing it to the accommodating Jamahl.

Pretending he was scanning the two fake licenses, the wise bouncer smiled and returned them proclaiming everything to be in order. After sliding quickly through the turnstile, Cindy shared with Chrissie that she and Jamahl had dated a few times so he always let her and her friends in even though he really knew their i.d.'s were fake. Even here, it helped to have the right connections she thought sadly.

The Zebra Club was quite a place. It was cavernous and multi-leveled with a sound system that'd give you a migraine if you stayed too long. The lighting was dim, broken only by the flash of colored laser lights shooting across the room, some of which reflected off of a mirrored ball rotating on the ceiling. Mechanically produced fog covered the dance floor on the lowest level, adding an otherworldliness to the place. Tan hemp cargo nets and stenciled old crates hung from the ceiling as though it was a loading dock, and replicas of big game heads hung mounted on the grasscloth-covered walls. The shapely cocktail waitresses all wore the same zebra-like material, cut with jagged edges that made them look like Wilma Flintstone or Betty Rubble, and their dresses were just as short here as in Bedrock. The plastic bones clipped in their pulled up hair rounded out their native apparel.

Chrissie was drawn back to reality by the grating Bronx accent of their waitress as she asked for their drink orders. Cindy requested a shot of Cuervo

Gold, a salt shaker, and a wedge of lime. Chrissie's order was more subdued, a pina colada.

Scarcely an hour had passed when she felt the firm grip of a hand on her arm and heard the crass demand that accompanied it.

"C'mon bitch, let's boogie," a black-garbed punker commanded as he spun her around to face him. She was repulsed by the skinny slime ball and his antics, and he smelled of booze. He had dirty spiked green and yellow hair, more pierced parts than she could count, and the red and blue tattoo on his underdeveloped arm read "Rape & Ravage". This was not what she'd hoped for when the night began.

Jerking her arm loose, Chrissie took one step back and scowled at her yellow-toothed accoster.

"Get your damned hands off me and get lost," she screamed, pushing him away.

Joining in, the fiery redhead cursed him even more only to be knocked to the floor by the brute. Turning back to his original prey, he cornered the now frightened Chrissie, backing her into the wall and forcing himself on her. As she resisted, he groped roughly at her breasts, tearing her blouse open in the process. Losing her footing as she struggled, the battered girl dropped to the cold hard floor, tearing her hose. As she lay there looking up through the man-made fog, her eye caught a speck of light reflecting from the shiny metal of a switchblade as it shot from its housing in the thin man's right hand.

His threatening movement toward her was halted suddenly and violently, courtesy of a blazing right cross to his ugly jaw that came from somewhere to the left of the tabletop that blocked her view. She could feel the weight of his body crumpling next to hers as she struggled to rise. Moving the table aside, the owner of the fist offered it to her in outstretched form, lifting her from the floor as though her one hundred and thirty pounds were but a feather. A second later, the powerful Jamahl was there, lifting him into the air like a sack of potatoes and rushing him out the side exit like yesterday's trash. By then, the tough redhead had gotten up, dusted herself off, and joined them.

Their savior was as ruggedly handsome a man as Chrissie had ever met. He was older, maybe thirty or so, with wavy black hair cut in military fashion. His face was tan, his eyes deeply set, and his jaw jutted squarely forward. He wore a collarless white silk shirt unbuttoned half way down his well-developed chest, a new pair of denim jeans, and a $500 pair of eel skin boots. On his right arm was a tattoo of a winged dagger. He could have been the Marlboro man.

"Are you ladies alright?" the hunk asked, looking directly into her staring brown eyes.

"Thank you, you saved our lives! No telling what that creep woulda done," Cindy exclaimed as she signaled for another tequila.

Holding her arms across her chest to support her tattered blouse, Chrissie added her gratitude.

"I think so, thank you. Thank you. You were terrific, a real knight in shining armor! I'm Chrissie and this is Cindy..." she said shakenly as she reached out her free hand.

"I'm Kevin, Kevin Reilly," he said with a grin. "It was my pleasure."

"Well, we'll just call you 'Batman', Kevin. The way you swooped in to our rescue. Wouldn't happen to have Robin nearby, would ya?" Cindy joked as she belted down her tequila.

"Sorry, Red, I'm here by my lonesome," he answered without taking his eyes from Chrissie's.

"Say, you look like you got roughed up pretty good. Can I offer you a ride home or something?"

"I rode with Cindy..." she began, out of reflex.

"But since I'm stayin', she sure could use a ride home, Batman," the worldlier girl interrupted. "Got your Batmobile parked outside?"

Chuckling, Kevin, played along with the gag. "Nope, that one's in the shop. Tonight I've got the Batcycle, all supercharged and raring to go!"

"I can't go home like this, my Dad'll kill me," Chrissie suddenly realized aloud as she looked down at her scarcely covered chest.

"Tell you what," Kevin said, "I'll take you to my place first. I've got a few of my ex-wife's things still and she was about your size. We'll get you all fixed up as good as new!"

She should have known better than to say 'yes' to such a provocative offer, but it made her knees tremble just to look at him. As she climbed onto the sleek and powerful motorcycle and wrapped her arms around his muscular chest for safety, she pushed her conscience from her mind. Roaring into the chilly night she felt more like a woman than ever, and she swore that for the rest of this evening she would be all the woman she could be. By the time the Kawasaki was out of sight of the Zebra Club, Chrissie Canfield had unwittingly lost any hope of protecting herself from what was to come.

CHAPTER SEVEN

Morning came late and hazy for a dazed Chrissie Canfield. She could barely open her bloodshot eyes, and when she did everything was a blur, including her fragmented memories of the night before. Closing them, she tried to remember what had happened after she'd left the trendy nightclub. She could recall the exhilarating ride to Kevin's on the fleet Kawasaki, and entering his first floor apartment after the handsome stud pulled the key from beneath the welcome mat. The sweet taste of the rum and coke he politely offered her after they went in also seemed vivid to her. Everything after that was a blank. Chrissie did her best to struggle to a sitting position, but her body wasn't responding. She felt drugged, like the time she did too many downers back in L.A. during the difficult first year of her teens. The warm but false sense of well-being that possessed her was familiar.

Straining as hard as she could, she made it half way up to a sitting position, then slid helplessly back.

Despite her best efforts, she drifted back into unconsciousness, oblivious to the brilliance of the morning sun which bathed her face. When she again awoke, the effects of whatever drug Kevin Reilly had given her had all but worn off. Her senses slowly returning to her, she rolled over to look at the cheap plastic clock next to the bed. It read one twenty two; from the daylight filling the room, she knew it must be afternoon. Squinting through still unfocused eyes she was able to determine this much - she was lying in bed, alone, and she was buck naked except for the lace thigh highs that had fallen to her knees and a black lace glove still covering her left hand. She still couldn't remember what had happened, but her imagination was working overtime filling in the possibilities.

"Ohhhh, my head! What in the hell happened?" she muttered to herself. Her throat was dry, and the words seemed almost incomprehensible to her ears. "Kevin? Kevin, are you there?"

There was no reply. Wiping the tears from her eyes that were starting to appear, the confused and ashamed Chrissie found her clothes in a heap on the floor, grabbed them up, and stumbled to the master bathroom. Dressing as quickly as she could, she faced herself in the mirror and cringed at the reflection looking back. "God, I look like hell," she mumbled in disgust.

Wetting a washcloth to remove her heavy makeup, she began wiping her face. Gradually, she began to resemble the sixteen year old virgin she'd been before last night.

She knew she couldn't wear the torn blouse home, so she opened the closet to search through the few clothes Kevin had told her his ex-wife had left. Opening the door, she couldn't help but wonder if he'd been wed to Imelda Marcos.

"I don't believe this. The damn thing's full!"

The large closet was packed to the hilt, filled with what appeared to be a full woman's' wardrobe. Even more confused, she began to rummage through the dresser only to find more of the same, and an odd photo framed in gold and black on the dresser top. She didn't recognize the smiling young couple in the picture, but the man was definitely not the handsome Kevin Reilly.

Chrissie helped herself to a pair of oversized women's jeans and a t-shirt, in order to minimize the explaining she'd have to do to her father when she reached home. She knew she could always return the clothes later. As she left the bedroom and headed for the door she was surprised to find the apartment nicely decorated with a decided feminine touch. It didn't seem at all like the rugged Kevin. Scanning the room for some further clue, she noticed a batch of mail sitting on the kitchen counter top. Rifling through each piece in rapid succession, she discovered everyone was addressed to a 'John and Penelope Morton', the same names she found on the front doorbell as she left the flat.

Walking in search of a taxi, Chrissie Canfield finally put enough of the pieces together to realize she'd woken up drugged and naked in someone else's apartment, not even Kevin's. As she waved at the first lemon colored cab she saw, she knew in her heart that something horrible must have happened. She just didn't know what. All she did know as she snuck into the canary yellow house on Elm Glen was that she was lucky as hell that her father wasn't home and wouldn't require an explanation she didn't have.

* * * * * * * * * *

It was nearing Halloween and the long anticipated election by the time Mark Canfield learned that his visa application had been killed by State Department intervention because of his wife's potential rise to the top of the government. He'd kept the trip from his spouse, knowing she'd disapprove and might even further complicate the situation. Kathy certainly wasn't going to use her connections to help send him to the battlefields of Bosnia. If he was going to get there, he'd have to come up with something on his own. Rather, he'd have to find somebody on his own who could help him beat the system.   It didn't take the determined doctor long to remember the most resourceful devil he'd ever known. Steve Svensen had been a miracle worker in med school. The smooth talking Swede had even gotten them into the Berkeley lab one evening so they could use one of the school's cadavers for a little extra studying before finals. Svensen was a bright rogue who played by his own rules and as far as Mark knew he'd never had one of his schemes blow up in his face. Mark had lost track of the witty blonde sawbones some years ago, but a few well-placed phone calls to fellow classmates produced a listing in Monterey. He wasn't at all surprised to find out that the old rascal was now a gynecologist.

It was about three in the afternoon California time when the call went through to Svensen's bay front condo. Svensen answered the phone himself, and in a few minutes he and Mark Canfield were making up for lost time like a couple of grad students.

"Sonofagun, Swede, the Medical Board actually allows you to practice your witchcraft on a bunch of helpless, naked women?" he asked.

"I lied about my character, what can I say? Plus they gave me extra credit on the exam for my extracurricular research on the subject, if you know what I mean," Svensen kidded.

Ten minutes of reliving the past and catching each other up on their lives went by quickly before the Georgetown plastic surgeon got to his point.

"Listen Steve, you used to be a pretty resourceful guy. Remember when you put together that fake driver's license for your sister so she could go bar hopping with us? You still have the artistic touch, old friend?"

"Oh, I might be a bit rusty, but I reckon I do. Guess it depends on whatcha got in mind."

Mark explained his predicament in detail to his old classmate and was pleased to get the answer he'd hoped for.

"Mark, send me a new passport photo and your current passport and let me see what I can do. I can't give you any guarantees, you know. It's been a while, but if I've still got the touch, I'll have it back to you in a week or so."

"Thanks Swede. I really appreciate it. It's real important to me," Mark said gratefully.

"Hey, it's your life. If you want to kill your fool self playing Florence Nightingale in Bosnia, it's your right. Just don't tell anybody I aided and abetted your stupidity!"

The click on the other end told him the conversation was over. Clearing his line, he immediately punched in the number Jerry had given him for his home. A few seconds later, the Pee Wee Herman lookalike was on the phone.

"Jerry, this is Mark Canfield. I'm in for January's trip. Should have my visa by the end of the month. Yeah, it'll be a great experience. I'm looking forward to it!"

Placing the receiver down, the usually placid Mark let out a sharp whoop as though he'd just hit a

World Series homerun. He was going to Sarajevo in spite of the obstacles. All this skullduggery was starting to make him feel pretty darned good about himself. Three hours later as he stuffed the fresh passport photo into the thick padded envelope and licked it, he thought the tangy taste of the envelope's glue tasted good. It tasted like adventure.

* * * * * * * * * *

The day before the November 4th election, an exhausted Kathy Canfield finally made her way home, spent and frustrated. The chill from the White House hadn't thawed much despite her tough stance with Mathers. Perhaps if she would have performed poorly in her debate with Farmer and hadn't jump-started the public and media frenzy again, things might have improved she thought. Well, she wasn't going to apologize for the never ending days of preparation, or for being photogenic, or for just generally kicking her opponent's butt in the debate. If the ticket carried the election tomorrow, it would be because of her contributions as much as Burlington's. She had to give the devil his due, though. The sixty-five year old Texan had put in some ungodly hours on the campaign trail, losing his voice twice and once being hospitalized for exhaustion. That had occurred only last week, and she was genuinely concerned for his health even though she didn't care for him personally. But he was a human being and a hard worker, and she'd been taught to respect those that knew how to keep their noses to the grindstone.

Coming home was even more pleasant because of Mark's surprising and unusually romantic efforts. Marva had dropped Kathy off in her driveway at about ten p.m. after picking her up at Dulles. All of the hoop-la and fanfare of the campaign was now behind her. There was no parade, no bodyguards, and thank God no reporters or photographers. Just the amber porch light beckoning to her like a lighthouse to a searching ship in a dense fog. Well, there *was* the homemade sign tacked to the garage door that read "Vice President Canfield Slept Here". And there *was* the red rose wrapped in a matching ribbon left in the protective rail of the front screen door. And there was Mark, waiting inside with open arms and a bottle of Dom Perignon, complemented by a crystal dish filled to the brim with chocolate covered strawberries.

"Welcome home, gorgeous. Care for a little post campaign orgy?" he said lovingly.

He was wearing nothing but a bathrobe and, as she would later discover, a pair of sexy tiger patterned briefs bearing a small red, white, and blue sticker that read "I Voted!" Underneath those words, he'd handwritten in "twice".

"Well, this is a pleasant surprise! Have I died and gone to heaven?" she asked.

"Nope. You're just home. The way it should be," he said as he pulled her into his embrace and kissed her longingly.

She wasn't sure what had gotten into him, but it really didn't matter. The effort and the love did. After all, it'd been some time since she'd seen him in more than passing, and longer still since he'd shown so much affection.

Mark didn't know exactly why himself. Perhaps it was the long separation, or maybe it was the growing respect and pride he'd developed for her during the campaign. Or maybe it was just how beautiful she'd looked on TV. when he and Casper had cuddled up on the lonely couch to watch the evening news each night. He really didn't know why, but something had rekindled the passions he hadn't felt in a long while, and he was just thrilled to be back.

When she dozed off in his lap on the antique beige couch where they'd made love, he gently carried her to bed. She looked tired but peacefully beautiful in the moonlight that shone through the lace bedroom curtains. His visa coup had left him in a better mood than he'd been in in a long time, and this evening he'd rediscovered the pretty brunette that had stolen his heart all those years ago. Climbing into bed next to her, he fell asleep with his wife safely wrapped in his arms. It was one of those nights that seemed as if time had stopped.

But it hadn't. The moonlight that'd bathed the bedroom in magic during the night, gave way to the morning sun. When Mark awoke, Kathy was already dressed and preparing to head out for the slow final day of the campaign.

"Morning, sleepy head! Didn't you get any shuteye while I was gone, or did you just wear yourself out last night?" she asked as she gave Mark a kiss, the morning paper and a glass of freshly squeezed orange juice.

"The latter, of course," he replied smiling with his eyes, as much as with his lips. "I really missed you, Kath. It's good to have you home."

"I love you too, Mark," she replied. "I know last night deserves more of a thank you than that, but I'm late. See you tonight for the party?"

"Of course...victory party you mean, right? Black tie, dancing, moonlight..."

"Shoes that're too tight, annoying reporters, bright camera lights. You know, that kind of party."

"Oh yeah. Must've been confusing us with a couple that has a real life. Sorry," he said ruefully.

With that, she left him alone to go about her day's commitments. It would be over soon, and regardless of the outcome, life would become manageable again. She hadn't had the time to read the Post before she left, otherwise she would have seen the headline blaring that the presidential race was considered the closest in thirty-five years. Mark shook the paper in half to read the rest of the article. It read that if the election went to the Republicans, it would be because of the woman who'd just made his orange juice.

"That's my girl," he said proudly to himself.

It felt as unreal and strange as seeing his wife on the tube in some old rerun. It had always seemed as though she'd had an evil twin that led this other life that was distant and glamorous, not at all like the relatively normal one they'd shared together. But then 'normal' *was* truly relative, wasn't it?

* * * * * * * * * *

By ten, Kathy had made it to the secure surroundings of her office. At noon she was scheduled to address a press covered ladies' auxiliary luncheon and then spend some time shaking voters' hands outside of a nearby polling place. She'd be home by six to change and pick up Mark. The limo would arrive at seven to take them to the Biltmore Hotel and the President for what they hoped would be a victory party. It would be the first time she'd see Burlington since San Diego, and the first time she'd speak to him since his forced ten second congratulatory call following her debate with Farmer. She was convinced Andy Mathers had put him up to making even that one solitary phone call.

Kathy was scanning the accumulated paper on her desk when Marva strolled into the inner office to rejoin her.

"Counting the hours, I bet," the aide said to her.

"And the minutes. You know, Marva, I've been so busy that I completely forgot to ask you about the child care bill. How's your arm twisting going?"

"There's a memo somewhere in this stack," she replied, thumbing unsuccessfully through the mountain of paper. "Anyway, you'll be pleased to know it passed the full Senate while you were in Wyoming. It's over in the House. The Speaker's assigned it to Congressman Jackson's sub-committee."

Workhorse that she was, the dedicated aide had burned the midnight oil in her boss's absence to try and keep the bill moving over Stewart Farley's opposition. Marva'd learned a few tricks over the years and had a pretty good reputation for getting things done amongst the capitol's staffers. Nevertheless, she was no match for the power of the speakership, especially when it was in the hands of the devil himself. Farley had buried the bill, and Kathy knew it the minute Marva told her who had a hold of it.

"Not as in Bart T.?" she asked Marva with a glint of despair in her voice.

"Afraid so. Old 'Bama Bart himself. I tried to talk his A.A. into sending it somewhere else, but he told me off the record that Farley's taken a personal interest in this one."

Congressman Bartholomew T. Jackson, 'Bart T.' to his constituents. He was known to be one of Farley's more loyal minions. In truth, the crotchety octogenarian from Alabama was less a Farley ally than a stooge. Talk on the hill was that the ruthless Ohioan had something on the dean of the House, something that was damning enough that when Farley said jump, he leapt like the senior citizen's Michael Jordan.

"Well, we know what that means," Kathy observed with disappointment.

"I've already talked to all the sub-committee members on your behalf. I lined up as many votes as I could. I mean, I called in fifteen years' worth of IOU's, I even cornered Congresswoman Younger in the women's head."

"Aggressive! How close are we? Or do I owe her an apology?" Kathy asked.

"Nope, and we're only one away. The opposition party members are on board and so's Congressman Patrick. The Democrats want to shove it down Farley's throat, and Patrick's wife threatened to leave him if he doesn't support it!"

"Who are you targeting?" Kathy queried.

"My secret. For today, at least. I think I can tie it up tonight. Anyway, I'll know by the party."

* * * * * * * * * *

Marva knew how important the bill was to Kathy and she'd die before she let her down. Still, she was one vote short of getting it out to the full Business and Commerce Committee. One lousy vote. She was banking on a positive result in today's election giving her the juice she needed to swing one more. After all, tomorrow she could be the chief aide to the Vice President of the United States - the presiding officer of the Senate and the person who would be a heartbeat from the presidency. She knew which member of the sub-committee she'd have to swing, and she'd already programmed the cellular number of the Congressman's chief aide into her hand held phone. As soon as the networks projected a winner, if it was Burlington-

Canfield, she'd be on him like lightning. She was sure she could tie down that vote before the day's end.

Time went quickly. At six o'clock eastern standard time, the network analysts were still projecting it too close to call. As Kathy, Mark, and an oddly subdued Chrissie frantically dressed for the party, Marva was already making her way to the Biltmore. She'd gotten a tip that the aide she'd targeted for the arm twist needed a ride, so she'd gotten him on the phone and offered one to him. Actually, she didn't really give him a choice. She'd left the office early, gotten gussied up as quickly as possible, and picked him up in front of his condo. As they crawled through the Washington traffic, she gave it all she had. It began innocently enough.

"Mel, have you had a chance to go over my boss's child care bill yet?" she'd asked him.

By the time they'd arrived, he'd have pledged his wife, his kids, his next born if need be to get her off his back. He seemed almost relieved to learn all she wanted was his promise to put the full court press on his boss at the evening's gathering. And to get back to her before the night was over. She'd had no doubts that he would.

* * * * * * * * * *

Back at the Canfield household, Mark had been planting the first seeds for his Bosnia trip. While dressing, he'd told Kathy he was going to a medical convention in Rome and would be staying for two weeks to tour Italian hospitals. In fact, his flight from Washington on Alitalia would actually land in Rome first before the relief group would be switching planes for the short leg to Trieste. They'd be met there by a Red Cross representative and would travel with him to

Zagreb, Croatia where they'd join a U.N. chaperoned convoy to Sarajevo. Assuming the embattled city was accessible, that is.

But that was two months away. Tonight was the big one, and as ambivalent as Mark had been about his wife's candidacy, the excitement of the moment was compelling. So too was his devotion to her. He was surprised how much he wanted her to win, mostly because she'd worked so hard for it and deserved it. But partly because his competitive juices were flowing now too.

The months of stress and loneliness were over. Tonight there'd be no personal or political attacks on Kathy or the family, it'd be a night of celebration. And his gut was telling him she was going to do it. He wasn't a particularly intuitive guy, but he felt it. Hell, no matter what happened, even if he was wrong, he'd have something to celebrate. He'd either be sleeping with the Vice President of the United States, or at least their lives would be normal again.

The long white limousine that Malcolm had sent pulled up to the Canfield house at precisely seven o'clock. It was their daughter who noticed it first.

"Mother, it's here," Chrissie yelled.

"Tell him we're on our way," Mark hollered back from the top of the wooden bannister.

Before the tuxedoed driver could get the door for them, Chrissie'd reached it first, playing doorman for her parents. She looked like she was going to her first prom in the pretty royal blue satin dress she and her father had picked out the week before. Her long silky brown hair was worn down and her makeup was lightly applied. Tonight she looked like a pretty teenager out for a good clean time with her family. She even showed signs of coming out of the funk she'd been in since the ugly night with Kevin Reilly. On the way to the hotel she playfully hummed 'Hail to the Chief', or at least it sort of sounded like it.

"I wonder how it would sound as a rap song?" she dreamed aloud.

"Don't get ahead of yourself, little girl. Your mother's running for Vice President, not President. And they don't have a song for that," Mark told her.

"Will we be moving to the White House if you win?" she asked her mother pointedly.

After a pause for reflection, Kathy looked at Mark and then at her inquisitive daughter. She answered laughingly, "You know, I never even asked that question myself with everything that was going on. I honestly don't have a clue, not a clue!"

The family laughed together in a way they hadn't in a long, long time. Kathy looked absolutely radiant tonight and the laughter made her even more stunning and alive. She was wearing a bright green cocktail dress that brought out the color in her eyes. She'd made the feminine decision to shun the politically correct suits, blouses and bows that Malcolm and Tex had kept her in. They made her look like a librarian. The dress she wore this evening left just a hint of cleavage uncovered, a not so subtle reminder to the world of her potential status as the first woman Vice President of the United States. As the lights along the highway passed teasingly across Kathy's face, Mark decided he liked the shorter hair style she'd picked up somewhere in the sweltering west during the campaign. It made her eyes stand out like emeralds in the night.

* * * * * * * * * *

As the limo pulled into the crowded circular drive of the Biltmore and assumed its position in line, Kathy pondered the time ahead.

"You know, Mark, I don't want to jinx this thing, but I feel like we've won it. It's funny, I feel this peace, this certainty. This bizarre sense of destiny."

He'd felt it too, this sense of being swept up in a powerful riptide, of divine intervention.

"I know, Kath. I can't explain it either, but I know what you're saying," he confided as he turned up the sound on the limo's small T.V. set.

CBS's Dan Rather was delivering the network's long awaited projection. "I've just been told that we have a winner projected in the race for the White House. It is now eight o'clock eastern standard time and voting booths have closed here on the east coast. Exit polls conducted for CBS have shown a late surge by the Republican ticket that insiders are crediting to the spiraling popularity of President Burlington's history breaking running mate, Senator Kathleen Canfield. CBS is now projecting that the President will be re-elected by a margin of five percent, making Mrs. Canfield the first woman in history to be elected by her countrymen - and women - to the second highest office in the land."

Inside and outside the limo pandemonium was breaking out. The Canfields burst into the same whoops and hollers that could be heard all over the outside of the hotel.

"You did it, baby, you did it," Mark screamed as he euphorically hugged his wife.

"Yes! Mother! I can still call you that, can't I?" Chrissie teased.

Their turn in line came a moment later. As they pulled to the front of the hotel, the limo's door was opened by a hulking man with a short haircut, and a conservative dark blue suit. Behind him were several more men that looked like they'd been cut from the same mold. The earpieces and the lapel pins made it clear they were with the United States Secret Service.

With only a faint smile, the one that opened the door politely introduced himself. "Madame Vice President, I'm Jack Cutter with the Secret Service. I'll be heading up your security detail," he said stoically. "If you and your family would follow us inside quickly, please."

And with that, it began. The Secret Service men surrounded the Canfields like a shield, sweeping them into the Biltmore through a barrage of lights sticking out of every type of camera imaginable.

"Geez, this is worse than the Academy Awards," Bill exclaimed to Kathy as they were guided towards the ballroom.

They'd gone to the Hollywood ceremony once, after her election to the Senate had generated a surprise invitation, but even that didn't seem this crazy. People were everywhere, screaming and yelling her name. "Kathy! Kathy," they screeched as though one name was sufficient, like Cher, or Prince.

There was passion in their voices, an almost desperate fervor as though she'd somehow freed them from their limitations, or from their problems by breaking the historic barrier. The air was filled with an indescribable enchantment as they were whisked through the picturesque hallways of the Biltmore to the grand ballroom and all its grandeur. The sparkling crystal chandeliers hanging from the carved ceiling were spectacular, as was the lighting which brought the patriotic wonderland and its red, white, and blue bunting to life.

Kathy had to scream into Mark's ear to be heard over the tumult. "This is amazing! When I was campaigning, I could tell people saw me as something special, but I never dreamed I'd get this kind of reception!

"No kidding! Now I know how Jackie Kennedy felt," Mark answered back, not at all sure she could hear him.

Michael Burlington was entering from the back of the room and working his way toward the stage as the Canfields passed through the entryway. The roar of the crowd was now thunderous as the two approached the steps of the platform from opposite directions to face each other for the first time in months. As their eyes met and they came together, there was a moment of awkward, frozen silence. Then the President smiled that toothy grin he used for public consumption and reached out to grab her hand.

"Congratulations, missy! It looks like we done tanned their hides," he crowed.

The look in his gray eyes was as cold as the feel of his palm. A bit like petting a shark, she thought. As she retrieved her hand and moved toward the rear of the stage, she heard Mark whisper in her ear as he moved beside her.

"Better count your fingers," he said. "If they're all there, check your jewelry."

Her acknowledgement was silent as they stepped back to the approval of the elated throng. The stage was full with the President's family, the Canfields, Lord knows how many Secret Service men, and a few other players including Bobby Joe Richards and the polished Ivy Leaguer, Andy Mathers. The short Texan made his way towards them, wiggling his way through the crowd on the platform.

"Madame Vice President and Dr. Canfield, how are y'all or do ah need to ask," he said excitedly as he shook their hands. "Congratulations!"

"It's good to see you Bobby. Mark, this is Bobby Joe Richards. He and Malcolm Tolliver headed up my part of the campaign. Bobby, is Malcolm here?" the new Vice President asked loudly.

"Nice ta finally meet ya, doctor," Bobby Joe said to Mark, shaking his hand. "He's around here somewhere. Listen, Andy asked me ta catch ya. The President's gonna make his acceptance speech and he'd like ya and your family ta stand behind him. When he's done, he'll introduce ya and raise hands with ya. He'd appreciate it though if ya ended it there. Ya know, didn't make a speech or anything."

Mark's face reddened at the chafing sound of the words and before he or anyone else knew what he was doing, his hands were firmly planted on the lapels of the smaller man's pin stripe suit coat. Not even the Secret Service men reacted quickly enough to protect Richards. When Mark addressed him, he had him on the toes of his wingtips.

"Bull! The only reason that pompous sonofabitch is standing here at all is because of this woman right here, you pint-sized little shit."

Kathy's firm hand on his wrist broke his grip as a Secret Service agent stepped towards them. Mark let go of the shaken consultant, but the fiery look in his eyes made it clear that his anger hadn't subsided.

"Hey, ah just work here, friend. Just a middleman! Ah'm sorry, ah truly am. Ah understand your feelings, really I do," Bobby Joe tried to explain as he stepped away toward safety.

Putting her hand on his shoulder, Kathy assured him she understood. "I'm sorry, Bobby Joe. I know it isn't you. We're all just a little fed up with this 'back of the bus' routine he's been putting me through."

But she didn't agree to honor Burlington's request. She wasn't sure herself whether she would or not. She'd just have to find out when the moment came and the spirit either moved her or it didn't.

Bobby Joe left them and Kathy kissed Mark lightly on the cheek in appreciation for his protective stand. She stood tall and erect as Michael Burlington approached the podium, waving to the crowd with both hands, and asking them to "simmer down".

"Ah have just been informed that the voters of this great nation have sent us a message courtesy of Mr. Rather. That message is..." he paused for effect, "four more years!"

The partisan crowd erupted back into a frenzy until he waved them down again. "Well, ah have a message for Governor Provelone and his associates in the Democratic Party, ma friends. Ah say to them...the eyes of Texas are upon ya!"

They went crazy again, and as they did, he went on to claim victory as if he were David and he'd just laid Goliath out single handedly - using a slingshot he'd made himself, and a stone he'd chipped from a boulder with a butter knife. He was an arrogant bastard, no matter how you sliced it, or what you sliced it with. It made it impossible to feel sorry for him even though he looked peaked from his hospital stay, and sounded short of his usually powerful bombastic delivery. The big man went on for another fifteen minutes, basking in the limelight.

"This jerk's got no shame, none at all," Mark whispered to Kathy. "I'm starting to regret not voting for the other guy."

Finally, Burlington wound up his speech with an obligatory mention of his running mate and stepped back from the podium to raise her hand in his. As far as Mark was concerned, this was the hand of the woman the Texan owed it all to, the woman he'd slighted for months and intended to put down again here and now, in her finest hour. Taking her thin hand in his, the President thrust their joined arms into the air to the delight of the crowd. As the photo op passed and their hands dropped, the spirit moved her.

Stepping toward the void Burlington left when he stepped from the microphone, Kathleen Canfield juked around the presidential carcass and up to the oak podium, taking the microphone in her hands. The lights and the eyes of America and the world focused on her. She had earned it and no one, President or not, was going to spoil it for her.

The roar in the ballroom doubled as those seated rose to a standing ovation and colored balloons filled the air. Pulling the microphone down to her full lips, she began to speak with an ease and authority that captivated the millions watching across America.

"Thank you, thank you," she began, waiting for the crowd to quiet. When they did, she continued.

"When I was a little girl growing up on a small farm in the Midwest, my father used to tell me that this was the country of opportunity. The country where any boy or girl, regardless of color or wealth, could someday rise up to become President of the United States. Well, my fellow Americans, today this country took a monumental step towards that ideal. Today we've moved a nation closer to where it should be, closer to a dream generations of Americans have fought for. We have risen, risen above, through hard work and a commitment to freedom from oppression by government or our own prejudices. But I stand before you today not as a woman Vice President, but as a Vice President who happens to be a woman. When that philosophy becomes second nature to us, then we will truly have won and secured our place in the history of the world! Thank you for your faith and support! God bless you all."

The room erupted again, and this time it went on for ten minutes straight. A reverberating chant of "Canfield, Canfield" began in one corner of the ballroom and moved slowly from left to right like 'the wave' at a packed ballpark. Only later would she learn that the maverick section where it all started was where the missing Malcolm Tolliver was seated.

* * * * * * * * * *

From a distance, Burlington's feelings weren't discernible, but up close you could feel the heat coming from the simmering Texan. The toothy grin was there for the press, but if he'd forced his teeth together any more tightly they would have shattered. Mark Canfield was smiling so broadly, his face was starting to cramp. He finally had to force the sides of his mouth downward just to relieve the pain. It made a great spectacle for his daughter, who was having a ball with the exciting evening. It was the moment of a lifetime for them all. It was also a great moment of hope and optimism for America. Kathleen Canfield no longer belonged to just them, but to a nation hungry for leadership.

As the celebration wound down about two o'clock that morning, the family eventually made its way back to the limo for the ride home. This time there was a Secret Service car in front and one in back, and the white rental limo had been replaced with a shiny black one with armor plating and bulletproof glass. Somehow, Marva had gotten the agents to tape a note onto the screen of the small television informing Kathy that she'd tied down the final vote to get the child care bill out of sub-committee. Next to it was a telegram of congratulations from young Bill that the aide had also gotten to them through the cooperative

119

agents. It'd been a long time since the world had felt this perfect to any of the Canfield family, but it'd been worth the wait.

A full moon watched over them as they rode home. A weary but happy Mark and Kathy Canfield celebrated in each other's arms, as Chrissie fell asleep on the long seat facing them. They talked excitedly about the political Disneyland they'd fallen into, and about their love for each other. As the limo made its way to the home they'd soon be leaving for loftier quarters, they both knew they'd rediscovered each other and success all at the same time. The world was indeed theirs for the taking.

CHAPTER EIGHT

The ensuing winter in Washington was particularly cruel and bitter. The record setting temperatures had forced a shortening of the inauguration ceremony, giving the miffed President the perfect excuse to keep his new Vice President out of the event. The icy cold seemed appropriately symbolic to the isolated Kathleen Canfield. So she did what she'd always done. She made the best of the situation.

January was spent moving the family into the Vice President's mansion on the grounds of the Naval Observatory, overseeing the redecorating, and setting up her office in a wing of the White House. Her necessary preoccupation with these mundane chores kept her busy from morning until night and, to Burlington's delight, out of the public eye. Mark joined in with what free time he had and seemed to be enjoying himself. He even briefly considered canceling his covert trip to Bosnia until a condescending Secret Service man mistook him for a mover rather than the Vice President's husband. He laughed it off at the time, but he dismissed the thought of canceling the planned trip.

By the end of the month, Kathy was settled in and Mark's bags were packed. 'Matt Fielder', as his fake passport read, was ready for his humanitarian adventure. If he found redemption of his manhood in the process, then so be it. That would be all the better.

On the Thursday morning of his flight, his thoughtful wife drove him to Dulles Airport. To be more accurate, her driver drove and she and a contingent of Secret Service agents accompanied him in the government limousine now assigned to her. As far as the group knew, Mark was flying to Rome for a medical convention on new techniques in plastic surgery and an extended tour of Italian facilities. No one was the wiser as he kissed Kathy politely on the cheek and said goodbye.

"Kath, I'm gonna miss you. I wish all these damn photographers weren't hanging around so I could say goodbye properly."

"It's ok, hon," she said. "It's only two weeks and I'm so buried right now, it'll go by in the blink of an eye. You take good care of yourself and don't worry about us. Chrissie and I'll be fine. I love you."

"I love you, too," he said quietly.

With that she hugged him and threw caution and political correctness to the wind. It was a good kiss, Mark thought, one that would get him through the next fourteen days. The whoops and howls of the crowd in the airport caused them to blush, but it was worth it to them both.

Boarding the Italian airliner, he settled into a cozy window seat on the new green and red Boeing 767, joining Jerry and the other already boarded volunteers for the long flight to Europe. He was feeling proud and even a little bit naughty over his deception. He had sworn Jerry to secrecy and he had readily agreed. The skinny anesthesiologist seemed to be having fun with his new highly placed friend over it.

"Matt, buddy! Matt Fielder, how have you been? How's the wife doing? How about your brother Cecil?"

"Knock it off Jerry. It could really hit the fan if this got out," Mark said quietly but sternly. He wasn't at all sure that he could put up with the annoying man for the duration of the flight, let alone two weeks.

"Sorry, man, just kidding. It's kind of neat really, sort of cloak and dagger."

"I know, but I need your help to make it work, alright? Make like Cosby to my Culp, will you?"

Jerry scrunched up his nose over Mark's choice of spies. "Sorry, pal, don't do Jello. How about Felix Leiter to your James Bond?"

"Works for me," Mark replied without really listening.

He fell asleep easily despite the annoyance of Jerry's monotone chatter with the elderly Italian woman sitting in front of them. It would be the only good sleep he would get for some time to come.

* * * * * * * * * *

Kathy and Marva had built quite a network for gathering information during the long campaign in order to overcome the lack of cooperation from the President and his staff. Expanding and refining it became their focused priority as the slow frozen days of winter rolled into February. Those that signed on silently to the Vice President's clandestine organization became known informally around the office as 'The Canfield Underground'. They were as cautious as if they were with the CIA, as in fact some of them were. Her popularity and Burlington's lack of it, combined with the general knowledge around the capitol of the President's abusive treatment of his Vice President, served as excellent recruiting tools. In short order, the two women had closed the information void that Burlington had created with only a few bases uncovered. There were their contacts in the State Department, the Pentagon, the National Security Agency, the CIA, the FBI and so forth. In certain cases, the underground members came from high up, such as J. Thomas Gower, the longtime head of the FBI. The sartorial trend setter always had been a rather independent sort and had maintained that posture and his job through three administrations. Most people looked on him as the heterosexual GQ version of the second coming of old J. Edgar himself. Even his shortening of his first name after assuming the position served as a reminder of the bureau's glory days. Kathy had known him for years and had been forced to rebuff the lady killer's advances on more than one occasion. She had personally sought his help after the election and he had gladly offered it. Not only did Gower want to ingratiate himself with the beautiful Vice President, but he thought the crude Burlington an unrefined pig unworthy of the office. Besides, he loved to exercise his power and there was no more challenging opponent than the man at the top.

It was becoming more apparent daily that the job of Vice President came with virtually no job description. Her frosty relations with the Oval Office ensured that whatever assignments were sent her way were ponderous and low level, or ceremonial fluff. She could wait a thousand years before being called upon to cast a tie-breaking vote in the Senate, so it boiled down to her deciding what course to chart for herself. But first there was unfinished business. Stewart Farley had successfully bottled her child care bill up in the Business and Commerce Committee. Under the guidance of its new author of record and Kathy's old friend and Senate colleague, Michigan's Senator Constance McBride, the bill had picked up steam before the vengeful speaker had squeezed the right body parts of just enough good Members of Congress to have it tabled. Parrying this latest move would be difficult, even with every weapon at her disposal, she knew. She simply didn't have the right maneuver figured out yet, but she knew it would come to her. It had to. Perhaps the devious and all-knowing J. Thomas would have some creative suggestions.

* * * * * * * * * *

It was nearing dusk in Washington when Marva Franks finally got to the 'in' box on her immense new walnut executive desk. The mysterious manila envelope that had been secreted amongst the evening's inter-office mail stood out like a sore thumb to the ever observant woman. There were no stamps, no markings to denote who had sent the large envelope, only the Vice President's name and a notation of 'personal and confidential'. Concerned with the remote possibility that it could be a letter bomb, she shook it gingerly, then trimmed off a corner with a sharp new pair of scissors she'd just requisitioned, so she could peek inside. Her sigh of relief was audible when she saw only a handwritten note and some photographs within its dark confines. Feeling that she'd gone as far as she could in good conscience considering the confidential intentions of the sender, she delivered it promptly with the rest of Kathy's mail to her even larger desk. As she entered the office, she noticed the cuckoo clock had been hung in exactly the same relative spot as it had been in the Canfield Senate office. It felt like home, she thought, as she placed the stack of papers in the gold-plated top box on her boss's desktop. Kathy was leaning back in the plush navy blue leather chair reading a set of surreptitiously obtained briefing papers on satellite observations of troop movements in Bosnia. The gold rimmed glasses sat in their usual position midway down the bridge of her slightly turned up nose. She barely noticed the new additions to the mounting piles of paper in front of her.

Without lifting her eyes, she spoke to Marva with the weight of her new responsibilities ringing in her voice. "Mar, the CIA seems to think that movements on the ground in Bosnia are sure indications the Serbs are mounting another push at Sarajevo. This must be why Burlington's increasing military commitments over there."

"Isn't Bill in the Adriatic as part of it?" the aide asked.

The question hit a soft spot. "Yes, he is," Kathy replied. "I'm sure he's very good at what he does, but I'd feel a heck of a lot better if he was doing it somewhere else!"

"Well, maybe our troops being sent will scare 'em off and we won't have to use force," Marva reasoned.

Young Bill was smack dab in the middle of what could easily become the most volatile war since World War II, and Kathy was worried. During her days in the Senate, she'd supported U.S. participation in the U.N. peacekeeping force but this was different. Burlington was looking at offensive strikes from U.S. carriers to fend off the impending advance, to break the backs of the Bosnian Serbs, forcing them to the negotiating table with a more cooperative attitude. And the Russians were talking tough about counterbalancing the effort. If things got out of hand, Vietnam would look like a walk in the sun, and she knew there wasn't much she could do about it from her current vantage point. Twirling to return to her office, Marva remembered the mysterious envelope that had grabbed her attention and curiosity only moments before. The day would end a bit better, she thought, with one less mystery hanging over her head.

"Oh, by the way, there was a rather funny looking envelope in the inter-office mail addressed to you. It was marked confidential, but it didn't have the usual routing info," she informed Kathy. "I hope you don't mind, but I clipped the corner just to make sure it wasn't explosive or anything."

Kathy's maternal instincts extended to those she was responsible for outside her family as well as within. "For God's sake, Marva. You're no bomb expert! Why do you think there's a Secret Service agent stationed outside at all times? Leave that sort of thing to them!"

Her tail had been properly tucked between her legs by the boss and she knew it, but that didn't keep it from hurting. She should have known better.

"You're right, you're right, I'm sorry. Won't happen again. It's on top of your 'in' box, though, if you're interested," Marva said apologetically.

Her self-deprecating remorse tickled the tired politician, as did her persistence. It was clear Marva wasn't going home until her nagging curiosity had been satisfied.

"Really has you intrigued, eh? Well, knowing you I might as well go ahead and open it or the next thing it'll be another corner and another..."

Setting her reading material aside, Kathy stretched forward across the expanse of desktop that separated her from her manila target. Retrieving it, she slipped her fingers into the missing corner and slit the envelope open from side to side, then held it upside down, emptying it in front of her.

She regretted that choice the instant the glossy color photographs hit the desk's green leather writing pad in full view of her thorough and observant aide. Some things weren't meant to be shared, and it was clear the lurid pictures staring back at her fit into that category. She didn't recognize the other men and women in the photos, in fact their faces were conveniently hidden from the camera, but she couldn't help but identify her naked daughter whose face was all too clearly displayed in every photo. Along with the rest of her body. She couldn't make out which limbs belonged to which deviant amongst the contorted display of hedonism, but she could tell that the all too visible leather and lace painted an uglier scenario than she could have imagined in her worst nightmare.

"Oh, my God," was all she could mutter weakly as she quickly pulled the pictures from Marva's line of sight and shoved them back into the plain brown wrapper they came in. "I can't believe it."

"What do they want?" Marva stammered in shock.

"What do you mean, I, I..."

"It's got to be blackmail of some kind. There was a note with the pictures, what does it say?" Marva asked.

She was as mortified as the distraught mother before her and she was embarrassed, humiliated for the both of them. Stepping behind the desk she placed a reassuring hand on Kathy's shoulder. It was all she could think to do.

Kathy reached back into the envelope and retrieved a small slip of paper. In red lipstick was one word, in capital letters followed by an exclamation point. The six characters of the alphabet hit her as if they'd been a six shooter. 'RESIGN!' it said. Nothing more.

"My God, I'm so sorry Kathy. So sorry." It was the first time she'd ever referred to her by her given name, yet it was the only way to address her at this moment.

"Marva, would you please have the car brought up? I need to talk to my daughter before we do anything. I know I can count on you to keep this between us," she said, knowing full well she could trust the unflinchingly loyal Marva with her life, if need be.

* * * * * * * * * *

The ride home was as painful as the one she'd taken three years ago behind the curtained hearse that carried her mother to her final resting place at Forrest Lawn. This felt *like* death, cold and empty, powerful and omnipotent. Impossible to overcome or to change. Kathy was absolutely numb, too numb to rationally deal with her daughter. Too numb to even think clearly. If only Mark were here, he'd know what to do. If only...

As the limo pulled to the front of the secured mansion she now called home, she answered that question for herself. If only Mark were home, he'd... scream, yell, and go looking for his gun like any other red-blooded father. After further thought, she realized it might be best this way. Perhaps she could handle this and he would never have to know.

Kathy did her best to appear normal as she stepped out of the car and walked past the posted guards to the heavy front door of the residence. It took her acting training to get it done, but with the aid of the inky darkness, she did. Once the door was safely closed behind her, the act ended and her facade gave way to her anger and worry. The government servants had all gone home and Chrissie was nowhere to be seen. There was no shoulder to cry on, no solace to seek other than the purr and nudge of the blue eyed Casper who'd answered her cry. Clutching him to her breast, she drew every ounce of love and support from the big cat he had to offer. It would have to do for now.

The antique wall clock in the living area of the quaint old mansion had just finished its St. Michael's chiming of ten o'clock when Chrissie came strolling through the front door. She didn't get very far.

"It's a little late for a school night, don't you think?" Kathy said with maternal authority. She was leaning against the doorway of the study, wearing a pretty pink silk bathrobe, and had a glass of bourbon in the left hand of her crossed arms. She was not drunk though she had a right to be. She was simply settled.

"Oh, hi mother. I'm sorry, I must've lost track of time," she replied with a hint of deception in her voice.

"Why don't you join me in the study, Christina?"

She phrased it like a question but her tone of voice and her use of her daughter's full given name made it clear it was not. Chrissie recognized she was in trouble and obediently followed her mother into the expansive wood paneled room. Off to one side of the study was a beautiful old round table that once belonged to Ben Franklin. Her mother had pulled a chair out from it and stood with one hand on the chair back, silently commanding her to sit. On the table top lay a brown manila envelope with one corner missing.

"What's that?" Chrissie asked as she sat.

Staring into her eyes, Kathy looked at her with a look that was half anger and half anguish. The ambiguity carried over to her voice.

"I was hoping you could tell me."

The teenager reached for the envelope that held the missing memories of that 'Twilight Zone' of a night she'd suffered through those weeks before, the night she'd forced deep into the recesses of her mind. Opening the envelope with her left hand she reached in and extracted its contents. They were upside down and she had to flip them over to see them. As she did, and realized what they were, she dropped them in shock, sending the photos and the note scattering across the Persian rug beneath her.

"Oh, my God," she cried out as though she'd been shot. She began to tremble and rock as she drew her arms to her chest in a near fetal position, unable to deal with the devastating pictures. Kathy did not move to comfort her.

"Oh, my God, indeed! What in the hell happened to you," she screamed.

Sobbing, Chrissie did her best to explain. "I'm not sure, mother, really I'm not. I don't remember everything, but I'll tell you all I can."

Between sobs and sighs, the teenager told her everything she could recall from the night of hell, which now sounded worse than Kathy had imagined. Once the teen had learned she wasn't pregnant, she'd thought she was in the clear, older and wiser as a result, she told her mother. Now the other shoe had dropped, and it was big enough to fit Shaquille O'Neal. This was of such a disastrous magnitude that it threatened to disgrace not just her daughter, but her whole family. She knew it could force her from office and leave the both of them as a small but notorious footnote in American history. Chrissie told her she would have rather been pregnant with triplets.

Finally, the mother overcame the politician and Kathy pulled her daughter into her arms.

"It's ok, we'll figure something out. The important thing is you're alright. Physically, anyway," she said to Chrissie. "We'll figure something out tomorrow."

They held each other for support for a good half an hour without another word. When they fell asleep together in front of the study's fireplace, cuddled up in an old blanket, they did so out of emotional exhaustion, rather than any other reason. Kathy had slipped into slumber with a prayer on her lips and a desperate hope in her heart. She had *no* answers. She had *no* idea what she would do when the sunlight came.

But come it did. Locking the damning photographs in her briefcase, Kathy saw her distraught daughter off before she left for the White House. She called their doctor to arrange a house call, one of the prerogatives of office, and asked the housekeeper to look after her. Then she was off, to the office, to Marva, and hopefully to a solution. Calling her aide from the limo, she had her clear her morning's calendar. She also approved Marva's recommendation, developed over *her* sleepless night, to invite J. Thomas Brower to stop by the office this morning. Whoever had the photos was in a position to ruin her anyway. Taking a risk on the FBI head didn't seem to worsen the odds much, and it was a cinch she couldn't go to anyone else, certainly not to the President.

When the dapper fed arrived, Marva showed him immediately to Kathy's office, closing the door behind her to leave the two of them alone. This was one meeting Marva didn't mind missing, not in the least.

"Good morning, Thomas, thank you for coming over on such short notice," Kathy said sweetly as she extended her hand.

"It's my pleasure. I'm at your service," he replied flirtatiously.

Showing him to a seat and pouring him a cup of coffee from the Sterling silver set on the table, she began to confide in the one person that might be able to help.

"Tom, I'm in a bind, a big one. I have no one else to turn to for help. My husband's somewhere in Rome, and I haven't been able to reach him. I'm not sure he could do anything anyway. Frankly, it's out of both our leagues."

"What is it, Kathy?" he asked with excessive familiarity.

Withdrawing the brown envelope from her burgundy leather briefcase, she handed it to him reluctantly and waited while he perused its contents. As he shuffled past photo after photo she felt as though she were standing naked before him herself. It was the greatest humiliation she'd ever endured, but she saw no choice apart from giving in to the blackmailer and resigning. That she was not yet ready to do.

Before Gower could ask, she volunteered the painful information he would soon request anyway.

"It's my daughter, Tom."

He looked up with only a hint of sympathy in his eyes, and said simply, "I see."

The next thirty minutes were spent recounting what she'd been told by her daughter the night before, and responding to the fed's machine gun line of questioning. Finally, he summed up the course of action he wanted to follow.

"Kathy, I'll need to talk to your daughter. I'll need to have her look at some photos. And I'll need to run these through the lab," he said, holding up the pornographic pictures.

"Tom, you can talk to Chrissie, but it's got to be just you, I don't want it going any further," she said. "And for now, I'm going to hold onto the photos. I don't want them to become the day's entertainment for the boys in the lab."

"I understand. Look, I'll stop by your place this evening at say, six? And you bring the photos. I'll bring some mug shots for Chrissie to look at and a fingerprint kit. I'll process 'em myself."

She'd forgotten that J. Thomas had been with the agency all his life and had worked his way up. He might be rusty, but she was confident he could still lift a print or two if there were any.

"Six it is. And thank you, Tom. Thank you for everything."

"No problem," he said smiling as he pulled on his overcoat. "You can owe me one."

With that sobering thought, he left. Kathy wasn't sure that she wasn't jumping out of the frying pan and into the fire. She could read Thomas Gower like a comic book, and the sexual innuendo he used she knew was intentional. If she'd had another choice she might have made it, but she did not.

And then Marva entered the office with another piece of bad news.

"I know this is the last thing you need to hear right now, but I finally got through to the hotel in Rome," she said with a note of alarm in her voice. "Kathy, Mark's not there. He checked out this morning."

"Is he coming home? Maybe Chrissie got a hold of him and he's coming home early."

"I don't think so," Marva said. "His luggage was sent to the airport alright, but not for a return flight. He hopped an Alitalia connector to Trieste, Italy. I don't want to alarm you, but that's right across the border from Croatia."

"I don't understand..." the Vice President stammered.

"The desk clerk said he overheard them saying they were going to Sarajevo as part of some Red Cross deal. And there's more. The reason it took me so long to track him down is he's traveling under an assumed name. I found out he applied for a visa last year, but State disapproved it because of the security risks of having the Vice President's husband in a war zone. He must've gotten a phony visa and gone anyway."

"Great! I'm being blackmailed, my daughter's been gang raped, and my husband and son are somewhere in the middle of a war," she cried. "What's next?"

She collapsed into her chair and looked as if she were on the verge of fainting. In a flash, Marva was gone and back again with a glass of cold water and a towel. The Red Cross would have approved, Kathy thought, as Marva wiped her clammy brow with the dampened cloth. After a few minutes, the color slowly began to reappear in her cheeks.

"Do you want me to inform State?" Marva asked. "They can call the embassy and put out a search party."

"No Marva, Mark must've wanted to do what he's doing pretty badly to have gone to all this trouble. As long as his identity is secret he won't be under any more danger than any other thick-skulled American," she reasoned. "But do me a favor and ask the underground to keep us as well informed as possible on changing events over there. If things start falling apart, I may want to reconsider."

Widening her eyes, Marva swallowed hard and offered whatever help she could give.

"If there's anything I can do, you know, anything. Please let me know, any hour of the day or night."

Mustering a faint rise in the corners of her lips, she thanked her for her offer and then thanked God for her. Marva was the best, absolutely the best. If they kept their heads about them they would get through, she thought. Mark was bright and stronger than she in some ways. He'd be fine, and if somehow Tom Gower could pull a rabbit out of his hat, she and Chrissie would be too. Chrissie. In all the hullabaloo she'd failed to consider what she must be going through. If she was telling the truth, she'd been drugged and gang raped as part of some sordid blackmail scheme to force her mother out of office.

"Damn, Dr. Mandell's back in L.A.," she muttered to herself. The family's therapist was a good one, and Chrissie had gone to him before. But these events weren't the kind a young girl could discuss with a sixty year old man, doctor or no doctor.

Punching the intercom number to Marva's office, she called in her offer to help.

"Mar, do you think you could find a top flight local shrink, female and outside of government, that you could trust to keep quiet?" she said into the box.

"Give me an hour," she replied.

Day seemed to move into night at an unreal pace, like one of those accelerated time film clips where the sun rises and gives way to the moon in a matter of seconds. Once again, Kathy Canfield felt caught up in a vortex, in a whirlwind of events outside her control. And she had a strange, uneasy feeling that there was more to come. More of this, she could do without.

Tom Gower was punctual, arriving at six o'clock sharp in a nice navy blue blazer with a light yellow button down shirt and gray slacks. As always, his jacket pocket was adorned with a coordinated silk scarf. This evening's color was, of course, a pale yellow to go with his cotton shirt.

"Thomas, thank you for coming. I'd like you to meet Chrissie. Perhaps you two can make yourselves comfortable in the study," Kathy said.

"That'd be fine. Hello Chrissie, Tom Gower. How are you holding up?" he asked as he extended his hand.

"Surviving, but that's about it. Do you think you can catch the guy that did this to me?" she asked plaintively.

"We'll see. I'll certainly do my best, I can tell you that. Can't have rapists and blackmailers running around trying to topple the government, now can we?"

Kathy left them alone in the study with the envelope, leaving the door open out of a sense of propriety. Also because she wasn't real sure she should trust Gower with a sixteen year old, particularly after he'd filled his eyes and mind with the sexual fantasy the blackmail pictures represented. Chrissie felt awkward and embarrassed, but less so than if her mother had been by her side.

* * * * * * * * * *

It took Gower only a matter of minutes to dust for fingerprints and to lift the ones he found. He knew the likelihood of finding anything of use was remote, especially considering all the handing the photos had received by Kathy and her daughter. But there was always a chance. Dusting off his hands, he pulled a notebook from his polished monogrammed black leather satchel and opened it, placing it on the table in front of the young girl. After he'd heard Kathy's description of the dastardly Kevin Reilly, he'd gotten a hunch and retrieved a book of known contract operatives for the CIA from top secret FBI files. Even the CIA didn't know about them. After Chrissie mentioned the tattoo of a winged dagger on his arm, he knew his hunch had been right. Flipping to a page two-thirds of the way into the notebook, he pointed to a photo at the upper corner of the page.

"Do you recognize this man?" he asked her.

She didn't have to say a word to him. He'd been trained to be observant and he couldn't help but see her shudder as she focused her brown eyes on the page.

"That's him," Chrissie exclaimed. Her finger pointed straight at a photo of Kevin Reilly, except the name beneath the photo identified him as one Miles O'Keefe. Gower knew him as a former CIA field agent, now retired and working as an occasional independent for the company. He'd done work in South America under the Reagan administration and had been considered one of the best. When he resigned and went independent, it was generally considered a career move to provide him more freedom to operate as he saw fit, rather than a segue into retirement. He would have no selfish motive, Gower knew, and besides he worked only for money and lots of it.

Someone had retained him as a hired gun to set Chrissie up to get to Kathleen Canfield. Who, he wondered? Someone high in the intelligence community? Someone acting on the orders of someone in government? How high could it go - to the President? Would Thomas Burlington really go this far to rid himself of his Vice President now that he'd used her to get elected?

The infinite unanswered questions brought the 'G-man' out in him. He was so excited about the suspense and challenge of getting to the bottom of this great new mystery, that he accidently slammed the notebook closed on his own finger.

"Damn," he yelled as he pulled back. "Getting dangerous in my old age."

The commotion that followed came from all directions. As Gower's pager began beeping in the study, the sounds of a helicopter approaching filled the sky around the residence. In the living room, the phone began to ring and a moment later the sound of walkie-talkies could be heard squawking from outside. When Kathy joined Chrissie and Thomas in the study to look out the window, he was on the phone checking in with FBI headquarters, responding to his page. Pulling back the heavy draperies that covered the high windows of the study, Kathy saw the pulsating lights of a helicopter as it descended onto the grounds of the property. As Gower hung up the phone, one of the servants entered with Jack Cutter of the Secret Service. Still looking out the window, Kathy could now make out the markings on the chopper as it landed. It bore the now familiar seal of the President of the United States. What in the world was Mike Burlington doing here unannounced at this hour, and by helicopter, she wondered?

Turning, she asked the question aloud, to anyone within earshot that might know the answer.

"What's going on? Why's the President here?"

Cutter looked at Gower and Gower looked back at Cutter as though they were trying to decide who should reply. After a moment's silence, Cutter accepted responsibility and spoke. There was anguish in the agent's normally steely voice.

His answer overwhelmed her.

"Mrs. Canfield, the President's just been airlifted to Bethesda Naval Hospital. They think he's had a stroke and they're not sure if he's gonna make it."

Gower finished the picture for her. "Kathy, he's in a coma. The chopper was sent to bring you back to the White House because you're next in the line of succession. Until he dies or recovers, you're the acting President of the United States."

Within minutes Kathleen Canfield and her daughter were darting through the light snow on the front lawn toward the dark green Marine helicopter, hair flying every which way from the powerful blasts of the chopper's whirling blades. They were surrounded on all sides by armed and anxious Secret Service agents, mindful of the importance of successfully retrieving their prey. Lifting off, the copter's rise into the cloudy black sky was illuminated by the half-moon above, creating a compelling sight for those that stayed behind as Kathleen Canfield flew across the Washington skyline to her destiny.

CHAPTER NINE

Somewhere over Italy, Mark Canfield was putting his magazine away to take a look at the airport below. He'd flown enough to know that runways came in all sizes, and with the flight from Rome being especially bumpy in the winter weather, he was growing concerned. The outline of the airfield in Trieste appeared alarmingly small as he stared at its lights through the moist portal window. With the plane circling above the fog awaiting clearance to land, he fidgeted and began to worry about the landing conditions. Next to him, Jerry was digging his fingers into the arm rests of his seat.

"Excuse me miss, but are you sure we can land safely in this weather?" Jerry nervously asked a flight attendant.

In a calm, heavy accent, the pretty, olive-skinned Italian tried to reassure him.

"I'm sure the captain will not try to land if it is not safe. If so, he will return to Rome. Do not worry, this is American DC-10, it is safe."

141

"Well, that makes me feel better. Mark, how many crashes of American planes have we had back home this last year?"

"Oh, I dunno. Five or six that made the news that I know of," Mark calculated.

"Forget I asked. Miss, could I get a whiskey please?"

The plane grew quiet, and Mark noticed the anesthesiologist eyeing the nearest emergency exit, trying to figure out the fastest way to open the latches on the door. As the attendant brought Jerry his whisky, Mark dug into his jacket pocket for the tiny airline-sized bottle of vodka he'd squirreled away from the Washington to Rome flight. Neither man wasted any time in downing the soothing liquors.

Twenty jittery minutes passed before the airliner's loudspeaker system crackled to life, followed by the pilot's deep voice. They couldn't understand much of what he was saying at first since none of them spoke Italian. Fortunately, the pilot followed up his spiel with an English translation.

"Ladies and gentlemen, we have been cleared to land in Trieste and are beginning our approach. It may get bumpy on the way down so please keep your seatbelts fastened and extinguish all cigarettes. Thank you."

The plane's descent was like a roller coaster as it rode from updraft to downdraft and back again. Then suddenly, as the plane descended to one hundred feet from the ground and the landing gear dropped into place, the buffeting miraculously stopped. Gazing anxiously out the window, Mark could see the runway lights through the thinning fog beneath the jet. As the massive wheels of the DC-10 touched down, they seemed to almost caress the pavement with no more than a brief squeal. It was as though a big hand had plucked the jetliner from its approach and set it down gently on the ground.

"Yes! What a landing," Jerry whooped. "I love this pilot!"

"Nothing like a prayer and a vodka to see you through a crisis," Mark mused.

Yelling over the applause erupting in the compartment, Jerry added, "Give the guy credit, man. That was a friggin' miracle! I've never had a landing that smooth, and in these conditions!" He released his death grip on the arm rests and the blood began to flow back into his whitened knuckles.

There was no covered access from the plane to the terminal. The hundred or so passengers deplaned down a set of rolling stairs right onto the snowy tarmac of the airfield, making their way as quickly as they could across the windblown fifty yards that separated them from the terminal. Some slipped, some slid, and some fell, but all made it through the dirty glass doors to the relative safety and warmth of the building. Once inside, the relief team patted each other on the backs and headed for the baggage station.

When they reached their destination they were met by a craggy-faced man of about fifty, bundled up in a dark gray scarf and a darker gray trench coat and fedora. In his hands was a hastily crafted placard that contained a crude crimson cross with the words 'Red Cross' beneath it.

"Welcome, welcome! I'm Serge Malkovic, from European Red Cross. Grab your bags and we go. Is midnight and you must be tired," he said gleefully in comprehensible English.

His black plastic eyeglasses, like his garb seemed out of style by American standards, but somehow they looked right on his rosy wind-burnt face. The jolly Serge helped them find and claim their luggage, negotiating animatedly, and successfully, on their behalf with an overzealous baggage clerk. Maybe it was jet lag or just general exhaustion, but the group looked more like Moe, Larry, and Curly than a medical team as they stumbled from the terminal through the snow to the fleet of Yugos waiting outside. They squeezed like a group of frat pledges into the three miniature cars, then began their trek toward the Italian-Croatian border.

The road was narrow and windy, with intersecting turns and odd looking European direction signs every few minutes pointing the way to 'Yugoslavia'. The former Soviet semi-satellite had broken into several countries four years ago, but the Italian authorities had yet to change the directional sign references on their side of the border. Thirty or forty minutes through the intermittent snow and the lights and warning signs of the border checkpoint came into view as they turned a corner. Mark could recognize the familiar red and white stripes of the gate arm and the silhouettes of two uniformed guards.

"Excuse me Serge, but is that a machine gun hanging on that guy's shoulder up ahead?" Mark asked with concern.

Jerry confirmed it before the Croat could reply. "Shit, it sure is!"

"Not to worry. Is normal for border here. Just be 'cold' and everything is fine."

"I think you mean 'cool', Serge," Jerry said.

"Sorry, how you say? 'Cool.'?"

"Cool."

The caravan pulled to a halt in front of the guards, and Serge rolled down his window to address the first of the two. Both appeared to be in their early twenties, though at first glance the olive drab uniforms made them look older. Mark and Jerry agreed the vestments resembled the Soviet uniforms they'd seen in the movies and on television. That, combined with the ominous looking machine gun, the nation's communist history, and his very American face, began to make Mark feel increasingly vulnerable. When the older of the two baby-faced soldiers ordered the group out of their cars and into the guard station, a bead of sweat formed on his brow. It couldn't have been more than thirty degrees outside.

"Can anybody tell what's going on?" Mark asked to no one in particular.

"Nope. Sounds like they're speaking Russian to me," a woman said.

Jerry chimed in with his two cents worth. "It's similar, but not quite the same, I don't think. Unfortunately, I can't make it out either."

The discussion between Serge and the guard seemed pretty serious to the group, none of whom spoke Serbo-Croatian. The language, like the uniforms, had a distinct Russian flavor to it. Finally, Serge returned to them to explain.

"He wants you sign register and hand passports for check please. There no problem, just long time before he sees Americans here!"

"Whew!" Wiping his forehead, Mark let out a sigh of relief. It felt better to hear a few more coming from the others as they handed their passports forward.

"Had me worried there, old man," Jerry said to Serge. "Felt like Mexico for a minute. Visions of one way prison doors were starting to run through my head!"

"Took the words right out of my mouth," Mark added as he passed his forged document to the guide.

One after the other, the group filed forward to sign the register and pose for the guards as they compared their passport photos to their persons. Having scribbled his alias, curiosity got the better of Mark Canfield so he thumbed back through the book looking for names with the familiar 'U.S.A.' under the heading 'country of origin'. He found only a couple and they had Slavic surnames next to them. The young man was right, their presence was a novelty in the war-torn region.

The bureaucratic dance took some twenty minutes. As they turned to leave, Mark heard a young voice he couldn't understand call to him from behind. To his surprise, the younger of the guards approached him and grasped his right hand, leaving something in his palm. He smiled and said something, but the doctor couldn't understand a word. Opening it, Mark discovered a small hand carved wooden cross hanging from a necklace of wooden beads.

Serge placed his hand on the soldier's shoulder in appreciation. "He want you to have. Say God be with you in travels to help our people."

Mark thanked him with a bow of his head and immediately placed the gift around his neck and the lump in his throat. He touched it often as the caravan continued through the late European night toward the capital city of Zagreb.

Morning had broken when the jar of a bump in the road woke Mark from his cramped slumber in the front passenger seat of the Yugo. Through blurry eyes he saw that Jerry and one of the female team members, Debra Hansen, remained entwined asleep in the tiny back seat. Serge sat next to him, surprisingly wide awake behind the little steering wheel. The fog coated landscape surrounding them was full of tall barren trees that seemed to grow out of the fog, resembling strange mutant oaks. The scene was straight out of an old vampire movie Mark thought, before remembering that Transylvania was a very real region of Romania not so far away. He felt a sudden chill and wasn't at all sure if the locally made car's heater was failing or if the eerie surroundings were the cause.

"Good morning, Doctor Fielder," Serge chirped.

"Morning. Where are we?" Mark asked, rubbing his eyes.

"We be Zagreb in thirty minutes or so. How's sleep?"

"Well, it's not a Seely Posturepedic but it'll do," the doctor replied wryly.

Glancing at Mark with a puzzled look on his face, the Slav asked in confusion, "What seal pasture eating?"

Mark bellowed at the misunderstanding. It was the most gut-wrenching laugh he'd had in ages. It felt great to be away from it all, to just be himself, not a movie star or politician's husband or a great physician, but just one of the guys. It made him feel younger; it was like summer camp.

"Sorry Serge. Just an expression. I slept fine, really. How soon after we hit Zagreb are we hooking up with the U.N. escort and heading out?"

"There be time for breakfast and maybe shower, but convoy leaves at ten," he said. "Road into Sarajevo is open one week, cut off next. We want to go now before more dangerous."

"Man, that's not much time. Guess the sightseeing'll have to wait 'till afterwards, huh?" Mark teased.

Serge's weathered skin cracked as he laughed and said graciously, "For what you do, I give you personal tour of my country for long as you want when you return. Long as you want! Even show you old Roman forum where lions eat Serge's ancestors!"

Mark chuckled dutifully at the joke, but it underscored the awing sense of history he'd felt since his arrival. In the states, if a house is a hundred years old, they call it an historical monument. In Europe, it's considered new and the odds are about even the original owner still lives there.

Before long the rear-seaters were coming to and the train of cars was maneuvering its way down the cobblestoned one way streets of Zagreb.

"Didn't put shocks on these cars did they?" Jerry yelled from the rear as he covered his head to protect himself.

Serge continued to play the gracious host, pointing out various landmarks as they went by. One familiar sight seemed to fill him with particular pride.

"You know, we get McDonald's here soon. Going to open over there," the Croat bragged, pointing across the street.

Mark recognized the site from news reports. The near-completed golden arches were no more than a hundred yards down the street from where a Serb mortar attack had killed and maimed dozens a few months ago, littering the shopping district with body parts and debris. He couldn't let it go without mentioning it.

"Soon you'll be able to walk through the dried blood on the pavement over there and get a Big Mac. Worth dying for, isn't it?"

"War is crazy my friend," Serge said. "Might as well have hamburger before you go!"

The familiar sight of the American flag waving proudly over the American embassy finally came into view. Milling around in front were several khaki clad soldiers sporting the powder blue armbands, dickeys, and helmets of the United Nations. Parked around the corner from the men was a huge white armored personnel carrier with the letters 'UN' painted on the side, and a huge black dent on its rear.

Leaning over to Jerry, Mark asked, "What's that black stuff on the back of that thing?"

"Looks like shell damage. I'd say it got hit by a small mortar or something."

"We're not in Kansas anymore, are we Toto?" Mark said sarcastically.

The danger that had previously seemed so abstract suddenly seemed very real. His adrenalin began pumping.

Serge parked across the street from the old embassy building and the others pulled alongside. The relief team and its drivers began unloading their gear under the watchful eye of a giant bronzed horseman sitting atop his steed with sabre drawn, staring down at them from a nearby courtyard.

"Is old army general from long ago," Serge told them when he noticed their interest. "Or old famous horse, I forget!"

"Sort of the Croatian Mr. Ed, huh?" Mark said to Jerry.

"Bad as those Yugos ride, I think they shoulda stuck to that mode of transportation," Jerry complained. "My butt's killing me and not one of you damn doctors is a proctologist. Just my luck!"

The Slavic drivers helped with the luggage, enabling the crew to make it across the street to the waiting military contingent without getting run over in the heavy traffic. The tall Frenchman that introduced himself as their leader was a jaded and cynical man on the tail end of a twelve month stint of frustrating duty in the Balkans. Colonel Jean Pierre Martinee stood a good six feet tall and had a soldier's square shoulders and physique. Unlike the others, he wore a powder blue beret rather than a helmet to cover his thinning black hair; his thin moustache looked so stereotypically French that it added a touch of unintentional humor to his otherwise humorless countenance. The Colonel spoke nearly flawless English, albeit with a strong but dashing French accent.

"Welcome to Croatia, ladies and gentlemen. Gateway to the Adriatic, the world, and to the war. I am Colonel Martinee, your host and tour guide for your winter adventure to Sarajevo," he said with a straight face. "We will be departing at oh ten hundred in the chariot over there. Don't be late."

The Frenchman went through the motions of shaking hands with the men in the group but showed a spark of interest in only the women. Nurse Candy was attractive enough as most twenty-five year old blondes go, and Jean Pierre showed a glint in his middle-aged eye for her. It worked out to the benefit of the entire group when his less than cordial attitude improved and he invited them to join him for breakfast at a nearby sidewalk cafe. The food was wonderful as was the delightfully rich coffee with whipped cream they served. The waiter even spoke broken English and seemed excited about the rare opportunity to use it, but there was a tension in the air toward the U.N. soldier.

"Is it me or are the people around us giving us the evil eye?" Candy asked as she glanced at an old couple nearby.

Serge volunteered an explanation, saving the Colonel the trouble. "People don't understand why world has not stopped war, and saved their sons. They think U.N. is a joke and have given up hope."

"I can't argue with them," Jean Pierre admitted. "Most days I don't understand what we're doing myself. Most days it seems as though we're just referees in a shooting gallery. A good day is when we don't get caught in a crossfire or taken as hostages."

"How bad is it in Sarajevo?" Mark asked.

The rugged soldier winced at the question. "It is bad, doctor. Sarajevo was a beautiful city like any other large city in the world, filled with happy hard working people. When were the Winter Olympics there, ten years ago? It was at its most beautiful then. Now, it looks like Beirut. Not a building left undamaged in the whole town, fifty percent of them or more will have to be torn down and rebuilt, and that's just the city."

He hesitated and drew a deep breath, then continued. "The people are in despair. You can't find a family that hasn't lost someone. If it's not a mortar or cannon shell, it's a sniper's bullet. Those bastards will shoot a newborn baby if they get a clean shot."

Serge supplemented the analysis with this bit of wisdom. "There is no mercy, no humanity in war. Almost none. People like you are few, but you give hope, you give reason to believe tomorrow be better."

"Now all I have to do is get you there in one piece! Feeling lucky today?" the French Colonel asked rhetorically.

With that, the rock of a man rose, and within minutes the 'Sarajevo Six' as he began to call them, were on their way to Sarajevo in the stuffy confines of the personnel carrier. Mark would have felt safer if he hadn't remembered reading about the recent deaths of those three U.S. diplomats in one of these things after it tumbled from a crumbling country road. An hour into the trip and he was hanging onto his wooden cross and praying the driver was sober and the roads were firm. He should have prayed for a trip free from enemy attack.

The shrill whistle of the mortar shell as it approached could be heard several seconds before its impact, giving the veteran driver of the personnel carrier just enough warning. The armored vehicle lurched as he hit the gas, leaving the dangerous projectile three feet short of its intended target. Striking the muddy country road just behind it, the explosion sent its rear end two feet up and into the air. The seatbelts kept the inhabitants from flying out of their seats, but it still felt like an 'E' ticket ride as the carrier came back to earth with a thud, digging its treads into the soft earth. As they caught, it took off, hurtling through the fog that still hung lightly above the Croatian soil. Then there was another shriek, and another. It seemed like the explosions were coming from all sides.

"Keep your heads in your laps," the Colonel yelled.

The driver needed no orders. He'd begun evasive maneuvers the minute he'd gotten traction. The carrier could reach over fifty, so they had the horsepower to escape, so long as their luck didn't run out and the Belgian driver kept it on the road.

Their luck held. The explosions slowly fell behind them then ended altogether. As they reached and crossed the Croat controlled checkpoint at the Bosnian border, Mark noticed a faint smell of urine in the closed compartment. He couldn't determine the source, but he knew he'd come close himself.

"Damn, what was that," a shaken Jerry asked the Frenchman.

"Whatever it was, it was way too close," said another.

The Colonel smirked at their reactions, but the look on his face told them even he had been concerned for their collective lives.

"By the size of the explosion, I'd say they were mortar rounds. Too small to be heavy cannon fire. Plus this sector was supposed to be secure, so I doubt they could've gotten anything too heavy this near the road," he explained.

"How would this thing've held up if they'd hit us?" Mark asked.

The smirk grew to a smile. "Let's just say our travel plans would've been changed, mon ami."

Jerry and Mark looked at each other as if to say, "What in the hell are we doing here?" Adventure was starting to look more like danger to them now, which Mark decided, was at least a sign they hadn't lost all of their sanity. At least not yet. The rest of the trip was uneventful, unless of course you count Jean Pierre's comforting of the frightened young nurse. Although a self-professed Christian, the near death experience had left her vulnerable to his overtures and so she rested her head on the Colonel's shoulder through the remainder of the trek. Checkpoint after checkpoint slowed them, but also reassured the group that the roadway was safe and in government hands. As they chugged into the outskirts of war-ravaged Sarajevo, the sound of gunfire welcomed them to the city, the ping of snipers' bullets ricocheting harmlessly off the armor plating. That made it clear to them that this would be no picnic. It was also definitely *not* summer camp.

Rolling to a halt, the carrier's diesel engines shut down and a crewman opened the side hatch letting in the first meaningful natural air and light they'd experienced since morning. It was nearly six p.m. Bosnian time, according to Mark's new plastic watch, and it appeared from the limited view he had that dusk was settling in on the town. Thank goodness he'd at least had the intelligence to leave the Rolex at home, he thought.

The dry Colonel's next orders lightened the moods of the weary travelers. "Ladies and gentlemen, please check your seats to be sure you have all your carryon luggage. We have arrived," he joked dryly. "Thank you for flying with the U.N."

The air was cold and damp, the view one of devastation and death. Walking from the carrier to the bombed out building that served as Red Cross headquarters, Mark Canfield stepped around a shell crater in the paved roadway. A puddle of what looked like dried blood lay to one side of it. He'd seen mayhem during his emergency room internship in his youth, but he'd spent the last twenty years on nose jobs, tummy tucks, and liposuctions. There was a huge difference, he knew, and he began suddenly to wonder whether he would be able to handle it.

"Man, I had no idea it was this bad," Jerry exclaimed as he surveyed the hollowed buildings. "Somehow, on a twenty-seven-inch screen, you lose the magnitude of it all."

"I know, Jer, I know. I hope to God the medical facilities aren't as bad. I don't think I can reconstruct a face with bailing wire and duct tape," Mark said.

"Yeah, it's probably worse in your line. I can always just fill 'em with booze or whack 'em on the head."

There wasn't a man or woman among the relief team that didn't have the look of a zombie in their sunken eyes. Jean Pierre wasn't foolish, he knew there was work to be done tonight, but he also knew there'd be a full day's work tomorrow and the next day as well, so he bid his charges a good night and excused himself so they could get some rest.

The accommodations were rough. There was a generator providing limited electricity, but no running water. That had to be brought in from a nearby well that was occasionally subject to sniper fire. There were squeaky, rusted metal cots with musty mattresses that saved them from sleeping on the cold, damp floor. Thankfully, at least the blankets appeared new and clean. The men's and women's sleeping areas were separated by a wall with a gaping hole and a blanket nailed over it to restore at least visual privacy. Tonight though, it wouldn't have mattered if there had been lecherous intents on either side of the wool divider. Everyone was sound asleep by seven o'clock.

Morning snuck up on the group like a ninja, stealing away the extra hours of sleep their bodies cried out for. When Mark groggily arose in response to Jerry's nudge, he dressed quickly in the khakis the Red Cross had issued them back in the States and a white parka he'd been given by Jean Pierre the night before. That too bore the markings of the Red Cross, a hopeful signal to snipers in the trees and hills to aim elsewhere. Jerry and Mark joined the others in front of the building, waiting to be pointed to what they expected to be a chow line. By the time the Colonel meandered up to them a little before seven, they'd made a pact to eat the first living thing they saw moving. Fortunately for the soldier, it had been just cheap talk.

"Ready for breakfast, my friends? I think we're having oatmeal and that American army favorite, how do you call it...spam?" Jean Pierre said with a sly grin. It was the first time he had smiled.

They hoped he was kidding, but he was not. The three course meal was rounded out with a piece of stale bread and a glass of goat's milk. 'Breakfast of champions' Mark called it. Wisecracks aside, they ate it, not because it was good, but because they were hungry enough to eat worse.

Their first look at the hospital wasn't any more encouraging. The medical facility looked like something out of a horror novel. The operating room, Mark's primary focus, was dirty and only slightly warmer than the outdoors due to the heating unit's reliance on the on again off again generator. It was dusty and much of the equipment was inoperative, the result of damage from perennial bombardments and lack of maintenance. It took the better part of an hour, but when they were done the 'Sarajevo Six' had identified acceptable instruments or crude substitutes that they felt would work.

"It's a good thing they don't have malpractice over here," Mark told his colleagues. "Or we'd be duck soup for the local lawyers."

"Don't worry, doctor, there are fewer lawyers here than there are physicians, and most of them are now privates in the military."

The quip came from the head of the Red Cross medical team in Sarajevo, British surgeon Dr. Douglas Lloyd-Davies. Mark had read about him in Time Magazine. He'd been in Sarajevo for over two years, a two week volunteer stint that had never ended. He'd become a bit of a cause celebre in the medical community, a male Mother Theresa in a white smock. He was particularly recognizable by his wild mane of gray streaked black hair. It made him look bizarrely like the Bosnian Serb leader, Radovan Karadzic. In another time, he could have made a decent living as the strongman's double.

"Dr. Lloyd-Davies I presume?" Mark said as he extended his half-frozen hand.

"One and the same. And you are?"

"Fielder, Dr. Matt Fielder. Plastic surgery."

Jerry bit his tongue to keep Mark's secret. He'd sworn he would, at all costs, and he too was enjoying the cloak and dagger ruse. It added to the excitement for the normally mousey beanpole.

Introductions followed for all. Then the work began. It had been quiet in the area for a month, but with a lack of medical staff, the injured were still stacked up in the hospital, hoping for treatment. The group joined Dr. Lloyd-Davies and a handful of other international practitioners that were already there. Breaking into four surgical teams, they began what would be a ten hour day.

"My god, Doug, what happened to this kid?" Mark asked in horror as his first patient was wheeled in.

He was a badly disfigured six year old who'd gotten in the way of a Serb shell. One ear had been almost completely severed and had been simply cleaned and bandaged to his head. The jagged edges had started to heal together on their own, producing a badly disfigured result.

"He was in the wrong place, at the wrong time, doctor. Just like all the rest of them."

They worked feverishly without a break, from one patient to the next. Any self-doubts Mark had had about his ability to perform were left on the frigid cement floor of the operating room. There was no time to think about anything but the work at hand and he wasn't about to let these people down when he had the God given talent to help them. So he didn't. And they didn't. By the time the tireless physicians had cleared the operating room late that night, over two dozen patients had undergone the knife in their care.

"Buy you a cup of coffee, Doctor?" the weary Lloyd-Davies said to a stooping Mark.

"Only if it's decaf. I don't want to miss a minute of sleep tonight," he replied.

"Well then, decaf it is, yank!"

Adjourning to the makeshift dining room across the way, the two surgeons joined a British nurse and a German x-ray technician. A Japanese-made boom box sat on a shelf playing an old Eric Clapton tune. Somehow the enterprising medical volunteers had jerry-rigged it to get the BBC out of London.

Lloyd-Davies did the courtesy of the introductions. "Matt, this is Dr. Nancy Lansford. She was handling table number one today. And this fine young kraut is Hans Warnemuende, x-ray technician extraordinaire. Don't worry, he speaks English. This my friends is our new yank face fixer, Matt Fielder."

"My pleasure," Mark said politely. "Get any good programs on that thing? Say, isn't the Super Bowl on tomorrow, or is it the next day?"

There were no takers for that question. American football was an oddity that had never caught on in Europe.

"What's that, super bowl? Is that what your Jolly Green Giant eats his Wheaties out of?" the dry Brit asked.

Mark was starting to realize that it was humor that helped keep these people going here in the war zone. Serge, Jean Pierre, Lloyd-Davies. They all had that same cynical sense of humor. It was starting to feel like a *M.A.S.H.* marathon to him.

Sporting talk soon gave way to the music as the foursome enjoyed a bottle of white chardonnay the Colonel had smuggled with him from Zagreb. The music on the British channel was mostly familiar to Mark, and he began to tap his fingers to the beat. When a Harry Connick, Jr. tune filled the air, he was more than happy to accept Nancy's invitation to dance.

"I love this song! Matt, would you dance with me please?" she asked.

"Well, I'll warn you, I'm no Fred Astaire, but I'll do my best," he replied.

He was a world away from his life as Mark Canfield, and she felt good in his arms as they slowly whirled across the cement floor. She wasn't beautiful by customary standards, but she had a full figure and a pair of fawn brown eyes that were soft and open, inviting. Her pale skin went perfectly with her wild and wavy chestnut hair which she wore back from her face, sloppily rubber-banded behind her head. Within the confines of the ugliness of Bosnia, she was a jewel, or so Mark thought as the alcohol worked its spell.

"Well, Dr. Fielder, you're not that bad," she whispered into his ear as she moved her arm across his shoulder. "Not bad at all."

The warmth of her breath in his ear, and the sweet scent of her perfume made him giddy. If he kept his eyes closed, he could almost imagine he was seventeen again and at the prom with Mary Lou Lydecker.

His trance was broken before the tune had finished when an announcer rudely interrupted the regular station programming. Mark and Nancy stepped back from each other as a special news bulletin was announced. It was there Mark Canfield learned the shocking news, over a foreign radio station in a foreign land while dancing with another woman.

"We interrupt this program for a special news bulletin. The White House has announced from Washington D.C. that President Michael James Burlington was hospitalized at six o' clock p.m. Washington time today after collapsing from what doctors are describing as a stroke. No word has been released on his condition, but observers are bracing for the worst. It has been reported that newly elected Vice President Kathleen Canfield has been flown to the White House to assume all powers of the American presidency. Mrs. Canfield was the first woman to be elected to the Vice Presidency in American history, and now it appears after three short weeks, perhaps the first woman to serve her country as its President. We will keep you informed of further developments as they occur."

The chilling announcement seized the attention of everyone in the room, but no one quite as much as Mark. He stood there helplessly, with his mouth gaping open, unable to move or speak. "I'm dreadfully sorry, Matt. Rotten luck I'd say. Always a shock when one of our leaders is struck down, no matter how it happens," Lloyd-Davies said, trying to console the American.

"Look at the bright side, Matty, your country's finally caught up with ours, putting a woman in charge. Bet she'll do a bang up job," Nancy said lightly.

"Got to agree with that," Mark muttered under his breath as he waited for his heart to start again. When it did, he excused his rattled self as courteously as he could. "I'm sorry, it's a bit of a shock. I'd better go let Jerry know. See you all in the morning, and thank you for the dance, Nancy."

With that, he left, jogging towards the dilapidated barracks with a thousand thoughts running through his mind. His head was so addled by the turn of events that he didn't even hear the cannon shell whistling down on him. The sound finally registered when he lay flat on his stomach in a mud puddle, blown from his feet by the nearby impact and explosion. The shell had hit the parked personnel carrier they'd ridden in, sending it up in flames and showering the area with metal and debris. Rising from the mud, he heard a voice yell to him from not twenty yards away. It was the French Colonel, beckoning to him from the safety of the entryway of an old wine cellar. Slipping in the muck, Mark threw himself in that direction, reaching the doorway as the second shell blew through the roof of the kitchen facility next door. The force tossed the American doctor through the doorway and down the flight of stairs on top of the Frenchman.

"Damn, yank, get your bloody ass off me," Jean Pierre yelled from under the weight of Mark's body.

Hitting his head as he rolled down the stairs, Mark slipped into unconsciousness with one vision still in his head - his wife standing in the Oval Office with the weight of the world on her shoulders wondering where in the hell her mate was when she needed him.

"Sergeant, get on the radio and find out what in the 'ell is going on," Jean Pierre screamed to one of his troops as he drug himself free. "The Serbs' heavy artillery was supposed to be ten miles back!"

As the others made their way to the relative safety of the cellar, chaos reigned throughout the city. Nancy and Lloyd-Davies finally made it from the shell-struck kitchen, though in the weak light of the cellar it appeared to Jean-Pierre that her lanky legs were covered in blood. The German was nowhere in sight, buried beneath the rubble a hundred yards away.

As the Colonel watched the British doctor tend to Nancy's wounds, the sergeant reported back with what he'd learned.

"Sir, HQ says the Serbs have launched an offensive on our position. It's big, real big Colonel.

They said intelligence believes it may be the largest movement of troops and weaponry of the war."

"We're under attack? Not a harassment action, but a large scale attack?" the Colonel asked.

"Oui, mon Colonel."

Colonel Jean-Pierre Martinee lit up a broken French cigarette and took a deep puff. If intelligence was right, it was a cinch his life would be over a long time before cancer could get him. If they were right, every man, woman, and child in Sarajevo would be at risk before the week was through. As shells continued to fall and shake the ground beneath them, only one thought hung in his mind. He hoped they were wrong.

CHAPTER TEN

As the first artillery shells were striking Sarajevo, the presidential helicopter carrying the Vice President was touching down softly on the well-lit White House helipad. Stepping from the chopper in the cold moonlight, a still stunned Kathleen Canfield was greeted under the whirling blades by an unusually frenzied Andy Mathers. She knew the older Burlington had been like an uncle to the younger family friend and aide, and it appeared to her that he was in a state of shock over the President's sudden collapse.

"Andy, I'm so sorry, are you all right?" she asked worriedly, touching his arm lightly with her hand. "How is he?"

"We're all pretty shook up, it happened so suddenly. We don't know any more than that he's unconscious, in a coma of some kind."

His voice sounded as though it were shaking, and it was impossible for her to tell if the jacketless Mathers was reacting to the frigid weather or the chaotic events.

163

"Exactly what happened, Andy?" Kathy asked, hoping he could shed some light on the tragedy.

Mathers tried to explain between chattering teeth, folding his arms to keep warm as they rushed through the Rose Garden toward the rear entry of the Oval Office.

"We were in an emergency Cabinet meeting concerning what intelligence believes are Serbian preparations for an all-out assault on Sarajevo. Things got pretty hot when we started debating options. One minute the President was yelling and arguing his point about the need to launch an all-out defensive counterattack, and the next he was on the floor. He hasn't been the same since he was hospitalized for exhaustion. I guess it was just too much."

Reaching the White House, they entered the Oval Office through the French door the Marine guard held for them. To Kathy's surprise, inside by the President's desk stood Stewart Farley and the Chief Justice of the Supreme Court. Both were dressed casually, and Farley's chubby left palm was resting on a bible in the elderly justice's hand. His right hand was raised into the air.

"I hope I'm not interrupting something," she said, with a delivery as icy as the frigid Capitol weather. "Unless my memory is flawed, you're still one more stroke away from that chair."

"Well, Mrs. Canfield! Glad you could make it. We didn't know how long you'd be and we have a crisis at hand that requires immediate leadership. Experienced leadership," he answered arrogantly.

Kathy moved swiftly and angrily to face the pompous President wannabe, stopping six inches from his pointy nose. She reacted instinctively, cooly taking the bible from the Chief Justice and removing it from Farley's reach. For a moment, they stared each other down like a couple of gunfighters at high noon. It was the elder judge that broke the tension.

"Mr. Speaker, now that the Vice President is here, my constitutional duty is to swear her into office under the emergency provisions governing the line of succession. If you would, please," he said in a commanding tone as he stepped between them.

Infuriated, Farley brought his lips to her ear and whispered so no one else could hear his threat or the hate with which he delivered it. "You're in over your head, young lady! And I'm gonna hand it to you on a platter!" Storming toward the door, he paused and turned. "You know, missy, there's a lot more to governing than smiling pretty for the camera. I'm going to enjoy watching you learn that." And then he was gone, leaving her alone with Mathers and the Chief Justice.

The swearing in took but a minute, far too short a time for anyone to properly brace themselves for the weight of the world as it rested itself upon their shoulders. Setting the bible aside, the solemn magistrate shook her hand and then said a small prayer for her and for the nation. And then he too was gone, leaving the new President alone with her predecessor's shaken Chief of Staff.

"Andy, I want you to know I pray to God he'll recover, and recover quickly. This was never a position I thought I'd find myself in, or ever wanted to be in. Frankly, I wouldn't have agreed to run, had I believed this would happen. It's important to me that you know that," the new President said to Mathers with a crack of emotion in her voice. "Farley's right, you know. I'm not equipped for this."

Andy looked at her with great affection in his eyes. "I doubt seriously that such vulnerability and humility has graced this office in this century. I've watched you for over six months now, and I can't think of anyone I know that could be more qualified to step into a president's shoes. You're bright, you listen. You're calm and fair, but forceful when you need to be. It's been a long time since I've seen someone stand up to Farley like that. And you hold the soul of the American people in your hand. There's no greater gift in public life, it happens maybe once in a generation that a political figure has the talent and charisma to lead a nation by sheer force of personality."

"Thank you, Andy, but..."

"No buts. The chain of events that brought you here has been extraordinary. How can it not be fate, or destiny? Your entire life has been preparation for this moment. Trust your instincts," he advised. "And understand that your lack of passion and interest for this office is not a disqualification. To the contrary, it's the greatest qualification you could have. It's what'll keep you grounded, and that I dare say, would be something this grand old house hasn't seen for a long time."

Kathy smiled at the good looking aide and gave him a big, warm hug. "Thank you, Andy, I needed that. I'll also need you by my side from here on in so I can take advantage of your knowledge, wisdom, and counsel."

"I assumed you'd want Marva to serve as your Chief of Staff," he said, surprised.

"I'd appreciate if you'd remain and take her on as your assistant. You've got more experience here, and it'll make for an easier transition, both now and especially when the President returns. I'll need you both," she said earnestly, as she held his hands.

"Of course, if that's your desire. Shall I get her in here?" Andy asked.

"Please. And I'd like your advice on where we go from here."

For the first time today, he smiled. It felt good to have her trust, particularly considering Burlington's past transgressions, and his growing attraction to the former starlet. "The Cabinet's still assembled in the Cabinet Room. I suggest we join them and get you brought up to speed on the Bosnia situation. An attack seems imminent and we have a decision to make on how we're going to respond," he suggested.

Kathy nodded in agreement. She waited while he quickly called Marva, and as soon as he finished the call they were off side-by-side together for the Cabinet Room down the hall. The walk was short, but it gave him just enough time to caution her on the resistance she could expect from some of the members of Burlington's hand-picked team.

Strolling into the Cabinet Room, Kathy recognized the familiar faces of the various secretaries of this, that, and the other departments and agencies of the federal government. The beige-walled room was well lit by its brass chandelier and wall sconces, making the leaf green and gold-trimmed draperies and like-colored carpeting appear all the more majestic, particularly with the snow-flocked Rose Garden visible through the windows. Sitting at the head of the gorgeous mahogany pedestal conference table was National Security Advisor Eb Danielson. Kathy approached and stood before him in silence, waiting for him to relinquish the dark brown leather and brass tack-studded chair. An uncomfortable moment later, he did. Andy took his usual seat to the President's immediate right.

Looking straight into the eyes of each man and woman seated around the long table, she addressed them for the first time as head of the government.

"Ladies and Gentlemen, the Chief Justice has just sworn me in. Until President Burlington has recovered sufficiently to reclaim the duties of his office, and I emphasize 'until', I'm the acting Commander in Chief. During this difficult time, I and the American people will be depending on your full cooperation and support. We can't succeed without it," she told them. "Andy has informed me generally about the Bosnian situation. I'd like you to fill in the details for me, bring me up to speed if you would, please."

Her words were simple, direct, and forceful. And they were delivered with the apparent confidence and ease of a person who knew she was right where fate wanted her to be. Inside, she was a wreck wallowing in her own insecurities. Regrettably, at least one member of the Cabinet was perceptive enough to sense that.

"Excuse me, Kathy, but we'd already reached a decision before you joined us. Eb was just preparing to contact the head of the Joint Chiefs of Staff to authorize a retaliatory response." The condescending words came from the sharp tongue of Secretary of Defense Paul Atkinson, scowling crankily as always.

Kathy's reply was polite, but they could all feel the keen edge it carried. "Well, Paul, I appreciate that," she said. "Perhaps you can fill me in on exactly what decision you've reached and why."

"Kathy, time is of the essence and we really don't have time to bring you up to speed starting at square one," Atkinson replied. This time, he was downright disdainful.

"Madame President," Andy said to Atkinson.

"Excuse me?"

"Madame President. I believe that's the proper way to address the President, not by her first name," he said firmly.

168

The few seconds that followed were filled with a tension you could bounce a quarter off of. But Mathers made his point, and his assertive show of support served to adjust a few attitudes.

Atkinson's didn't change too much, but even a little can go a long way in the right situation. "My apologies. Eb, why don't you kick it off, I'm sure another thirty minutes won't make much difference."

Discussions went on for over an hour-and-a-half, with Kathy asking question after question, many of which surprised the Cabinet members by their incisiveness. The 'Underground' had served her well, as had her conscientious study of the issue. By the time the summary of options had wound down, the Cabinet members had retraced every step they'd taken with Burlington earlier in the evening, and Marva and General Martin Tarrenton, the head of the Joint Chiefs of Staff, had joined them. The clock had just struck midnight when a secured phone rang from the corner of the room. It was the burly General that picked it up.

"Um, hmm. You're certain. Thank you, General. Please stand by the phone, Jack. I'll get back to you shortly." Setting the receiver down, the military chief looked directly at Andy. "It's started. We have confirmation on the ground that the attack began at about nine p.m. our time. Communications are spotty, so we don't have much in the way of casualty reports. We do know a hospital was hit in the initial shelling, and we do know that Croat and Muslim forces are in route to bolster the city's defenses."

Kathy took the initiative of speaking first. Her thoughts were so focused on her duties that Mark's possible presence at the destroyed hospital hadn't yet entered her mind. "General, what are their prospects of defending the city without expanded U.S. support?"

"Madame President, our best projections are that their chances are virtually nil. I don't believe they can hold out for more than six or seven days if we don't bring our air power in the Adriatic to bear on the Serbs' heavy guns and armor."

Looking at the faces around the table, she saw Secretary of State Edward Blankett nod in agreement. So too did the Secretary of Defense, but it was the rotund Blankett that brought the discussion back to the principal stumbling block: the growing threat of intervention from the Russians.

"The Russian President let us know again this afternoon that any U.S. escalation will be matched by his country. Our psych analysts at the CIA believe that the threat is legitimate."

"And we all know how public sentiment's running," added Danielson. "The polls indicate they'll recall the entire government if we dive into this thing."

Pressing her fingers to her chin, Kathy remembered her history lessons on World War I, and how the disastrous conflict was precipitated by the assassination of the Austrian Archduke Ferdinand while he was in Serbia. The last thing anyone needed was for her to direct an action in that same region that would set the fuse for a third world war.

"It would seem now's a good time for me to ask for that decision you reached before I joined you, Paul," she said to Atkinson. Continuing, she took great care with the words that followed. "I'd like to know what this Cabinet's best *recommendation* to me is."

Atkinson bristled, but by this point in the long evening he'd grudgingly accepted the sanctity of the Constitution and Kathy's rightful place at the head of the table and the government. His reply was restrained. "It is our *recommendation* that we first notify the Russians of our intent and then launch limited air strikes from our carriers in the Adriatic against their armor and heavy artillery. We feel that if we time limit the offensive to somewhere around seventy-two hours that they'll ultimately decide not to intervene. Hell, it'll take 'em that long just to get their forces over there."

"And what are casualty figures estimated at?" the President inquired.

"We estimate ours to be minimal so long as we restrict the operation to air and naval power. Enemy casualties on the ground are projected at somewhere in the neighborhood of a thousand given our surgical strike capabilities," the General responded.

"And if we stand pat?" she followed.

"Much, much higher, maybe a hundred thousand, with about seventy-five percent of the casualties being civilians, Bosnian Croats and Muslims in Sarajevo."

And at least one very special American, she suddenly realized. My God, Mark was there! If she didn't approve the counter-offensive, he would die! If she did, Bill and the others on the Kitty Hawk would be placed in harm's way. The world's biggest diplomatic and military problem had just become very personal.

"Is there anything else," she concluded. "No? Well, I want time to consider this carefully. We'll reconvene at three tomorrow afternoon. Please keep me apprised of any developments between now and then. Thank you, ladies and gentlemen."

Before another word could be said, and there were clearly more on the way from Atkinson, the new President had risen and left the room. Marva followed her while Andy stayed to gather up his briefing papers.

"Andy, does this woman have a clue what she's doing? There's too much at stake here to have some diva in the Oval Office dragging us into World War III," Atkinson fumed.

Mathers looked up from his papers at the Secretary, nearly piercing him with his gaze. "Paul, don't make the mistake of underestimating this woman. And that goes for the rest of you too. She's the real deal, she'll listen to us and she'll make the right call. And she'll get the public behind it, whatever it is."

Atkinson looked back at him with serious concern in his eyes. "I hope you're right, Andy."

* * * * * * * * * *

Nearby in the Oval Office, Kathy was asking Marva to close the door. "Marva, Mark could be dead, I mean how many hospitals are there in Sarajevo?"

"Can we confide in Andy?" Marva asked. "Between Mark and the blackmailer, we need some major help."

Damn! She'd forgotten about that too. The blackmail problem had taken on whole new proportions. It now threatened not only to destroy her, but to undermine the government during a world crisis. She needed her integrity intact, by God, if she was going to lead the country into war, even a limited war. The stakes were higher now, much higher.

"Mar, I think we've got to fill Andy in. Would you do it please? And let's set up a status meeting with Gower tomorrow just prior to the Cabinet meeting. Include Andy and you in that. Oh, and please chat with Andy about his thoughts on doing a national television address from here tomorrow. Seems to me the country could use some reassurance after getting the news about the President's stroke."

"Done," her aide said concisely.

Rubbing her eyes, Kathy felt the after-effects of the adrenalin rush she'd been on all night. She was exhausted. Right now, getting some sleep was tops on her presidential 'things to do' list.

"One last thing, Marva. Do you think you could line up a place for me to sleep tonight? And would you have someone pick up some of my and Chrissie's things from the residence so we can get by here awhile?"

An hour later, the long and amazing day came to an end for the new President in the green-trimmed Lincoln Bedroom of the White House. The walls of the famous room were a soft beige, tastefully garnished with dark green and gold-trimmed draperies and similar colored carpeting. It was furnished with American Victorian antiques dating back to 1850, the centerpiece of which was a magnificent rosewood bed that measured some six feet across and about eight feet in length. The head and foot boards had been carved by a gifted craftsman and included replicas of birds, grapevines, and flowers that took her breath away. Once her fascination subsided, she was fast asleep within minutes after laying her head on the fluffy pillows. For the next five hours, she wrestled with nightmares of death and destruction. Her family's and the world's.

Daylight seemed to come in minutes, bringing with it the burdens of the presidency and her fears for her family. Kathy was awakened by the knock of one of the White House servants on the bedroom's old wooden door.

"Yes," she called out wearily without lifting her head.

"Madame President," came a voice through the door. "Mr. Mathers asked us to inform you that he and your daughter are waiting for your presence for breakfast, ma'am."

"Just a minute," Kathy called back.

Pulling herself from bed, she pulled on the guest bathrobe she found in the bathroom and went to the door. On the other side was an older black man dressed in a white servant's uniform. He looked like he'd stepped out of a time long ago when social norms were very different. In his arms were what Kathy recognized as her makeup bag and her favorite royal blue suit.

"Ma'am, your daughter picked this out for you. I'll just wait here until you're ready so I can escort you to the President's Dining Room," he said.

"Thank you...may I ask your name?" the President queried.

"Oscar Jackson, ma'am."

"Well, thank you, Oscar. I appreciate it. Give me about thirty minutes and I'll be with you."

Kathy went about getting ready as she had a thousand times before. Outside, the old servant stood patiently without complaint. After all, it had been over twenty years since one of his presidents had shown him the courtesy of asking his name as though it meant something and was worth remembering. Sure enough, when Kathy emerged a half an hour later, the first words out of her mouth were, "*Oscar*, you can show me to the dining room now." *Too bad she's a Republican*, he thought to himself as he led her down the hall. She was alright. He wouldn't at all mind if she'd stick around for a while.

* * * * * * * * * *

The ornately decorated dining room was one of several in the White House. As large as it seemed

when she first walked in, it was apparently the
smallest of the lot according to the knowledgeable
servant. The walls were covered in scenic light blue
wallpaper depicting events from the Revolutionary
War, including George Washington's entry into Boston
in 1776. The windows were framed by beautiful
draperies made of blue and green silk damask,
garnished with gold-fringed green silk valances. The
dark hardwood floor was covered with a Turkish
Hereke rug on which sat the most exquisite Sheraton
pedestal dining table, ringed by eight New York
Sheraton chairs. Sitting at the end of the long
mahogany table were Andy Mathers and Chrissie. The
Chief of Staff looked like he'd been up all night. In
fact, he had.

"Good morning, Madame President," her
daughter perkily teased. She was enjoying the
excitement of the White House, but then she wasn't
aware of the precariousness of world events, or the
possibility that her father may have been killed. At
least not yet.

"Good morning," Andy said quietly.

"Good morning. Any news on the President's
condition, Andy?"

"Nothing new. They still have him graded
'critical'," he answered sadly.

"I'm sorry. Well, we'll just have to keep
praying for him. I assume Marva brought you up to
speed," she said, referring cryptically to the blackmail
situation.

"Yes, she did. Perhaps we can chat after
breakfast?"

Kathy agreed and watched with interest as
Andy ravaged the omelet and toast he had in front of
him. As they enjoyed the White House chef's best, she
thanked Chrissie for her choice of the blue suit and

175

discovered to her surprise she'd voluntarily taken on responsibility for getting them settled in temporary quarters at the White House. The show of accountability wasn't something she often saw from her daughter and it pleased her. Finishing his meal, Andy confirmed arrangements had been made for a six-thirty p.m. address to the nation and promised Kathy a draft of the speech by lunch. Excusing himself, the aide and his dark circled eyes headed off to work leaving the mother and child alone.

"Chrissie, there are some things I think you should know. They're very difficult, but it involves the family and I think you have a right to know," Kathy cautioned her.

"Yes, mother?"

"Baby, we think your father went to Sarajevo in Bosnia with some other doctors to help the people there. The city is under attack and we have information that a hospital was severely damaged in the initial shelling. We're trying our best to find out about your Dad, and I'll let you know as soon as I find out."

Chrissie broke into a whimper, and Kathy stepped from her seat to put her arms around her. "I'm sure he's ok, honey. At least he's with a bunch of other doctors."

"Can you get him out, mother?" she asked with a child's expectation.

"I don't know, Chrissie. It's not quite that easy, it's not like I can just send a bunch of Marines over there to rescue him."

"That's not true, mother. You're the President. You *can* do that," the teenager cried.

Odd as it sounded, her little girl was right, technically at least. She *was* the Commander in Chief of the military and did have far reaching powers over the services. But she also didn't have the luxury of putting her problems before the country's.

Downing the last bit of coffee from her china cup, she bid goodbye to her daughter and set off for the Oval Office. It was regular business hours now, and activity in the hallways was heavy. For most of the White House staff, a glimpse in the hall was their first personal view of the beautiful new President that would soon fill a chapter in the history books. From the office chatter, it appeared no one was disappointed with the charming new boss, but then the often rude and haughty Burlington was an easy act to follow in many ways.

When she reached her desk, Andy and Marva were both already there discussing the blackmail scheme. Everyone loves to play amateur detective and they were no different. Marva shared their best guesses as to the blackmailer's identity.

"Andy's confident neither the President nor any of his people were behind it," she began. "We both think Farley's the one with the axe to grind, and now he's got everything in the world to gain. If you were forced to resign, he'd automatically assume the presidency."

"True enough," Kathy reasoned aloud, "but how could he set it up?"

Andy proceeded to share what he knew of Farley's background. "Some time ago, he was an Army intelligence officer in Vietnam. After he was elected to Congress, he chaired the sub-committee that oversees the CIA. I'm sure he met a number of 'spooks' as a result, maybe this 'Kevin Reilly' character was one of 'em. How about we call the Director of the CIA in here?"

"No, Andy. I've entrusted investigating this to Tom Gower. If he decides that's wise we'll let *him* do it. But I suppose it can't hurt to bounce your thoughts off of him when we meet at two-thirty."

For the next hour the three discussed the various options on dealing with the Bosnian situation that had been outlined the night before. The more they talked, the more uncomfortable Kathy was becoming with the responsibility of having to make a decision that could jeopardize the lives of thousands, maybe millions if the Russians got involved. Funny, the crazy things that creep into your mind at the oddest times. She suddenly remembered the little girl that used to hide her father's axe on the farm so he couldn't kill a chicken for dinner. She abhorred death at any level, and the thought of sending any mother's son into combat turned her stomach. The fact her son would be among them if she authorized the action underscored the horror of the choice she had to make. But she would have to make it.

"Andy, what if we call the Russian ambassador in here and I make a personal plea to him to either use their influence to stop the Serb attack or in alternative to at least stay out of our way?" she suggested.

"Nothing to lose, really, as I see it. If they can't or won't then we're no worse off. We still have the hope that the seventy-two hours will be just short enough to keep them from diving in."

It was the best course they could come up with between them. They agreed they'd run it by the Cabinet, and if there was a consensus, then she would meet with the ambassador at five before her televised address. Andy was told to include that approach in the draft of the speech and to arrange to have the ambassador on standby. In the meantime, the remainder of the day would be committed to informing congressional leaders on the rapidly changing events.

That series of meetings came and went in quick succession. Before Kathy knew it, the time had come for her to meet with Tom Gower. Preparing for his arrival, she pulled the blackmail photos from her briefcase and sat them on the desk. If only he had a lead of some kind...

"Good afternoon, Madame President," Gower said to her as he entered with Andy and Marva.

"Hello, Tom. Please tell me you have some news," she pleaded.

The three pulled up chairs in front of the big desk and sat down. Gower wasted no time in beginning.

"Well, there are three sets of prints on the photos: yours, Chrissie's, and an unidentified third set. The third doesn't match anything in the international computer database."

"What exactly does that mean, Tom?" Andy asked him.

"It means they belong to 'Joe Citizen', a person never arrested, never in the military, who never worked for the government. It could even be the prints of the guy who developed the film. It means it doesn't help us."

Kathy tried desperately to cling to her hopes. "Tom, do you have *any* leads?"

Gower looked miffed at the new President's expectations for immediate results, but he reminded himself of the pressures she was under. "We're searching for the mysterious Mr. Reilly. I expect a call here within the half hour from the field agent I put on him. We believe we know where he's at. If we're right, we'll either have him or at least some clues to tell us who he's been involved with. We're also checking bank and phone records, etc. If you're asking me who I suspect at this point, if I had to pull a name out of the air it would be Stewart Farley."

Andy and Marva looked at each other as if to say, "heck we figured that out and we haven't been running the FBI for twenty years!"

Gower continued, "We have information on Mr. Farley that he's unaware we have. I can't yet link him to this, but I can tell you something like this is not beyond his character."

Kathy felt the perspiration flowing. She'd hoped for more from Gower. She'd hoped for a miracle.

"Thomas, this is in confidence and can't leave this room. There's a strong possibility that we'll be entering the war in Bosnia within hours. We expect it to be on a short term and very limited basis, however, there's also the possibility that it'll bring the Russians in. The last thing this country can withstand right now is chaos at the top of the government. If that photo gets out, it'll undermine me with the public at a time we need their full support. If I resign, either voluntarily or under pressure, Stewart Farley steps in. I'm sure you'll agree he's the last person this country needs in the driver's seat at a time like this."

Gower understood and agreed wholeheartedly. He knew Farley could never maintain public support under the weight of the Balkan conflict, and the secret the FBI head held in his possession persuaded him that Farley should not reside in the White House.

"Madame President, I assume time is of the essence," Gower said with proper presumption.

"Yes, Tom, it is. Very much so."

"Then let me say this as carefully as I can. If it *is* Farley, I have the ability to neutralize him. That's all you need to know. But I do want your personal consent."

Every eye in the room grew larger. Marva spoke for them all when she asked for clarification of exactly what he meant by "neutralize".

Gower reacted with indignation at the obvious implications of the question. "People, please! I'm not the CIA! I mean the information I have on Farley is as damaging to him as the information somebody's trying to use against you. I'm talking standoff, stalemate, not 'hit'."

Kathy stood up and walked to the window, eyeing the beautiful White House grounds. This was definitely not her style, but her alternatives were few. "Tom, if you don't have information clearing Farley within twenty-four hours, do it. I don't want his head, I just want him to back off. And I want the film."

"Understood," he said with a sadistic smirk on his face. "It's as good as taken care of."

The buzz of the intercom interrupted them. It was Gower's call, which he took on an extension on the other side of the room. He was looking cock-sure when he returned a few minutes later.

"We found him. They're holding him at a rundown motel the other side of town. We should know more before my twenty-four hours are up."

Kathy thanked him for his loyalty and help and saw him to the door. It was now five after three, and they were late for the Cabinet meeting that would decide the country's response to the Serb offensive. Walking down the hall in the direction of the Cabinet Room, the trio was intercepted by Mathers' harried secretary, who ran after them in order to give him a small slip of paper. On it was a strangely cryptic message. It read simply "homerun".

"What's that?" Kathy asked quizzically.

"Good news! Real good news," he beamed.

"How good?"

181

"We've received intelligence information that your husband's alive. I don't know what shape he's in, but at the time of this message, he was still with us!"

Her eyes moistened, but she knew Mark was anything but safe. It was way too soon to be counting eggs in baskets.

"Thank you, that's great to hear. Mar, would you do me a big favor and tell Chrissie before you join us?"

The Cabinet meeting was much more subdued than the previous evening's, somber like a wake, with the world seeming to move closer to war with every tick of the clock. The new President's presentation of her plan was brief and to the point, and the Cabinet quickly reached consensus that it was the best of the lousy alternatives on the table. As they broke, Kathy asked them to remain until after her meeting with the Russian ambassador so she could brief them on his reaction.   Anatoly Roschenko was a chameleon. Like most in the Russian leadership, the former communist had made himself over into a reformer after the breakup of the Soviet Union. And like most of the others, he was about as sincere as a snake oil salesman on that score. He was old-school, a former high ranking KGB official who walked with the same overweight waddle that Leonid Brezhnev had had. A beefy fellow, he resembled an old Soviet bear, particularly when he drank, which by all accounts he did often. As he ambled into the Oval Office at a fashionably late five after five, it appeared he'd already been intimate with a bottle of Vodka.

"Good evening, Mr. Ambassador. Thank you for coming on such short notice," Kathy said staidly as she greeted the hefty diplomat. "It's a pleasure to finally meet you. I regret it's under such circumstances."

"Thank you, Madame President. On behalf of my government, I extend welcome to you in your new capacity. And may I say, you are much prettier than your predecessor," he replied smoothly through a thick accent.

Andy showed Roschenko to a chair, renewing his acquaintance with the man he'd dealt with for four years as Burlington's Chief of Staff. "Mr. Ambassador," he said dryly, "there's a chill in the air. I hope we can warm it before we all freeze."

The President took her seat behind what was now *her* desk, and narrowed her bright green eyes as she addressed him. "Mr. Ambassador, we cannot afford miscommunication at this very dangerous time, so I'll be direct. The United States has been patient and restrained in our dealings with the Bosnian Serb leadership. We will not, however, permit the current offensive against Sarajevo to proceed thus permitting the slaughter of tens of thousands of civilians. I have asked you here to inform you that at four o'clock this afternoon I authorized our forces in the Adriatic, operating under U.N. and NATO resolutions, to launch a seventy-two hour air and naval campaign against Serb forces attacking the city. I am asking your government to exercise the same restraint we have shown in the past, and to refrain from acting on your threats to involve your country militarily in the conflict."

The old Russian bristled. It was bad enough he'd had to adjust to perestroika and the new order, but being bullied by an American woman flaunting military force, President or not, politely or not, was too much.

"Mrs. Canfield, you are new to this office, perhaps you do not understand what you do. The Russian people do not back down. You must know we will retaliate as if your attacks were against Russian soil. You are starting world war. But do not make mistake, we will send our ships, our planes if you do this."

The poker game had begun, and with the highest of stakes.

"Mr. Ambassador, please communicate what I have told you to your government. All we ask is seventy-two hours, no more," she said strongly, rising to shake his large hand thereby signaling the end of the meeting. "Thank you for coming."

As the Russian approached the door, he paused and turned to face the American head of state. "Madame, President, the next time we speak, we will be at war. The blood of many will be on your hands." His gait was straight and brisk as he hurried away to report to his superiors.

Neither Kathy nor Andy said a word for the better part of a minute. Finally, Andy broke the silence with a desperate plea. "Dear God, if ever the world needed your helping hand, it's now."

The clock struck six as the President and her Chief of Staff knelt together in prayer on the sky blue carpeting of the Oval Office. Within three cycles of its brass hands, they'd know whether or not they'd been heard.

CHAPTER ELEVEN

The President's address to the nation was a dynamic one, or at least so Bill thought as he stood in the Kitty Hawk's overcrowded rec room and watched it on the satellite feed with a hundred of his shipmates. Space in the iron-walled room was so tight he could tell what deodorant the sweaty young officer next to him was wearing. He'd only known for a few days about the chain of events that'd catapulted his mother into the presidency, and it'd seemed like a dream until now. The picture of her on the tube in front of him made it all real, *too* real considering her words.

"...and so at four o'clock this afternoon, after consultation with the Cabinet and congressional leaders of both parties, I authorized U.S. forces in the Adriatic to launch defensive actions to protect the innocent civilians of Sarajevo from slaughter. I have urged the Russian leadership to refrain from following through on their threats to intercede against our forces and have advised them of the seventy-two hour limit placed on our action. I remain optimistic that they will ultimately see the wisdom of restraint and not send this limited humanitarian action spiraling toward world war." She went on to say how she understood the feelings of mothers whose sons were being placed at risk above foreign soil, noting that her son too was a part of the U.S. forces of 'Operation Survival', her new name for Burlington's 'Operation Backbreaker'.

There was only one problem for Bill Canfield. The first wave of F-14's had left the Kitty Hawk a half hour ago, without him. He'd been grounded by the ship's captain as soon as the news came across the wires of his mother's rise to the Oval Office. He wasn't sharing the risks the other pilots were and that infuriated him. He wanted to fly, he wanted to help protect these people, even without knowing that his father was among them. Storming from the room in frustration, he bulled his way through the narrow corridors toward Butch Norton's quarters at the other end of the carrier. He was breathless and covered in perspiration by the time his knuckles rapped on the wall of the Lt. Commander's room.

"Yes?" Norton growled in response.

"Sir, it's Lieutenant Canfield requesting permission to enter."

"Permission granted. Come on in, Lieutenant."

Stepping through the privacy curtains, Bill snapped to attention in front of the undershirt clad squadron leader. "Request permission to speak with you, sir, concerning my grounding."

"Lieutenant, that wasn't my decision," Norton answered in sympathy. "If it were up to me, son, I'd have you up there. You're too good to sit down."

The compliment helped, but it didn't solve his problem. His growing desperation was apparent as he pleaded with Norton. "Thank you, sir, but you've got to help me. Please talk to the Captain on my behalf. I

186

can't sit on the sidelines while the other guys take all the risks, just because of my *mother*. Please, sir."

Norton looked pained and helpless. He understood Bill. Hell, ten years ago he was Bill. "Lieutenant, I've already fought that battle! The old man nearly busted me for pushing the point this morning. It'd take a frickin' order from the Secretary of the Navy himself to get you back in the air, boy," he yelled in mirrored frustration.

"Or an order from the President?" Bill asked.

Norton smiled, amused at the lad's creative problem solving. "Well, I reckon that'd do it. You know, I might be able to get you a few minutes on the ship-to-shore phone down in communications."

"Thank you, sir," the flyer said, with newfound hope in his voice. "Thank you."

Getting to the communication center was easy, but getting a call through to the President isn't, he discovered. Not even when the President is your mother. It took nearly forty minutes of transfers and holds before a string of skeptical voices put Bill through to the new President's Assistant Chief of Staff. Marva recognized the youthful but manly voice immediately.

"Bill, how are you? Let me get your mother for you son, she's right here."

"Bill? Is that you?" asked Kathy, sounding every bit a mother and not at all like a president.

"Hi mother. Thought maybe you could use a direct report from the action out here," he joked.

"Bill, I've got my hands full at the moment, are you okay?"

"Well, I would be if I could get up in the air. They've grounded me because of you, mother," he informed her.

"Maybe that's best, Bill. If you were captured, they'd have a field day."

"That's possible, but what about what you told all those other mothers? I don't *want* special treatment, and you won't be able to keep the public's support when they find out I've been held back. This is what I do. I need to be able to do it. Please, get them to reinstate me," he begged.

If ever there'd been a battle between head and heart, this was it. Every fiber of her being was crying out to keep her son from harm's way, but that was not his wish, and he was right. She had no moral authority to protect her flesh and blood while risking other American sons and daughters. And given Mark's imprisoned status in the besieged city, the Canfield family stood to benefit more than any other American family if the air attack succeeded in breaking the Serb offensive. It was time that young Bill be apprised of his father's plight.

"Bill, you're right, of course. There is something you should know though, son. We're virtually certain your father's in Sarajevo right now as part of some Red Cross relief mission. I'm not crazy about having both of the men in my life in the middle of this thing."

His reaction was impassioned. "God mother, what in the hell is he doing in there! If anything, that's all the more reason for me to go. At least if I can get up in the air I'll be able to help Dad. As much as I can, anyway."

And then the chiming of the office clock began anew, an annoying reminder of the dwindling time.

"That damned clock," Kathy thought to herself as she tried to find the words and the strength to utter what Bill wanted to hear. With every 'tick', time seemed to be running out on her, and on her family.

"Mother? Are you still there?" Bill asked the silence. "Hello?"

"Bill," she finally gasped, "please take care of yourself. Don't take any crazy chances. Please promise me that."

"Of course, mother," he said to her calmly. "I promise. You'll take care of it then?"

"It'll be done. Love you, Billy."

His reply was barely audible, but she understood why. He wasn't alone. "I love you, too, mother. Goodbye." And then there was a click, and he was gone.

Marva was beginning to understand her pretty well, Kathy thought as she hung up the phone. That reassuring hand had again found her troubled shoulder.

"He'll be okay, don't worry. Tarrenton was telling me that air losses in the Gulf War were almost nonexistent, and that the anti-air equipment around Sarajevo's even less effective than what they had in Baghdad. And remember, Bill's an exceptional pilot," she said in an effort to soothe her worried boss.

"I know. I know. I gave him my word, Mar. Would you see that the order gets to the Kitty Hawk's Captain?" Kathy said with an emptiness in her voice and a sadness in her eyes.

Marva nodded and headed off to the Cabinet room to pass the directive on to General Tarrenton. The aide couldn't help but think that Kathy must be feeling a lot like Abraham as he prepared to offer up his only son Isaac. There'd been a look of bleak resignation on her face, as though she'd peered into the future and seen the worst.

* * * * * * * * * *

Back on the U.S.S. Kitty Hawk an hour later, a second strike force was preparing to launch. This time, Lieutenant Bill Canfield was a part of it. Climbing up the tiny metal footholds of his F-14, he gave a thumbs up sign to his communications officer, and lifted himself into the tight cockpit of the fighter. His adrenalin nearly carried him clear over the other side of the plane, like an excited cowboy accidently jumping over his saddled horse. Once strapped into his seat, he began working his way through the pre-flight checklist he'd gone through a hundred times before. This time, he went a little more cautiously than usual making sure there would be no oversight that would jeopardize the promise he'd made to his mother. By the time the LSO had given him the green light to launch, he was positive he'd never been readier. With just a little bit of luck, and a heads-up performance by his skittish colleague in the back, he was confident they'd be able to deliver their ordinance without taking a hit from the out-of-date ground-to-air weapons they'd be facing. With that assurance, he gave the LSO the thumbs up sign and felt the sudden release of the jet shove him back into his seat with enough force to pull his cheeks back toward the carrier that quickly fell behind as he guided the F-14 skyward.

They'd been assigned a heavy artillery battery as their primary target on this sortie, and a tank battalion as the secondary. With the sophisticated guidance systems of the Maverick missiles and AGM-62 glide bombs he was carrying, there'd be no excuse other than cloud cover for an unsuccessful mission. If the weather reports back on the Kitty Hawk indicating a one hour break in the usually dismal weather were correct, then the mission was a done deal. His first combat sortie was looking good, as Butch Norton came over the radio to address them fifteen minutes into the flight.

"Red Rover leader to squadron, targets approximately ten minutes out. Disengage safeties and arm ordinance. Repeat, disengage safeties and arm ordinance."

Flipping the series of switches that armed his weapons, Bill eased back on the stick and felt the computer triggered wings of the F-14 open as he and the rest of the squadron slowed to attack speed. Suddenly, radio silence was broken by a priority message from the E-2C Hawkeye flying above to coordinate the attack.

"Red Rover, this is Eagle Eye. We have bogeys inbound on your position from three o'clock low, do you copy?" came the startling warning.

Norton's surprise was evident in his reply. "Come again Eagle Eye. You say bogeys? We were led to believe they didn't even have a weather balloon in this sector."

"That's an affirmative, Red Rover. Radar indicates five fighters inbound. By radar signature and air speed, we believe they're MiG-23's."

"Shit!" Scarecrow yelled into the intercom. "We're not even carrying air-to-air. We're sitting ducks!"

Bill had done his homework and he knew that the older Soviet-made Floggers heading their way couldn't match the F-14's speed and maneuverability in a dogfight, if the squadron could get that close without first being decimated by whatever air-to-air missiles their opponents might be carrying.

"Eagle Eye, this is Red Rover leader," they heard Norton say. "Please ask Homeboy to equip and scramble backup. We are not equipped to defend, over."

"We copy, Red Rover leader. Stay loose, help is on the way!"

Their adrenalin began pumping like the Alaska Pipeline, set off by the realization that their first combat mission was going terribly awry. The experienced Norton knew he had to settle his men-children down before the MIG's arrived. "Red Rover leader to squadron. Boys, it looks like the Russians've slipped a wild card in on us and loaned some old fighters to these guys. We're approaching target, so we're goin' in to complete our mission. After you've dumped ordinance, rendezvous back at ten thousand feet. They won't have us in missile range for three or four minutes, that's enough time to get it done and the lighter load'll give us a fighting chance to evade while we're waiting for support. Stay calm and good luck. And remember, this is what you've trained for!"

Shadow Canfield tried to reassure his nervous radar information officer. "Scarecrow, stay cool, man. I can handle these characters if you just stay cool and call out the approach and the breaks, buddy. Just like maneuvers."

This was what Bill lived for, the opportunity to compete, to prove he was the best. His heart beat faster as the MIG's neared, because he knew the advantage they were conceding the Russian aircraft was a significant one. With five fighter's firing inbound missiles, there was far too much chance of flying out of the path of one right into the path of another. His flying was going to have to be tighter and more precise than ever, and his reactions were going to have to be quicker than lightning. One miscalculation, one stroke of bad luck, and they'd become a fireball his father could see from the city below.

Pressing forward on the stick and dropping his flaps, he began his approach to the target with

Scarecrow working overtime to lock in the weapons. As the heavy artillery came into view on the jet's powerful cameras, Scarecrow gave him the go ahead to release the glide bombs on the locked target. Bill could feel the F-14 rumble and jump as the weight of the heavy bomb casings dropping away from the aircraft propelled it upward. It was as though the plane was caught in an updraft. Breaking right, he made a snap decision to go for broke and pointed the nose of the heavy fighter toward the secondary target, the tank battalion whose guns were mercilessly pounding the defenseless city below. Scarecrow confirmed a direct hit on the primary target, as the delayed sound of the AGMs exploding onto the artillery pieces reached his ears. Suddenly, he could see the tank battalion dead ahead, rising up from the middle of a clearing. He could also hear the high-tech plane's alarm buzzer screaming out, announcing the approach of an enemy missile.

"Shadow, we have an inbound AAM at five o'clock, two miles out," Tommy announced anxiously to his pilot. "Must be using the cheap stuff or they woulda fired from further out! Prepare for a hard right on my signal."

"Keep it tight, pal, I'm on approach. I don't want to break off unless I have to," Bill replied.

Brunarski had to lift his visor to wipe the sweat from his eyes. His life was in the hands of some flying Rambo! He was nuts, absolutely nuts, he thought. All he could do was beg, and keep his eyes glued to his radar console. He suspected the first wouldn't do much good with 'Wild Bill' Canfield, so he focused on the second.

"Don't do this to me, man. This ain't no game, that thing's coming down our heat trail awful fast!"

"Just keep it tight. I can make it to target and get missile lock, before it gets here," Bill insisted.

The next thirty seconds felt like thirty days to Tommy Brunarski. The blip on his radar kept getting closer and closer. As he turned his head to make visual contact, he could see the smoke trail from their pursuer. It was less than a mile out. And then, as if things weren't bad enough, the warning alarm sounded again. This time his radar told him the threat was from the ground. Anti-aircraft missiles had been launched at their F-14 and at their wingman's. They were now being squeezed from two sides, and Bill was still staying his course. Before the panicked Scarecrow could beg him one more time to break away, he noticed the tanks finally coming into view on his monitor screen and felt the shudder of the aircraft as Bill released the laser-guided Mavericks.

"Thank God, now get the hell out of here! Break up and right!"

Bill pulled back on the stick and gave the powerful bird full throttle, breaking hard right at the same time. As he did so, Tommy jettisoned a series of flares to distract the guidance systems of the approaching weapons. The MIG-fired AAM roared by their starboard side not much more than fifty feet away, momentarily blinding Bill as the smoke of its exhaust crossed the climbing jet's path. As he rolled the plane over, the second threat, the ground-to-air missile, passed beneath the jet's underbelly, another near miss.

"Give me the coordinates to the MIG's, fast. We've gotta close to gun range so we can engage," Bill screamed to his buddy.

"Hard left thirty degrees and hold. I've got two bandits sixty seconds out at full throttle."

Bill began looking left and right for his wingman, but he was nowhere in sight. He didn't know whether he'd been shot down or if he'd just lost him with his roller coaster maneuver. Not everyone could hang with Shadow Canfield's version of 'Mr. Toad's Wild Ride'.

"Red Rover One to Red Rover Two, position please," he said into the radio, and then repeated it as they bore down on the MIG's. There was no reply.

Closing to a half mile, two against one, the alarm system again sounded.

"We've got two inbound AAM's. Releasing counter measures," Scarecrow screamed into the intercom.

Unless they had pretty current armament, a head-to-head shot was a million to one at this range Bill told himself, especially with the flares and chafe Tommy had just tossed into their flight path. He could see the propellant trails as the missiles approached, but he bit his lip and held his course against all natural instinct. From this angle, it looked close. Real close. As they neared, he shut his eyes for a second until he heard the rushing sound they made as they passed by both sides of the jet's fuselage. He felt the sharp pain of his teeth cutting through his lip and the warmth of his blood as it trickled from the side of his mouth.

"Eeeee hahhhh!" he bellowed out to release tension. Jerking back on the stick, he put the agile fighter into a steep vertical climb as the MIG's whistled past below. As quickly as he'd pulled back, he pushed forward, hitting the plane's brakes and flaps and throwing it over into a vertical dive on the trail of the Russian-made fighters. The first rolled left and he followed the second to the right, matching him turn for turn, maneuver for maneuver until he had him in gun range. Clicking the weapons system to 'guns,' he pressed the cap of the stick and watched the first burst of tracers strike out in vain for the enemy plane. With the second round, the F-14's guns found their target and plumes of smoke spewed from its damaged engines as it rolled lazily left and downward, finally spiraling faster and faster toward the earth. Like a well-oiled machine, Scarecrow was already calling out the coordinates of the second MIG closing behind them. Hitting the brakes and pulling up again, Bill missed colliding with his opponent by no more than a few feet, sending the jet spinning out of control as the alarm went off for what seemed like the hundredth time. A series of anti-aircraft missiles had been fired at them from below, only this time the jet wasn't responding to his control. The jet wash from the MIG had propelled them into a spin.

After a few panicked, confusing seconds, control returned and he was able to level out and spot the MIG out the left side of his canopy as an errant Serb missile struck it, ripping it apart in a ball of flame.

Less than a few seconds later, before either Bill or Tommy could get their bearings back, their F-14 was struck violently by a second of the deadly anti-air missiles. It hit the rear of the plane, splitting it in half. Tommy died instantly. Somehow, instinctively through the spinning chaos, Bill's fingers found the handle to the ejection mechanism. The carefully packed charges blew what was left of the canopy away from the jet and fired him upward and out just as it began its fatal arc toward the ground. He lost consciousness for a moment as his body was thrown from the seat like a rag doll. Coming to only seventy-five feet from the ground, he found himself dropping into an orchard of some kind, dangling from his camouflaged parachute. Reacting to his training without a conscious thought, he bent his knees and absorbed the impact as his body carried through the branches of a tree before hitting the ground hard and rolling forward to a stop. Bill was dazed, too much so to enable him to effectively determine whether or not he'd been injured in the ejection. The sounds of voices from over the next hill acted like needed smelling salts, however, and in an instant he was hobbling after his open chute, gobbling it up in his arms and burying it in the nearby shrubbery along with his helmet. Ducking into the brush, he kneeled and peered out across the orchard, spying a platoon of Serb soldiers advancing over the ridge toward him. It was apparent they'd seen his chute and were headed his way, rifles at the ready.

It was his worst nightmare, and he knew he couldn't let himself be captured, certainly not as Bill Canfield. So he tore off his dog tags and the name patch from his flight suit, and buried them in the snow and soil. It was then that he heard the ruffle of the brush not ten feet behind him. Certain he was about to be captured or killed, he quickly drew his .45 caliber pistol from its shoulder holster and whirled about, ducking as he went. He nearly scared the lunch out of the dark haired young girl that faced him.

"Don't move," he ordered her with a quiet panic in his voice, pointing the pistol before inquiring if she spoke English.

"Not perfectly, but pretty good," she replied to the shaken aviator. "They're coming this way, hurry, we need to go."

And with that, she grabbed his hand like an angel of mercy and led him off through the orchard and the nearby woods to a small farm on the other side. As they neared a stone building that looked to Bill like a century old barn, an older man stepped from around the side with a beat up old rifle cradled in his arms. There was fear in his eyes when he saw them and anger in his voice as he yelled at the girl. She seemed to be arguing back with great energy until the man threw his hands in the air and headed into the barn with her and Bill in tow. Kicking away some mildewed straw from the damp floor of the old place, he revealed a half rotted wooden door in the floor with a circular iron handle. He and the girl pulled it up and shooed him inside, where he curled up with the musty old wine kegs and who knows what else. Once they closed the door on him, it was pitch black. Were it not for something scurrying across his boot, he would have been sure he was alone.

"Be patient, you will be safe here for now. I will come for you when they are gone," the girl told Bill through the wooden door, as she covered it with straw. He wasn't sure if she could hear him when he told her, "thank you," in return.

Time crawled by like an inchworm, but it gave him an opportunity to calm himself down and assess his condition. His head was bleeding and he had a splitting headache, maybe even a concussion. His left shoulder felt separated from hitting the canopy on ejection, and his right knee was badly sprained from the landing. He hurt, but he would live, at least from the injuries he'd sustained so far. But then again, the day wasn't over yet.

When it was quiet, he tried his emergency radio, but the weather and the walls of his protective shelter seemed to be preventing communication. Sustaining himself on a candy bar from his survival kit, Bill passed the time trying to figure out how to explain his predicament to his mother. After all, he had failed to keep his promise to the Commander in Chief.

Several hours went by before the girl and the man returned to let him out and invite him into their home for a basic dinner of bread and chicken. Bill quickly learned that her name was Marija and that the older man was her uncle with whom she'd lived since her parents were slain by the Serbs the year before. Once inside the tiny farm house, the man offered a pair of baggy clothes to Bill and went outside to bury the uniform that could cost them their lives if discovered. Dinner was actually an enjoyable experience for the young pilot.

"It is stupid war," Marija told Bill over the meal. "No side is right and all sides have committed crimes on the battlefield. It is waste of human life, and for nothing but prejudice and ethnic pride."

She went on to explain how all cultures had co-existed in the former Yugoslavia, without major difficulty, until the country crumbled into separate nations, fueled by pride in heritage. Croatia had been one of the first to declare its independence, and the rest had followed like falling dominoes. Somewhere in the process, people that had once been friends and colleagues, even husband and wife, had been separated by ethnic lines, she explained to him. Any impure lineage became suspect. In fact, Marija herself, was a Croat countess by heritage, but that meant nothing in the new order and hadn't since titles were abolished after Tito's rise to power over the former Yugoslavia decades ago. The fact that her father had been Hungarian made her life even less secure, particularly in Bosnia. Still, even though she didn't have a crown or a castle, it was wonderfully romantic to Bill to be rescued from certain doom by royalty, even if she did wear a peasant's clothes.

She was pretty, in her own way. Her hair was a dark auburn like his mother's, only thicker and

wavier. Her dirt smudged face was strong, but
sufficiently feminine to convey vulnerability when she
allowed it to. And somewhere hidden under the
disguise of the clean but faded dress was an awfully
nice figure, he imagined. As they talked together late
into the night, he forgot for the moment about his
plight, about the death of his friend, and about the
danger that surrounded him. Either the blow on his
head had been harder than he'd thought or she was
attracted to him, too. When she showed him to the
barn for the night, he kissed her on the cheek in
appreciation for her help. It was her that returned it
with a kiss on his lips.

The night was surprisingly quiet with only the
distant sounds of explosions serving as ugly, unwanted
reminders of the war. His dreams that night were filled
with thoughts of her, rather than thoughts of death. It
was, indeed, a pleasant relief from what had been and
what was to come.

Over the next forty-eight hours, Bill learned
much about Marija, about the various ethnic groups of
the region, and about life in Bosnia. He also learned
that his emergency radio had been irreparably
damaged during his bailout, leaving him cut off from
any reasonable chance of rescue. After discussion with
the girl and her uncle, he'd decided to wait out the last
day of the American air strikes, and then begin making
his way into Sarajevo. If his colleagues on the Kitty
Hawk and the rest of the task force in the Adriatic did
their jobs, there was a good chance that the Serbs
would be beaten back and that Sarajevo would soon be
safe, much safer at least than the open vulnerability of
the little Bosnian farm. It had been an absolute miracle
that it hadn't been destroyed during the war, but
apparently it had been passed over by most of the
ambitious Serb troops more intent on taking the big

city ten or twenty kilometers down the road. Fortunately for them, Marija had explained, the one Serb patrol that had come across their home was led by an old schoolmate of her uncle's, and he had mercifully spared them and their property and moved on. Nevertheless, she had been hidden away in the wine cellar so as not to tempt the accomplished rapists and murderers amongst the old friend's rag-tag troops.

By his third day with them, Bill was helping his hosts feed the chickens, pick up their eggs, and repair the roof of the stone and plaster-walled chicken coup as American warplanes streaked by only a few miles away. His injuries made it difficult, but he wanted to repay their courageous generosity. He knew their already fragile lives would end violently if they were caught sheltering him.

The end of the day came before he knew it, and with it came a glass of wine and Marija's pleasant company on the porch of the small farmhouse. The sounds of war had died down, and the sun was actually peeking through the gray skies as it began its plunge below the horizon.

"Oooh, is getting cold, is it not?" Marija said to him teasingly, as she nuzzled up closer to his body on the old cedar bench. She lifted the blanket she'd brought outside with her up to their necks, and as she did Bill pulled her closer to him until he could feel the beat of her heart pounding against his chest.

"That's better isn't it," he smiled. "You know, the sunset's so incredibly beautiful. Funny, but it's the first time I've actually seen the sun since I've been over here."

She came even closer to him until they were indistinguishable as separate people. Then she whispered into his ear, "Bill, you are so different from any man I know before. I meet Americans when I go to college in Belgrade and later in Sarajevo long time ago, but they were so, how you say... arrogant?" She kissed him softly. "You are not, and even though you are soldier, there is peace and love in your eyes. For so long, I have seen nothing but hate in the eyes of men."

When they turned their heads and peered into each other's souls, they each saw love looking back at them. It was instantaneous, almost from the moment they'd met, and in the war-torn world that surrounded them, no one had time to waste.

"Marija, I feel the same way. I've never met a woman like you, so strong, so brave... and so naturally beautiful. You are very special," he said, kissing her first gently and then with passion.

Suddenly, the cold had ceased to be a problem to them. It felt crisply warm to the new lovers. As she led him to the barn, the war stopped momentarily, as did time, or so it seemed as they made their way through the mud and snow to their centuries old hideaway. Their clothes tore away quickly under the privacy of the worn wool blanket, and for hours they made ardent, romantic love on their bed of straw. Afterwards, laying with her snuggled in his arms, Bill wondered why his mother had hated farm life. It seemed pretty good to him.

When she finally left his arms to return to the house, he could not sleep. He felt lonely without her, and the prospects of leaving in the morning for Sarajevo alone made him as gloomy as the grey skies above. Maybe he could stay an extra day he thought as he eventually drifted into slumber. Or two, or...

The roar of the jet's afterburners tore Bill from his sleep as it flashed through the early morning skies above the defenseless little farm. The distinct whir of its turbines was the same frightful sound he'd heard from the two Russian-made MIG's as they'd blasted by his F-14 during the dogfight three days before. It was barely daybreak as he rushed to the creaky barn door in time to see the shiny warplane banking upward above the tree line at the edge of the field. It was hardly two hundred feet off the ground as it began its climb, with the tiny farmhouse in clear view of its pilot and its weapons, courtesy of the rising sun. Spying the plane through the barn's doorway so as not to be seen, he watched it drop air speed and turn slowly into an approach that was taking it right back toward the farm at attack altitude.

"That bastard's gonna fire!" Bill cursed. In a fraction of a second, he could see the flame and smoke of the two missiles the Serb pilot had just launched, as though he were complying with Bill's prediction. Bolting full stride toward the farmhouse, he could see Marija and her uncle coming through the doorway as the missiles streaked down. The explosion as the warheads struck knocked them all to their knees, and obliterated the adjacent chicken coop. Bill glanced skyward at the fighter's underbelly as it pulled up and through the cloud of chicken feathers. The underside of the wings were bare, the pilot was out of missiles, he'd shot his wad. If they moved fast, and if there were no ground troops in communication with him, they would be alright.

Reaching his two friends, Bill yelled desperate directions to Marija. "Hurry to the barn, he's out of missiles! If we can get there before he comes around again, we've got a chance!"

They started to sprint as fast as their legs would carry them, but the old uncle was past a sprinter's prime, and they had to go back for him. Bill tried to persuade Marija to leave the old man to him and flee for the safety of the stone barn, but she was stubborn and wouldn't budge. They were stumbling and sliding on the treacherous earth and still fifty yards from refuge when the MIG leveled off for its second pass.

Its tracers pounded into the frozen earth like a hot butter knife, with each round inching closer and closer to the fleeing trio. The young pilot's stomach sank as he realized they were not going to make it. Shrieking, "Get down!" at the top of his lungs, Bill shoved the two Bosnians down and into the snow, throwing his body over the pretty Marija to protect her from the blazing rounds as they buried themselves into the ground around them.

The jet passed over its frightened targets and as it did, the old man rose to his feet and started again for the barn, but there was no sound of footsteps other than his own. He turned and looked over his shoulder as the roar of the jet turbines waned in his ears to see what had happened to his niece and the American flyer. They lay motionless on the ground, and he could see the sharp contrast of their crimson blood as it oozed from their bodies onto the stark white pallet of the snow covered earth.

CHAPTER TWELVE

The first day of the offensive was a chaotic one at the White House. The meeting with the Russian ambassador had left Kathy with barely thirty minutes to familiarize herself with her speech to the American people which was about to be nationally televised from the Oval Office. Even though a teleprompter had been set up, she needed to learn the lines well enough so as not to stumble over them. What she was about to announce to the public concerning the seventy-two hour action was not likely to be popular, and she was going to need all of her skills and powers of persuasion in order to turn the tide of public opinion. As Marva touched up her makeup for her, she hoped that the country would grant her a honeymoon period and the benefit of the doubt on her very risky decision.

When the red lights on the television camera came on, she sat up straight and looked into it with an open vulnerability that made her seem as though she were having a conversation with her best friend. She was forceful in defense of her decision, and reassuring

205

as she could be concerning the transition at the White House.

Andy Mathers stood by watching her and the monitor alternatively, in awe at the magic relationship she had with the camera. It seemed to magnify every beautiful curve and smooth out every line in her face. Even her voice sounded more melodic over the monitor's speaker system. If Ronald Reagan was the 'Great Communicator,' Kathy was certainly the 'Marvelous Mesmerizer'. Her beauty, carriage, and strength of character made her the most fascinating and attractive woman he had ever met. When the lights went off fifteen minutes later and she removed the microphone from her jacket, he stepped toward her with his compliments.

"Outstanding, absolutely so!" he said to his President in glowing admiration. "If I were sitting at home watching, I'd probably be calling my Navy recruiter right now, asking where I could sign up."

There was a sincere respect in his eyes, and that touched her deeply. Things had moved so quickly that she'd had little time to entertain self-doubts, but the Chief of Staff's reinforcement would help her fight them off when they did creep back into her mind.

"Thank you, Andy. Guess all those acting lessons came in handy," she replied gratefully. Touching him gently on the side of his face, she made sure he knew how much he meant to her. "I want you to know that your support's appreciated, more than I can ever really properly thank you for. I couldn't have gotten this far without it, without you."

He smiled, inside as well as out. He wasn't a man who generally worried about what others thought of him, but he found her opinion of him very important. As the camera crew broke down the equipment and he watched her take time to thank them, all he could think was, "what a woman."

* * * * * * * * * *

Across town, J. Thomas Gower was feeling his oats, wallowing in his element like a pig in mud, back on the front lines. As he stood over a weary Kevin Reilly in the tiny kitchenette of Reilly's cheap motel room, he excused the two FBI agents that'd located his suspect and held him until his arrival, and asked them to step outside. It was interrogation time and he loved it, perhaps even more so because of Reilly's CIA training. He'd be a tough nut to crack, a challenge.

"Well, Mr. Reilly...I'm sorry, it's O'Keefe, Miles O'Keefe isn't it?" he said to him arrogantly, as though trying to impress the young man with his knowledge.

The tired Irishman had already endured some three hours of free-lance questioning from Gower's agents and it hadn't inspired his cooperation. "Hey, you can call me Ray, or you can call me..." The slap of Gower's hand across his face stopped him mid-sentence.

"Now Miles, let's not insult each other. You know who I am and I know who you are. So, why don't we try and treat each other with a little professional courtesy?" Gower suggested with an edge in his voice. His interrogation methods were definitely old school, a sharp contrast to his natty dress and progressive image. He obviously hadn't forgotten his training as a rookie agent under Hoover over thirty years ago.

O'Keefe was beginning to wonder what in the hell was up, why the head of the FBI would be detaining and personally grilling a lowly CIA contractor.

"Professional courtesy, huh? Ok, how about we start with what the hell this is all about?"

Gower wasn't about to cede control of the interrogation to his subject. "Miles, that's not really something you need to know right now. In fact, the less you know, the better your chances for a longer life, free of incarceration. Get my drift?"

The FBI head was getting heavy-handed with him, convinced that he alone stood between disaster and the national security of the country at this delicate moment. He had no shortage of ego and that was readily apparent to O'Keefe as he sat in the uncomfortable wicker chair, shivering in his undershirt in the chilly motel room.

"Yea, got it. So how can I be of service to my good friends at the FBI?"

"Well, you can start, Miles, by telling me what you can about your relationship with Mr. Stewart Farley."

"The Speaker of the House?"

"That would be him."

"Haven't talked to him in four, maybe five years."

Gower bit into the inference like a wild dog, reading between the lines. "So you know him?"

Miles was growing tired of the game, and he wasn't going to drag himself down for anybody. Cooperation and self-preservation were starting to look like one and the same.

"My old man served in intelligence with him in 'Nam. Met him at a fundraiser my Pop took me to once, and again at a closed hearing when I was full-time with 'the agency' and he was chairing the House

Intelligence Committee. Since then, I don't think I've bumped into him but maybe once or twice in passing."

"Oh, really? So good old Stu had nothing to do with your little escapade at the Zebra Club a couple of months back?" The shock on O'Keefe's face told Gower he was hitting home.

"What? Hey, what the hell business does the FBI have poking into my sex life?" he demanded angrily, rising from the chair.

Gower shoved him back hard with a well-placed blow to his forehead, and the off-balance stud tumbled back into his seat.

"Well, I guess that depends on who *you're* 'poking', Miles," Gower said caustically. "Time to talk."

O'Keefe rocked back and forth in his chair nervously, then seemed to roll over for his insistent inquisitor. "Alright, but I gotta take a piss first, okay?"

"Sure, Miles. Let it never be said I don't know when to bow to a higher calling."

Gower called to the two field agents to keep an eye on his soon-to-be talkative suspect, then stepped outside for a Marlboro. He was a step away from bailing the beautiful new president's chestnuts out of the fire, and closing the box on the slimy Farley, all in one motion. The deep drag on the cigarette filled the air with acrid smoke, but to the puffed up Gower it smelled like the sweet aroma of success.

The crash of breaking glass from the side of the first floor room startled the relaxed Gower, causing him to drop his Marlboro. As the red hot butt melted into the snow, so too did his chance to get to the bottom of the blackmail scheme. Reacting to the noise, he bolted around the building, slipping and sliding as he turned the corner in time to see the younger of his two agents falling from the small broken bathroom window in vain pursuit of the escaped agency spook. Regrettably, O'Keefe was nowhere in sight and the sound of a motorcycle engine winding out from the rear alley told them they'd lost their prey.

"Sonofabitch, you idiots can't even hold onto a guy with his pants down!" Gower hollered in frustration. He was beet red with fury.

"I'm sorry, sir," the second agent apologized. "We didn't think the window was big enough for him to get through."

"Get after him, and find him, damn it! That is, if you plan on having a career to come back to!"

The humiliated young feds leapt into their government issued Ford, and sped off after the fleeing biker, but O'Keefe was already three blocks away, racing in the opposite direction to freedom. Gower walked back to his black Cadillac at the curb, angrily kicking a tire with enough force to crack the bone in his big toe. The pain forced a string of vibrantly colorful expletives from his mouth. Dragging his injured foot into the car, he tried to find the silver lining in the storm clouds that'd suddenly overcome his efforts. If nothing else, he thought, he'd confirmed O'Keefe's connection to Farley. If he had no more to go on by the same time tomorrow, then that would have to be enough. Hell, it was more than enough, he'd been looking for an excuse to take down Farley for years and now he had it, evidence or no. As he turned toward home, he knew his injured toe would feel much better in twenty-four hours. Right after he planted it squarely up Farley's backside.

* * * * * * * * * *

Daybreak brought day two of the three day offensive, and a nine a.m. meeting with the Cabinet.

The Washington Post and other print media were reporting mixed public reaction to her speech and Bosnia policy. ABC was reporting on its morning show that polling reflected that public opinion was shifting slightly in favor of the charismatic president. The encouraging news gave the meeting a more optimistic air and contributed to the unity that was starting to develop amongst Kathy and the Cabinet's members. Even Blankett and Atkinson were begrudgingly coming around to support her. The wagons had circled.

Kathy, Andy, and Marva had barely settled back in at the Oval Office after the meeting, when the odd sounding ring of the red telephone connecting Washington directly to Moscow filled the room. The antiquated phone system had been in place since the 1960's, and had been only slightly upgraded over the past decades. Andy couldn't remember the last time it had rang, in fact, he wasn't sure that it had in his four years on the job.

Picking up the receiver, Kathy answered the first way that came into her head. She was more conscious of how she said it than in what she said. "Hello, this is the President," she answered calmly.

Dimitri Karpov was a civilized man by Russian standards. The Russian President didn't fit the typical historical mold of his predecessors; he didn't drink and he didn't curse. In fact, he was generally a gracious and diplomatic gentleman gifted with a clever sense of humor that translated well to English, which he spoke fluently. The voice on the other end of the line sounded to Kathy like the one she'd heard on television and radio, but the personality behind it was different. Karpov was definitely showing the stress the events and his political foes were raining down upon him.

"Madame President, good morning. This is Dimitri Karpov," he began. "You have created quite a problem for us both, and all in less than a week on the job!"

This time measuring her words carefully, Kathy tried to defuse his anger. "Mr. President, it's a pleasure to speak to you personally. I regret that it occurs at a time of tension between our two countries."

"Mrs. Canfield, 'tension' understates it. You are on the verge of forcing us into world war."

"Mr. President, with all due respect, that will be your choice, not mine. I sincerely hope you will understand that a three day limited action to prevent the senseless loss of hundreds of thousands of lives does not warrant aggression by your great nation against the people and forces of the United States."

The Russian was anything but calmed by her words. "It was not us who took the first step in this matter, Madame President. The Serbian people have been historical allies of Russia for generations, and we will not abandon them."

"Mr. President, Dimitri..."

"There is little more to say. I have dispatched the Third Fleet from Minsk to the Adriatic. If your action continues, our ships have been directed to engage all American military targets involved in operations against the Serb people. The choice is yours, madam. Good day."

The click on the other end of the line carried the impact of a cruise missile. Kathy's confidence in her decision had just been kicked in the teeth, and sharing the conversation with her top two aides did nothing to restore it.

"Andy, you know him, what do you believe he'll do?" she asked with a nervous look in her green eyes.

"He's a straight arrow as far as I can tell. He's never struck me as a bluffer. I think we need to take him at his word," he said somberly. "We can confirm their naval movements via satellite, but we can't tell their ultimate intentions until the first shot is fired."

Her hand drifted thoughtlessly to her hair and twisted itself in and out of the strands hanging in front of her left ear. "Go ahead and get the movements confirmed as soon as you can. How soon can they get there from Minsk?"

"Full steam? Six, maybe seven hours before our seventy-two expire. Why don't I alert Tarrenton so we can hear what recommendations the Joint Chiefs might have? Perhaps we can either delay their ships, or cut the operation short."

"Let me know, Andy. And thank you."

He left briskly out the side door to his adjoining office to call the General. Alone with her boss following Mather's departure, Marva looked at her for some form of divine reassurance. What she got was the uncertain reply of an equally worried woman.

"How sure can you be that they won't follow through on their threats?" Marva asked.

"I can't be, Mar, any more than you or anyone else can. You know, I've searched this office high and low for a crystal ball, but I just can't seem to find it. It's a calculated risk, the best choice I can make based on the advice available and historical precedent. Let's just pray this is another Cuban missile crisis with the same ending."

* * * * * * * * * *

It wasn't what she'd wanted to hear, but it was the truth. If only Kathy hadn't played with her hair, Marva thought, then maybe she'd be feeling better about things. This wasn't the time for her to be showing her nervous human frailties. Not when Marva needed to see Wonder Woman behind the big desk.

* * * * * * * * * *

Down the street in the House Office Building, Stewart Farley was going nuts as he paced back and forth across the hardwood floor of his plush office. J. Thomas Gower's call had been mysterious, demanding. Something threatening was going on he felt. He just didn't know what, but his survival instincts were ringing like a fire station bell for a three alarm fire. The portly Speaker poured himself a generous tumbler of Jim Beam from the hidden bar in the back of the room, belted it down, and then fixing himself another. He'd known Gower for twenty years and never liked him much, probably more because of what they had in common than the ways in which they differed. Gower, like Farley, flourished in the no-holds barred world of Washington politics because of his raw thirst for power and the easy willingness with which he wielded it. While it gave the ruthless men a common ground, it also made them deadly rivals and adversaries. Farley felt in his bones that Gower was bringing the battle of his life to him. And he didn't know what or why, and that was driving him up the wall with the anxiety of a cornered rat.

He was slumped down in his chair, tie and collar askew, when Gower arrived and strolled cockily into his office, shutting the door behind him. Farley had a buzz on and was working on his third drink; he wasn't about to get up to greet the fed.

"J. Thomas, decked out slick as ever, I see. What is that, 'bout a two hundred and fifty dollar silk

214

tie?" Farley chided. "To what do I owe this very dubious honor, anyway?"

Gower didn't reply but instead walked casually over to the bookcase on the rear wall and hit the button that dropped the false front, revealing the bar. He'd been in Farley's office enough times over the years to know where it was. Then, without invitation, he poured himself a scotch and water and pulled up a chair in front of the Speaker's desk.

"Well, Stu, I'm here to deliver a message from our new chief executive. You could call it a mission of mercy, if you will."

"Oh really?"

"Seems somebody's been trying to blackmail our new Commander in Chief into resigning, Stewy, and I've been asking myself who might have the motive and opportunity to do something like that."

Farley coolly flashed an evil grin at the FBI head. "Blackmail, huh? Well, I like the style but I can't claim credit for this one, old buddy."

"Suddenly came to me that if she was forced to resign, you would succeed to the presidency, Stu. I figure that's a pretty powerful motive, and then low and behold I discover that you're connected to the guy who pulled the job in the field."

"And exactly who would that be?"

"Agency independent by the name of Miles O'Keefe. Ring a bell?"

Farley knew Gower to be no dummy and figured he wouldn't risk coming down on him without his facts straight, so he didn't deny it. "Barely know the guy, J.T. And so what if I do?"

Gower had played his hand as far as he could without bluffing, but it was time to go for the pot. "Well, I just finished talking with him, and he's fingered you as the one who retained him to set up

Chrissie Canfield, in a compromising position shall we say, to force her mother out."

"Bullshit, Gower! Total bullshit!" Farley exploded, as he rose in furious indignation. "That's a complete crock, and you know it!"

The six-foot-tall Gower rose to meet the shorter Farley eye to eye across the wide expanse of the desk. Placing his hands on its surface, he leaned over until he was an inch from Farley's pointed face.

"Well, if that's so, your resignation's gonna be a damned injustice, Stewy!"

The Speaker flung his icy drink into the fed's startled face, sending him back a step. Fortunately for Gower, the thirsty Farley hadn't left much in the glass. Recovering from the surprise of the moment, the FBI head took two quick steps around the desk, seizing Farley with his left hand and slapping him across the face hard with his right. The force drove him out of the chair and onto the floor.

"Now that wasn't nice, you pompous little shit! This is the score, and you can take it or leave it, but something tells me you're bright enough not to say 'no'," he told the stunned man lying before him. Reaching into his jacket pocket, his hands retrieved a video tape. Flinging it at Farley, he continued. "Try playing this, Stu. It's not my best work, I know, but you just can't get theater quality pictures on those damned cheap government surveillance cameras!"

The Ohioan's face turned white as though he'd just been outmaneuvered by the devil himself. As he picked himself up and rushed around the other side of his desk to the VCR, he knew he'd been had even before he hit the 'play' button on the machine. He knew what his weaknesses were and now it appeared Gower did too.

216

The whir of the machine kicking to life and the flicker of the T.V. soon verified his worst fears. There on the screen in what looked like a poor home movie was Stewart Farley in bed with a teenage male Capitol intern, and then another, and another. Someone had done an Academy Award winning job of editing the last two years of Farley's perverted sex life together into a 'best hits' collage. He was dead, and he knew it.

Turning off the VCR and pulling out the cassette, Farley ripped the tape from the plastic box, crumpling as much of it as he could out of exasperation. He knew Gower would have another copy secreted away somewhere, but it was good therapy.

"Exactly what do you want?" Farley asked the fed, with the sound of unconditional surrender in his voice.

"This is the deal. As soon as this Bosnia crap is over, you're to announce that you're retiring at the end of this term. If you don't, or if you don't follow through, or if the damaging photos of Chrissie Canfield come out and so much as cause her mother to lose a minute of beauty sleep, the tape's out to the press and I'll make sure you spend the rest of your sorry little life in prison. Clear enough?"

Farley tossed the cassette into the trash, and made his way back to his chair. He dropped into it like a sack of potatoes, defeated. "Well, J.T. seems like you've got my number and I don't have much choice, really, now do I? But just for the record, I haven't a clue what you're talking about on this blackmail thing."

Gower didn't trust the conniving politician; he never had, and now didn't seem like the time to start.

"Whatever, Stu. You believe what you like, but the deal's the same." Gower made his way to the door, and opened it, turning for one final word with his checkmated foe. "You know, Stewy, I never really liked you much. In the end, that's probably enough. Just knowing I won't have to see your pointy little face anymore, makes it all worthwhile. See ya!"

And with that, Gower left the crushed tyrant to sort through the ashes of his torched political career. As evening wore into early morning, Farley sat despondently in the office from which he'd once wielded tremendous power in the federal government. With another Jim Beam in his left hand and a Smith and Wesson in his right, he faced the first hour of his last day. He was uncertain how far into that day he'd be able to go, but he knew he had one last act of revenge to attend to first. Shaking, he picked up the phone on his desk.

"O'Keefe? Stewart Farley. I know, I know. How'd you like to even the score and make $50,000 for your trouble? Good, I thought you might. Here's the deal."

* * * * * * * * * *

Staff at the White House had been working through the night due to the crisis, and Kathy was still meeting with the head of the Joint Chiefs of Staff as midnight came and went. Satellite photos had arrived confirming that the Russian fleet had indeed sailed from Minsk, and a revised timeline placed them in the Adriatic in about twenty-four hours, approximately eight hours before cessation of the American action. General Tarrenton's report to the President was killing at least one of the options she'd been considering.

218

"And so, Madame President, we believe we're going to need the full seventy-two hours to break the Serb offensive. The weather's limited the effectiveness of some of our flights and our best projection is that if we break off the action four or five hours early, they'll be able to regroup and reinitiate their offensive in a few days. We need the time, or we might as well pack it in now, put our tails between our legs, and go home. That's not the kind of message we can afford to send to the Russians, especially with..."

The gruff officer caught himself and his voice trailed off leaving the sentence hanging.

"Especially with a woman in the White House?" Kathy finished.

"I'm sorry, all I meant is that the Russian culture is different, and their perception is more likely to be that decision making up here is less firm, less determined because of your gender. I simply meant to say that I feel it's unwise to do anything to confirm that perception."

"It's alright, General. I understand your point and agree. Don't worry, I don't take it personally."

"To make a long story short, I think we have to tough it out. We're still exploring options for slowing up the Russian fleet, and I hope to have our analysis to you by oh six hundred, er...six a.m."

Tarrenton arose and left the room, passing Andy in the doorway. The Chief of Staff was holding a piece of paper in his hand as he walked in, head slightly bowed. There was a look of consternation on his face and he had difficulty looking her in the eyes. He'd grown to care very much for this woman over the past several months, and he hated the difficult news he had to give her. He also hated being the messenger.

"Andy, what's that? Good news, I hope," she asked.

219

He knew that it was anything but. "I think you'd better sit down," he said gingerly. "We've received an incident report from the Commander of the Adriatic fleet. One of our air strike missions was surprised by a squadron of MIG fighters. They weren't carrying air-to-air missiles, and two of the F-14's were reported lost in the attack. The flight leader did report one parachute from the second plane, but the first was destroyed in the air with no survivors. Rescue attempts haven't turned up anything yet, apparently, they've been unable to raise the downed pilot on his radio."

Kathy lowered herself back into the chair behind her desk. "My God, Andy. Already? Do you have names?" she asked fearfully.

Andy couldn't bring the words to his lips, so he took the easy way out and sat the communique on the desk before her.

Placing her glasses on, she tried not to look at him as she focused her weary gaze on the paper and its message. Regrettably, she'd already seen the look on his face and it had communicated the worst.

The Pentagon report went on for five sanitized paragraphs detailing the incident as if it were a sporting event. At the bottom of the page was a brief listing of the airmen involved and their presumed status, much like an NFL team might list their injured or disabled. It was there that she found the name 'Canfield, Lt. William' next to the initials 'MIA'. Her heart sank like a rock and her chest heaved involuntarily. She fought hard to hold in her agony, not wanting to collapse in front of Andy and not wanting to lose her tenuous grip on her fragile hopes that Bill was still alive after ejecting from his crippled plane.

"I'm sorry, Kathy. If he's anything like you, I'm sure he's a tough kid, and I know he's well trained.

I'll bet anything he's laying low on the ground waiting to make contact with the rescue choppers while we speak. They'll find him, you don't think they're going to let the President's son go unrescued, do you?"

She bit her lip and looked into Andy's sympathetic face.

He could see the usual life was gone from the beautiful green eyes he'd come to love. In its place was an emptiness that went straight to the bottom of her soul. The thought that he shouldn't flashed through his mind and then out again by the time he'd reached her and pulled her into his arms. He held her tight as she broke down into uncontrollable moans and sobs, and she held him as if she were clinging to life itself.

Bill's misfortune alone would have broken most women, but Kathy was also enduring the uncertainty of her husband's whereabouts and condition, a blackmail scheme that could scar her and her daughter for life, and the weighty responsibility of leading the world to the brink of war. It was too much for her. It would have been too much for anyone.

As her mind shut down in defense, Andy consoled her, whispering "It's all right," over and over in her ear. He caressed her head and neck, first with his hands and then with his lips. His mouth made its way across her cheek, searching, longing, until stopping square on the softness of the full lips he'd dreamt about for months. Kathy was delirious in her grief and she did not push him away. In her pain, and with the comfort of her husband nowhere in reach, she drew herself closer and kissed him back, accepting the only comfort she could find.

CHAPTER THIRTEEN

It was noon in Sarajevo on the first day of the U.S. counterattack when Mark Canfield returned to consciousness after twelve hours of darkness. The hills surrounding the city were filling with flame and smoke as American air power pounded the previously unchallenged Serb emplacements. The remainder of that day and the next, the good doctor was no more than a bad patient, confined to bed with a concussion that had left his vision blurred, certainly too much so to allow him to participate in the round-the-clock surgeries that were going on in the next room. The able bodied had set up a makeshift hospital in the huge underground basement of what used to be Sarajevo's largest department store. The open structure had been largely demolished above ground, but the heavy cement basement floor remained intact, an unintentional but effective bomb shelter. Light and electricity was provided by a hastily relocated generator, and the limited amount of light that reached the subterranean room through small ventilation

222

windows in the perimeter walls. By day, the sunlight filtering through the gray clouds made its way through the windows, breaking the sense of confinement. By night, the flashes of explosions and cannon fire supplemented the light provided by the generators.

Mark lay under a sign he could not read that when translated read "Women's Lingerie". Next to him lay the pretty British doctor he'd allowed a dance such a short time ago. It would be Nancy Lansford's last. Her legs irreparably damaged in the initial attack, Lloyd-Davies had been forced to amputate one of her lovely limbs just below the knee in order to save her life. She remained sedated through that second day, all the better for Mark who had not a clue what he would say, what he *could* say when she awoke.

"Well, Dr. Canfield. I see you're about! How are we feeling today?" Lloyd-Davies asked his restless patient. The tireless physician had taken a well-deserved break from trying to mend the wounded and the dying in order to thoughtfully check on his battered colleagues.

Sitting up in the shaky metal bed, Mark acknowledged his friend's visit. "Much better, Doug. Think I've got my vision back. Any chance you can come up with a cup of coffee to help get the cobwebs out of my head?" he asked woozily, still under the influence of the medication he'd been given.

"Sure, yank! Got plenty of coffee but, just my luck, no damned tea. The bastards buried that part of the kitchen when they dropped that first mortar on our heads." The head surgeon's positive attitude remained intact, an uncanny character trait that had yet to fail him and that had kept his subordinates going hour after hour against the rising tide of casualties.

Mark wanted to get himself reoriented as quickly as possible so he could pitch in. The screams of agony from the nearby operating room under the "Men's Apparel" sign told him his skills were sorely needed to deal with a lot more than a tummy tuck. Chugging two cups of coffee and three or four Tylenols, he asked the raccoon-eyed Brit to fill him in on the situation.

"Not good, I'm afraid," he replied sadly. "We lost Warnemuende and Nancy in the first attack, and some of our medical supply shipment was still in the personnel carrier when it was hit. And, as you colonists say, business is booming!"

"How about the battle, how're we holding up?" Mark inquired.

The doctor raised his eyes and tilted his head. His body language told Mark that it was touch and go. "Well, we're a bit out of the flow down here. Colonel Martine came in a few hours ago to have a bullet pulled from his arm and then he went back out again, the damned French fool. But he did say that your American president had sent military support. Seems we've had your fighters overhead for two days now, making a heck of a racket they are, those noisy blokes!"

Mark steadied himself and pulled on his dirty pants, wondering if his son was among those overhead, and surprised that his peace-loving wife would commit the nation's military forces to the conflict. He wasn't sure how much help he would be to the rest of the medical staff in his present condition, but he had to try. Lloyd-Davies was so overwhelmed by the never ending flow of casualties that he wasn't in a position to argue. Instead, he helped Mark with his shoes and then put his arm around his shoulder to steady him on the way to the operating room. This was an extraordinary time and place, and extraordinary people were sorely needed to meet the challenges that the war had wrought. Amongst all the death and destruction, Mark Canfield became what he'd needed to be all along, what they needed him to be right now. An extraordinary man.

His sight and much of his coordination returned with the help of the coffee, but his cranium felt like he'd just been head butted by Mike Tyson, and his balance was still shaky.

"Think you can hold me up while I operate, old bean?" Mark teasingly asked his human crutch.

"Well, not me personally, but we'll find someone. Maybe two 'someones,' mate. You weigh a ton!"

After trying unsuccessfully to prop him up with two muscular volunteers, they finally exercised a little creativity and nailed a high chair to the floor next to the operating table, tying Mark into it with a torn bed sheet splattered with blood. That didn't matter much, because within an hour he was covered with the sticky red body fluid from head to toe as the medical assembly line churned body after body past his gifted hands.

"Nothing like a little British ingenuity, eh! That chair seems to be working just fine."

"My God, Doug, how many have you brought through here since I've been out of circulation?" Mark wondered aloud, realizing he couldn't see the end of the long line of wounded that wrapped around the wall to the escalator that went nowhere.

Lloyd-Davies hadn't been able to break his concentration long enough to count. "Don't really know, doctor. Last twenty-four hours, maybe a hundred? More than enough, let's say."

"Sweet Jesus..."

They worked through the day and through the night and then through the day again. On the evening of the third violent day, after a brief three hour nap, Mark's faculties came back to him and he returned to the operating table minus the high chair that had become the target of teasing amongst a medical staff hungry for the release a little levity provided. The humor in the dreary room was now bordering on the macabre, but they all understood why. In any event, it felt good to be back on his feet, a privilege he was mindful the attractive Nancy Lansford would never enjoy again.

As he made his way back to the operating room, the building shook ferociously under the strain of the cannon fire hitting the upper floors of the bombed-out department store. The ceiling above his head crumbled from the stress, with large sections of plaster and cement falling a foot from him as he braced himself in a door jam. Gathering his equilibrium and his courage, he darted through the dust, and through the rest of the narrow corridor to the operating room. Thankfully, there had been no additional damage there and all within were proceeding as though it were business as usual. His watch told him it was six p.m. of the third horrible day, but he saw little significance in that. Every new hour seemed like the last as the sounds of war continued unabated, and time seemed to carry little meaning. If he had known all that was happening around him, it might have been different, but he did not. As far as he was aware, there was no end to the conflict in sight, and even the brief lulls in the action resulted in no measurable impact on his world. Only an end to the long line of mangled human flesh that streamed endlessly before him would convince him that the clock had begun to tick again with meaning.

At ten o'clock, a grimy Jerry Lake tugged on his arm to signal it was time for a break. "C'mon buddy, you're starting to confuse livers and spleens, it's time for a siesta."

"Nah, Jer, I can't stop now, there's just too many of 'em," he replied, wiping his fuzzy eyes for the umpteenth time in the last hour.

"Go ahead, Matt," Lloyd-Davies said to him from the next table, referring to him by his alias, "he's right. You're hurting us more than helping us right now. Get a few hours of shuteye."

Jerry persisted. "Either come peacefully or I'll anesthetize you and stuff you in the morgue for the night!"

Their collective efforts persuaded the well-meaning plastic surgeon to get off his blistered and swollen feet. He was dead to the world and he had to admit he was starting to make mistakes, so he adjourned to an old mildewed mattress in the corner. His hospital bed had long since been lost to a much needier Muslim child who'd given up his right arm for the cause of ethnic purity. Mark was so completely spent that he slept straight through until daybreak, undeterred by the screams of the wounded, the roar of the fighters, or the concussion of the explosions around the besieged city.

Exhaustion had taken its toll on the entire medical staff, and they'd begun to extend their sleeping breaks out of necessity after a slip of another weary surgeon's hand punctured a middle-aged patient's aorta, nearly killing him.

When the light of day finally made its way through one of the small ventilation windows and struck his face, he awoke from his deep and chilly sleep. Looking to the operating tables before him, he was convinced his tired, bloodshot eyes were deceiving him. Strapped into the high chair he'd used, still nailed to the floor next to one of the metal tables, was a courageous Nancy Lansford, assisting in surgery not seventy-two hours after losing her own leg. Glancing around, he could see that only he and a young Bosnian doctor lay on the sidelines. Inspired by the moving sight of the incredibly gutsy Nancy, he shook his colleague from his sleep and pointed at the heart-wrenching scene before them. He didn't know how long the sandy-haired medical practitioner had been asleep, but he didn't care much either. If she could do what she was doing, then there was no excuse for anyone else to be anywhere else other than by her side.

"Wake up, pal. They need us over there," he said, pointing in Nancy's direction.

The Bosnian didn't speak English but there was no communication problem. He muttered something in Serbo-Croatian and jumped to his feet, with an expression that made clear he was as shocked as Mark. Both of them made their ways hurriedly to the last vacant operating table, opening it for business and joining the battle against the human pain and suffering that filled the confines of the room and beyond.

The two worked side-by-side until nine in the morning. Following a brief and fleeting ten minute break, Mark paired with the tireless Lloyd-Davies at another table. The gray-headed Brit was like the Energizer bunny, he just kept going and going. After a morning of talking to himself while he worked with the Bosnian, it was good to again share a little conversation with the camaraderie. It restored some of the humanity to the insanely inhumane conditions in the bargain basement emergency room.

"So how well do you speak the language, Doug?" he asked, in an effort to make small talk, referring to the complicated local dialect.

Stitching up a bullet-torn artery while he spoke, the Brit still found himself able to manage a shrug of his shoulders. "Oh, reasonably well they tell me, except for the accent which they say makes me sound like a Slavic fisherman who's been swilling too much vodka while at sea."

"So you can tell what they're saying when they're on the table?"

"All the same thing, my friend. They're all crying out to God, whether they're Muslim or Croat, or just about anything else on this earth. Their words are a little bit different depending on which they are, but not much. And I cry right along with them, every one of 'em."

It was then Mark suddenly realized how alone the cries in the room had become, they were no longer muffled by the constant explosions outside the medical compound. It was nearly ten in the morning on the fourth day according to his watch, and the steady sounds of war that had become as normal to them as the sound of the wind or the sea had dwindled to nothingness. More importantly, the endless line to the operating tables had slowed as well.

When he first saw the wounded young Bosnian girl as she was lifted to the aluminum table by a nurse and a frantic older Bosnian man, he thought nothing more than that she was another patient, hopefully one of the last. Her wounds were serious, the result of two large caliber bullets that had pierced her back. For the size of the entry wounds, the bullets seemed surprisingly shallow in her flesh, but one had lodged itself dangerously close to the girl's spine, and she was covered in enough blood for two people.

"Doug, ask this guy what happened, will you? I haven't seen wounds like these before," Mark commented as he probed the first bullet hole. The pretty brunette was delirious and mumbling incoherently. Had he understood her language, he still would not have been able to make out much of what she was trying to say. Jerry was frantically administering the usual anesthesia, but it hadn't yet taken effect. And the blood pressure cuff that Mark had strapped on her crimson-soaked arm was providing an alarmingly low reading, a sign of how much blood she had lost.

Lloyd-Davies spoke calmly with the excited man that had carried her into the makeshift medical facility. He was covered in sweat and blood and could hardly stand from the severe fatigue of carrying the girl's dead weight for some distance, but he himself didn't seem injured. Mark figured the blood that covered the scared older man must be hers, and yelled for a nurse to ready her for a transfusion.

"Candy, get a type on this girl would you please, and how are we doing on the blood supply?" he asked anxiously.

"I'll check right away, doctor," she replied, before stumbling off for a needle and a bottle of rubbing alcohol. The last of the clean needles had run out hours ago, and this half-assed sterilization technique was the best they could do under the dire circumstances in which they found themselves mired.

The supplies of plasma and whole blood they'd brought from Zagreb had been one of the few things they'd unloaded before the personnel carrier had been destroyed. Nevertheless, he knew the exceedingly high volume of wounded must have depleted most of it by now. Her survival could very well depend on what her blood type was and what was left, sort of a serologist's Russian roulette.

"The man says the girl's his niece and she was hit when an enemy plane strafed their farm outside of town this morning," Lloyd-Davies explained after conversing with the uncle.

"Ah, that explains it. High caliber machine gun ammo," Mark said to himself as he reached the first bullet with his forceps and began to gently ease it from the back of her shoulder.

The experienced British surgeon squinted his eyes in a puzzled expression as he began cauterizing and closing the wound while Mark went to the next one. "Looks like a twenty-three millimeter. That's odd yank, something like that should've ripped right through her. Unless it hit something else first, you know, like if she were in a house and the bullets went through the wall before hitting her," he reasoned. "Let me see if the old boy can give us a bit more."

He spoke to the worried relative again, this time coming away with the solution to the little mystery. "Looks like we're right. He and his niece were running for cover with an American pilot that was shot down near their farm. Apparently, the old guy fell and the younger two had to come back for him. He says that gave the fighter time for a second pass, but that the American threw himself on his niece to protect her. The damned slugs had to have passed through the poor bloke to get to her."

Mark winced at the news of the loss of an American life. "Well, if we can save her, the kid won't have died in vain. It's a cinch if these had hit her direct she would've been killed instantly."

Mark took one of the few sharp scalpels left and slowly cut an incision across the bruised flesh surrounding the second wound to enable him to better grip the remaining slug. The ever efficient Lloyd-Davies checked the x-rays that had just been brought to them by one of the volunteers, and grinned as he gave his colleague the news.

"The bullet's about an inch from the spine. We ought to be able to get it out without any serious risk of paralysis. This girl was one lucky bird, I'll tell you that."

Nurse Candy's news was unfortunately not as promising when she returned from her assignment. "Sorry doctors, she's an AB negative and we're fresh out. Nobody down here seems to have that blood type either, other than a couple of patients that're already a quart low. You want me to send a runner to the next building?"

Their patient's pressure was continuing to drop from the extensive blood loss, and Mark didn't believe she had much time if they didn't pump something into her fast. And his grade-A American blood just happened to be AB negative.

"Candy, *I'm* AB negative. Get the needle and tap into my left arm, and we'll do a direct transfusion," Mark ordered. "Doug, I'm gonna need your help. If it looks like I'm getting punchy, dive right in and pinch hit for me."

"Just don't keel over on the patient, doctor."

Mark had always believed that heroes weren't born, but rather that they were made, challenged and forged by the chances of fate as they tested individual character under the pressures of a crisis. Like those around him, Mark had risen to meet his challenge with nary a thought for his own well-being. The nurse borrowed his left arm just long enough to insert the needle into his vein while he clung carefully to the forceps with his right hand. The idealistic young Candy had changed over the past days. She was no longer so naive, and she seemed to look a lot older now, as she pushed her greasy golden locks from her sunken eyes.

His life forces made their way through the narrow plastic tube and hand pump into the veins of the dangerously weak girl. The amount of blood she needed to stabilize her deteriorating condition was twice what Mark should have given, but he gave anyway in spite of his colleagues' protestations, and eased the destructive lead slug out not a moment too soon.

"Pressure is stabilizing."

"Whoa there Doctor, you're starting to wobble," Candy cautioned.

Mark's face looked white as a ghost and his legs buckled as he fainted from the loss of blood, pulling the needle from his arm as he collapsed in a heap onto the frozen floor.

"Let's get him, Candy!" Lloyd-Davies yelled. "Jerry, give her a hand, will you? I'll close up, and you two take care of him, find him a steak or a liver or something. He'll need all the iron he can get!"

Mark regained consciousness ten minutes later but was too weak to get back on his feet. Through his persistent bitching and moaning, he was finally able to persuade the volunteer orderlies to move him next to the young girl whose life he had saved so he could keep an eye on her. For some reason he couldn't yet understand, there was something special about the smooth-skinned brunette. Maybe, he thought, it was because another American had given his life for hers, and he just didn't want that life to have been given in vain.

For the next hour, he stared at his recovering patient in fascination. He recognized his head wasn't completely clear, in fact he felt almost drunk from the blood loss, but he still felt there was something familiar about her. And then it hit him, the odd similarity in bone structure, and the same auburn hair.

Her features were not as sharp or as perfect as his wife's, she didn't have the benefit of skin conditioners and makeup, and she was younger, but there was enough similarity to make the connection. If he and Kathy had brought another daughter into this world, and if she'd been raised on the other side of the globe as this girl had been, then she would look like her, he envisioned. And if she were his daughter, he thought, he'd feel exactly like the worried uncle that kept vigil on the other side of her rickety bed.

By eleven, rumors of a cease fire had reached the hospital, giving weight to what the guns' silence had hinted to the embattled men and women within. The cheers went on for half an hour and a sense of hope sparked itself for the first time since Mark had arrived.

After about an hour of bed rest, he was able to get back on his feet, though he was still very tired and weak. He was at the girl's bedside along with her uncle when she awoke abruptly, screaming out in the language he could not comprehend. Her sudden and violent movements forced the two men to move quickly to restrain her in order to prevent the fawn-eyed beauty from tearing out her I.V. Mark hadn't picked up much of their dialect during the week, but there was one word she used over and over that he did recognize.

"Bill, Bill!" she shrieked in terror.

Mark's jaw dropped and the color that was just beginning to return to his face faded. "What was that? What did she say?" he asked the uncle as they held her arms.

The crusty-looking farmer didn't understand a word Mark said and could only shake his head in unintelligible response. But the girl, slowly regaining her senses if not her composure, understood the panicked father and answered in reasonably good English.

"The American that was with me, where is he, how is he?" she cried out to the pale physician.

"I'm sorry, honey, but you came in alone. Your uncle told us that the American pilot died trying to protect you from an air attack."

Marija let out a shriek that curdled his blood. "No! Not Bill, not my Bill!"

Mark's hands dropped to his side, motionless, and his mouth dried up like a raisin. "Young lady, what was the pilot's name, my God, tell me it wasn't Bill Canfield!" he moaned, reacting as though he'd just had the wind kicked out of him.

The distraught girl looked at him through teary brown eyes, remembering what Bill had told her about his father the doctor being in Sarajevo on a relief mission, and noticing the physical resemblance. She knew she had found him.

The pain in her eyes screamed out the answer he dreaded, the one he did not want to hear. When the merciless words came, they only confirmed the worst, and they struck like a knife through the paralyzed father's heart.

"That *is* his name. Are you his father?" she asked as she reached out with her right hand to grasp his.

Mark dropped to the floor in agony, stricken by the tragic revelation of Bill's death. Devastated, he buried his head in her lap and sobbed loudly for his lost son. Marija wept right along with him as she shared the story of the heroic deed that had been Bill's last. Lying on her side so she could reach Mark, she hugged him as hard as she could in her condition, much the way she had hugged his son less than a day before.

"I'm so sorry. I only knew Bill a short time, but I fell in love with him the moment we met." Mark could tell by the look on her face that she felt the loss too, and meant every word.

The two shared their outpouring of grief, drawing what strength they could from one another, until they could shed no more tears. Over the next two hours, they exchanged happy stories about Bill. Mark brought a pained smile to Marija's face when he told her how his boy had broken the living room window playing Frisbee with an old vinyl record one day when he was six, his first visible interest in flight. She returned the gesture, telling Mark how an awkward Bill broke half of the eggs he'd helped collect on the little farm.

Eventually, the conversation turned to recovery of the body, and Marija translated for Mark and her uncle in order to facilitate their effort. "My uncle says he will take you in morning to our farm. He says your son and you gave him back my life. He will carry Bill on his back alone, if need be."

The thought of fulfilling this final obligation to his son offered the shattered father some small sense of ease, knowing that he could do something, if nothing more than to ensure that he had a proper Christian burial. But it was this sudden realization that gave him his only meaningful solace - his skillful saving of Marija's life on the operating table had preserved his son's sacrifice. That soothed his broken heart.

CHAPTER FOURTEEN

In her shock and torment, Andy's embrace seemed to ease Kathy's suffering, and for a moment it felt right. But only for a moment. Thoughts of her endangered husband and her marriage vows to him flashed through her confused mind even as her lips touched his. Her senses returned abruptly to her, and she gently pushed him away from her heaving bosom, and looked into his disappointed eyes.

"I'm sorry, Andy, I don't want to mislead you. I love my husband dearly and I'd never do anything to hurt him," she explained, with an embarrassed look on her tear-covered face.

"It's alright, I apologize. I shouldn't have, I know. I just couldn't help myself."

"It's okay. We're all under a lot of pressure and not quite ourselves these days. Let's just pretend it never happened, alright?"

That was not the enraptured aide's preference, by any means, but he was not some roguish Don Juan, and she *was* the President of the United States. And there were more important things to attend to than his starving libido.

"Of course. Well, it's getting pretty late, I suggest we both get some sleep. The Russian fleet'll be nearing our task force in the morning and we're going to need our wits about us," he said, using their work as a shield against the painfully uncomfortable situation.

"Good night, Andy. Say a prayer for us before you tuck yourself in, won't you?" she smiled, as she wiped a tear from the corner of her eye.

Alone in the spacious office, and feeling alone in the world, she turned off the desk lamp that was illuminating the dreadful incident report and made her way past the Marine guard posted outside her door. Her shoulders were slumped forward in a way they'd never been before, and her gait was uncertain, not at all steady. Heading in the direction of her daughter's room, she walked down the hallway that Lincoln had once strolled and made her way to the doorway of what was referred to as the Queens' Room. Her knock was soft, not by design, but because she felt as though every ounce of energy had been sapped from her.

"Chrissie? Are you awake?"

There was no reply, so she let herself into the darkened room, turning on the wall switch as she entered. The cut-glass chandelier lit up the majestically cheerful pink room as if it were daytime, illuminating the pink canopy-covered poster bed in which Chrissie slept. Kathy stepped onto the Hureke rug covering the room's old hardwood flooring, and made her way past the white carved wooden fireplace mantle to her bedside. "Chrissie? Wake up, honey."

"Huh? Mother, what's the matter? It must be midnight."

"It's after, honey, but I have some bad news

about your brother..." Kathy said quietly, as she wiped the remnants of another teardrop from her cheek.

Groping at the sleep in her eyes, Chrissie propped herself upright with the thick down-filled pillows so she could see her mother. In the bright light, the groggy girl could clearly see her mother's face, revealing her swollen eyes and the makeup running down her cheeks. Once again, words were unnecessary to communicate the tragic message.

"Oh, no! Bill's dead, isn't he? Please tell me he's not!" she shrieked, squeezing her mother's hand as the horrible thought entered her mind.

Kathy gave her all the encouragement the truth would allow. "Baby, they don't know. His plane was shot down yesterday over Bosnia and they believe he ejected. They saw one chute from the plane after it was hit, but they don't know if it was his or his partner's. They've listed him as 'Missing in Action' and have search and rescue units combing the area for him."

Tears flowed freely from them both. Kathy held her daughter as she had when she had first learned of the blackmail scheme, but this was different. This was not about a setback or an embarrassment, this was about the life of a son and brother and there was a finality to it that made them hold each other longer and tighter than before. Kathy laid with Chrissie until her worried daughter cried herself to sleep at two in the morning, then kissed her softly on her forehead and tucked her in snugly for the night. As she headed for the door, she caught a glimpse of herself in the mirrored portion of the 17th century trumeau hanging above the mantle, cringing at her own battered reflection. Her own efforts to sleep after she returned to the isolation of the Lincoln Bedroom were fruitless.

The third day began with no new news of Bill or Mark, and unpleasant reports concerning the situation in the Balkans. Tarrenton informed the President at seven a.m. that the Russian fleet was continuing its movement toward the Adriatic and projections still had them arriving before cessation of the American action. A confrontation appeared more inevitable than ever.

"Madame President, we suggest dispatching the Fifth Fleet to bolster our task force there. They won't be able to reach the region before the Russians, but the mere movement may cause them pause," the General advised.

"And I assume there's an equal chance that such an escalation will be met in kind. An eye for an eye, a tooth for a tooth?"

The stern military leader, tightened the furrows in his brow, and replied, "There is that risk, of course."

Kathy walked to the window that opened onto the Rose Garden. The gorgeous view had been speckled with a light snow, but its beauty was still evident, and the peace she had drawn from it many times over the past few days came to her once again. After a pause for reflection, she turned to Tarrenton.

"General, would you give me a moment alone, please?"

With a nod of his head the highly decorated old warrior acknowledged her request and left the Oval Office, closing the door behind him. Her eyes were locked on the scarlet telephone that connected her to Moscow, but her mind was searching for the words that could persuade the Russian president to turn his ships around. If she failed, the impending action would certainly spell doom for both nations, and indeed the world. After a few minutes of contemplation, she picked up the receiver and waited for the answer at the other end. The gravelly voice that answered belonged to the Russian president himself.

"This is Dimitri Karpov."

"Dimitri? This is Kathleen Canfield," she began informally, in hopes of establishing a working rapport with her counterpart. It took every ounce of self-control she had to subdue the quiver that fought to make its way into her voice.

"Madame President, I hope you are calling to tell me that you have come to your senses and are calling off your attack," he said firmly.

"No. To be frank, I'm calling to ask you to reconsider your position and call off your ships."

"Madame President, you should know I cannot do that. We have given our commitment to our allies, as you have."

"Then at least slow your ships, Dimitri. Hold them off until our operation is completed, then you won't be under pressure or obligation to intercede. I'll tell the American people and the world that we discontinued our action in respect for your concerns and our mutual desires for peace."

"Why lie? Simply call off your air power and I will turn our fleet around."

"I can't do that, my friend. My military advisors have informed me that if we don't follow through on our mission, the Serbs will be able to regroup in a few days with enough strength to reinitiate their attack and overrun the city, even with the Muslim and Croat reinforcements that are closing on Sarajevo. If I don't see the mission through, the city will fall and hundreds of thousands will die. That blood would be on both our hands."

"Madame President, do not think I take war lightly. My own son serves on one of the ships in the fleet I have dispatched. I do not want to throw his life away any more than you would want to sacrifice your son's."

Finally, she had discovered a common ground from which to work her magic. "Then you will understand the level of my commitment, Dimitri. I was informed last night that *my son* was shot down over Sarajevo the day before yesterday. As we speak, I don't know whether he's alive or dead. I don't want more mothers, or fathers, going through what I'm feeling right now, from either side. I don't want you to feel the pain of helplessness that I'm feeling right now, Dimitri."

There was silence on the other end of the line for a good fifteen seconds. When the Russian's voice returned, it was softer and carried a sincere sense of sorrow. "I am sorry, Kathleen. I sincerely hope your boy is alright."

"Slow your ships, please. If not for me and my son, then for you and yours. There is an old proverb in my country that goes, 'There is no such thing as an inevitable war. If war comes it will be from failure of human wisdom.' Be wise, my friend. For all of us."

"We have the same saying here. I can make no promises, but I will consider your words."

"Thank you, Dimitri. Thank you and may the good Lord be with us all."

When Kathy set down the hotline's receiver, there was a glimmer of hope in her emerald eyes. Perhaps her son's plight had opened up the hardened heart of the Russian leader and father. Maybe her loss was a piece of the greater puzzle which would pave the way to peace. No common man or woman could ever quite understand God's plan or his way of doing things, she had always thought. And now she knew that was true for presidents as well.

It was early afternoon on this tension-filled third day when Tom Gower phoned to inform her that his men had recaptured the escaped Miles O'Keefe, aka Kevin Reilly. This time his troops were bringing his suspect into FBI headquarters for a second round of Gower's personal questioning.

"You have my solemn word that I'll have everything he knows to you by six o'clock tonight. May I join you for dinner with my report?" he proposed suggestively.

"Sure Thomas, I'll see to it the arrangements are made. How did it go with Farley?"

"All you should know is that it was taken care of. He didn't admit to anything, but I'm fully confident that if it's him, and I believe it is, that you'll have no further problems. In fact, you can bank on it."

"Do you really need to talk to this O'Keefe character then, Thomas?"

"I don't like loose ends. Never have, never will. Just trust me on this one, Kathy," he said with his customary conceit. "You *can* trust me, you know."

About the only thing she knew she could trust Tom Gower to do was to make every effort he could to get her into bed. She only hoped he would be more successful at foiling the blackmailer than she knew he would be in his efforts to seduce her. Too bad he was the only one in town capable of riding to her rescue. Kathy knew she was leading him on subtly in order to maintain his assistance, and that sickened her when she thought about it as she leaned back in the indigo black leather chair. But in the overall scheme of events, this small transgression seemed hardly worthy of recrimination or regret. She did wonder, however, how many times her predecessors had felt the circumstances of office tugging at their moral fiber. As she joined Andy and Marva for lunch, she decided that it had probably been a weekly if not daily dilemma that had plagued her predecessors all the way back to George Washington. Theirs were, of course, different. She doubted that any of them had been required to dangle *their* sexuality to achieve an end.

Lunch with Chrissie was difficult and awkward. The teenager did not have a thousand other things going on to distract her from her worries about her father and brother the way Kathy did. And her youth left her ill-prepared to deal with the thought of death, real or imagined, particularly where a close family member was involved. Her sterling silver spoon found its way around her soup bowl a hundred times with ease, but it never made its way to her tight-lipped mouth. And Kathy did not have the words to ease her pain, for she too was frightened and worried for her men. During the entire meal, there was little conversation. Only the clanging of the dinnerware filled the room.

A few fleeting hours later, the antique grandfather clock across the Oval Office from Kathy's desk began chiming six. It was time to entertain the amorous FBI head in the small dining room down the hall. Holding on to all hope that Gower had successfully broken the blackmail scheme, she headed off for her rendezvous with the dapper fed.

When she stepped into the ornate dining room, J. Thomas Gower was already seated, awaiting her arrival.

"Tom, thank you for your punctuality. I'm on a very tight schedule this evening and it'll be of immense help in keeping me on time," she said, giving herself an early out, and sending a signal to Gower not to get his hopes up.

He rose when she entered the room, in deference to her gender, and moved to courteously pull out her chair. In the process, he cut off a startled Oscar Jackson who had just reached out to do the same, a routine he had followed for decades. "Of course, but don't object if I express my disappointment. I was looking forward to spending some time together," he said to her as he pushed in her seat. Gower looked a little sharper than usual, as though he had changed into a fresh suit and tie before dinner, and the sweet scent of his designer aftershave wafted through the room, an aromatic 'red flag' concerning his prurient intent.

"I'm sure you understand. With the Bosnia crisis, we're all working around the clock. But thank you for the compliment," she said sweetly, before bringing the conversation back to business. "Have you cracked the case?"

"I'm afraid I have," he replied with a raising of his left eyebrow, "and it may not be what we thought."

Kathy was tantalized by the open-ended reply, but she had neither the time nor the patience to play 'fifty questions' with him. As she took a bite of the orange duck that Oscar had served, she wiped her lips with her gold linen napkin and cornered Gower politely. "Perhaps you can be a bit more direct, Tom."

"Well, we shook down O'Keefe and his story suggests that Farley may be innocent of any involvement in this. Imagine that!"

"If he's not the one then who is?" she asked with a look of amazement on her face.

"Well, you may want to talk to your daughter again, Kathy."

His statement defied reason, and left her searching for an explanation. "Why?"

"If our boy O'Keefe is talking straight, and I'm pretty sure he is after what we put him through, then she knows a hell of a lot more than she's told either of us."

"Exactly what did the pervert tell you?" she asked with an edge in her voice.

"I'm not trying to play games, Kathy, but I think it'd be better if you got the full story from your daughter rather than me," he said with sincerity. "All I'll tell you here is that she was involved, and I don't think you really need to worry about the pictures ever coming out. Unless she decides to sell 'em to Penthouse or Playboy!"

"My God, Tom, what are you saying?"

"Just talk to her. If she doesn't come clean with you then call me at home tonight, and I'll fill you in. Your staff has the number."

Finishing her almond-covered green beans, Kathy left a good portion of the rest of her gourmet meal untouched on the china plate, then laid her napkin on the table and started to rise. This time, Oscar beat Gower to the punch, pulling the President's chair out for her before his competitor could move.

"Thank you, Tom, for everything," she said graciously as she extended her hand. "If I feel the need, I'll call you."

Gower raised her delicate fingers to his lips, and kissed the back of her hand in an effort to be gallant, as well as to keep the door open for future possibilities with the beautiful Commander in Chief. "It was my pleasure. I'm at your service, any time of the day...or night," he said coyly. Coming from someone else, the words might have appeared harmless. Coming from Tom Gower, she knew it was a blunt and clear invitation for an affair. Her way of dealing with it was to ignore it. With a smile and a turn she left the oversexed Bureau chief in her wake to contemplate his next cold shower.

The walk to her daughter's room was a short one, but the lovely pink Queens' Bedroom was empty, so Kathy dispatched Oscar to find her and bring her back to the Oval Office. On her way, she passed a dazed Edith Burlington in the hallway making her way toward her own quarters. It was the first time Kathy had seen the matronly First Lady since her husband's stroke had changed both of their lives.

"Edith, how are you and how's the President?" she asked the silver-maned woman out of genuine concern. Kathy had developed a strong dislike for the lady's husband, but she had always adored and admired her, if for no reason other than her tolerance of, and devotion to, her difficult husband.

"They say the next twenty-four hours'll tell, Kathy," she replied as she wrapped her cold, wrinkled hands around the new president's. "I heard about your boy. I'm so sorry, dear. I'll say a prayer for him tonight."

The two women hugged, and as they broke Kathy heard a muffled whimper from the sweet old woman. "You know, I'm not oblivious to Michael's faults," she volunteered, "but we've been together over forty years, and I love the damned fool. Not sure why, but I do. I can't imagine facing life without him."

"I think I know how you feel, Edith. He's a tough old bird, though, if anyone can beat it, he can," Kathy said warmly, as she balanced her condolences against her true feelings toward the comatose Texan. "I'll check in on you tomorrow and see how you're doing."

The grieving wives went their separate ways to bear their suffering for their loved ones as best they could, each in their own manner. With all the problems facing Kathy, there was still enough compassion left in her to cause her dehydrated eyes to mist as she walked away from Edith Burlington. There was just too much pain within these walls, she thought, as she turned the corner to her office. Just too much pain.

Kathy approached the entry to the Oval Office just as Oscar exited from another hallway with a frightened Chrissie in tow.

"Is it news about Daddy and Bill?" she asked hastily.

"No, it's not, but you and I need to have a serious talk, young lady."

Chrissie recognized the words and the tone of her mother's voice. She had heard it too many times before, and the conversations were never pleasant. Neither were the consequences she always faced when the talking was done.

"I take it I've done something?" she replied out of habit.

"That's for you to tell me," Kathy said dryly, as she shut the door behind her, leaving the two of them alone in the spacious office.

"What do you mean? I don't understand."

"I just spoke with Tom Gower. They caught your friend O'Keefe, Reilly, whatever his name is. Seems he talked pretty freely to Tom about what happened. He says Farley's not involved and that I should talk to you, that you know more about this blackmail thing than what you're telling."

Most teenagers have an instinctive talent for lying, but few have yet learned to lie *well*. Chrissie was no different, as she fidgeted and avoided looking her mother directly in the eye. "Honest, I don't know what you're, what they're talking about. I told you and Tom all I know."

"Don't lie to me, Christina. You can't even look me in the eye. What's going on?" Kathy demanded. "Don't you think I have enough to deal with considering your father and Bill and the war without having to deal with you?"

The volcano of pent up fury and resentment that had been welling up inside her for years erupted. "That's the problem," Chrissie cried out angrily, "you never have time for me! It's always politics, or Daddy, or Bill, but it's never me!" It was the first indication of her daughter's true feelings that Kathy had been exposed to since Chrissie's drug bust back in L.A. And then, she had been forced to read between the lines of her self-destructive actions.

"That's not true, you know I work very hard to spend time with the family. Why do you think your father and I moved everyone out here from California? You know how much criticism I took in the press over that."

"I don't recall anyone asking me what I wanted! Do you think I'd really rather be freezing my ass off here instead of sunning myself on the beach in Southern California with my friends? Gimme a break!"

"Christina!"

"Mother!" the angry young girl returned loudly in defiance.

"Don't you talk to me like that, young lady! Whatever problem you have with me we can work out. But first, I need to know the whole story on your involvement in this blackmail mess. If you've done anything illegal, and Gower gets to the bottom of it, you could be subject to charges."

"Oh, and wouldn't that just ruin your political career, Madame President?"

Kathy had taken all the abuse she was willing to take from her troubled teen. Raising her right hand, she brought it down hard across Chrissie's cheek with a loud 'smack'. She had never raised her hand to either of her children before, and her violent reaction upset her as much as it did her startled daughter.

"I, I'm sorry Chrissie, I didn't mean to," Kathy apologized as she tried to pull her into her arms.

Chrissie jerked away, covering the reddened side of her face with her hand. "Is that how you handle everything these days, with force? Send troops to Bosnia, beat your daughter. Being President has gone to your head!"

Kathy turned away and moved to a nearby chair. She did not sit down as much as she slumped into it. "Christina, I'm sorry for hitting you. And I'm truly sorry for whatever pain I may have caused you. Believe me, I've never wanted anything but the best for you. I've never tried to hurt or ignore you, baby."

Kathy wanted to cry, but she was spent. She had bawled her eyes out a half dozen times for a half dozen reasons over the last few days and she just didn't have anything left. And maybe that was her daughter's point. She didn't have anything left *for her*.

"Do you know how much I wanted your love and attention? Enough to make up this whole blackmail thing so you'd quit politics and come home and spend time with us, with me. And do you think it's easy being your daughter? I'm never gonna be as pretty, as smart, as famous. It makes me feel like shit! Maybe part of me just wanted to knock you down a notch, to embarrass you by being the perfect imperfect daughter."

"Baby, how did all this happen?"

"What, me resenting you, or the blackmail deal?"

"I'm starting to understand the first now that you've shared some of your feelings, so why don't you concentrate on the second for now."

"Easy. I went out with a friend of mine to a club and met this guy Reilly, or O'Keefe. I guess he uses another name because of the work he's in, well now I know what he does, but I didn't at the time," she explained. "We went back to what I thought was his place and one thing lead to another - booze, drugs, sex, and then some couple he was visiting came home and joined in. I was wasted, mother. That's not an excuse, I know, it's just an explanation."

"So what about the pictures?" she asked.

"I guess I passed out and somebody thought it would be cool to take a bunch of pornographic pictures to sort of, you know, remember the evening. I guess they posed me while I was passed out."

"How did you end up with the photos?"

"Kevin, er Miles. I guess his conscience got the best of him, so he got the film from his buddy and gave it to my girlfriend, and she gave it to me."

Chrissie paused as if she had said enough, but continued after her mother prodded her for more. "And then you won the damned election, and I didn't see you for weeks, and then the idea just sort of, you know, came to me about the blackmail thing. But after you became President, I changed my mind, that's why I never did any more with it. I was real proud of you, mother. I mean, I *am* real proud of you. And then there was Daddy and Bill. So I stopped."

Kathy was taken aback by the cutting confession. "I guess I never really knew how you felt. I've been so busy I just didn't take the time to notice, to see the signs. I'm so sorry, baby, I just didn't know, but I do love you so very much."

Chrissie's eyes began to water and she leapt into her mother's open arms. "I'm sorry, I love you too. It's just so hard sometimes. You're such an impossible act to follow."

"Baby, let me share a secret with you, I don't feel so perfect. Especially lately. To tell you the truth, I'm scared to death that I don't really know what I'm doing," she confided. "I'm terrified that through my ignorance, I may have killed your brother and driven your father to his death over there. I just can't let anybody else know, because they need to believe in me, in the presidency."

"Really? You're acting?" she asked, surprised at the revelation.

"Partially, I guess. I'm doing the best I can, but I'm afraid it won't be good enough. I don't want thousands of people to die because of my stupidity, just because the American people wanted a pretty face, a movie star, to ogle."

"You're being too hard on yourself, mother." It was as though they had exchanged roles, if only for a moment, with the embittered daughter sticking up for her.

"Maybe we both are, baby. Maybe we both need to support each other more, believe in each other." Chrissie laid her head on her mother's breast and Kathy rocked softly back and forth to comfort her, much as she had done when her daughter was a little girl. She had been home then, and that was the critical difference. For the first time, Kathy realized that there must have been many times her daughter had needed her just like this only she had not been there for her. She had been oblivious to it all these years, totally convinced that she was the model mother and wife. As she comforted them both with her body movement, the thought struck her.

"Chrissie, does your father know how you feel, I mean does he feel the same way?" she asked timidly, afraid of the answer.

"Daddy and I have talked a lot. I don't know that he would admit it, but I know he misses you tons when you're gone. And I think he went to Europe to do something special, so he could feel good enough for you."

"Oh, Chrissie."

"I really think so. He told me it was hard for him to, I think he said, 'live in your shadow'. He really feels like he's not good enough for you."

Kathy was simply stunned, she couldn't believe how blind she'd been. "I've been so wrapped up chasing my own dreams, that I've made yours and your father's into a nightmare. When we get out of this mess, I've got some making up to do."

"*Will we* get out of this?"

"I pray so, baby. The next day or two will tell. But I promise, whatever happens, I'll do everything I can to be there for you from now on. You're a beautiful, intelligent girl and I don't want to see your life messed up because of me," Kathy told her, as she wiped the tears from her daughter's brown eyes.

Chrissie lifted her head meekly. The exchange had drained the venom from her soul as if it were a boil that had just been lanced. "I'm sorry for all the trouble I've caused you, mother. I do love you," she sobbed.

"I know, baby," Kathy said, her voice trembling. Kissing Chrissie's dampened cheek, she took her daughter's head lovingly in her hands. "Be strong for me. Right now, you're the only one I can lean on, and I've got some serious leaning to do."

"I've got strong shoulders. After all, I'm a Canfield, aren't I?" she sniffed.

"Head to toe and back again, honey."

Their mother-daughter chat was interrupted by a buzz of the intercom and the announcement that

253

General Tarrenton was waiting with news from the Adriatic. Wiping the running makeup from each other's faces, the Canfield women made themselves presentable, and Kathy buzzed back to tell her secretary to send the stout soldier on in. When he stepped through the doorway, he had company. The Secretary of Defense was by his side.

"Gentlemen. How does it look?"

"Per your order, operations will cease at midnight our time, that's nine a.m. their time. We've got about five more hours to tie things up," the Secretary of Defense began. "General, please give the President your assessment."

"If the weather holds between oh seven and oh nine hundred..."

"That's seven and nine in the morning for us civilians," Atkinson interrupted.

"...and we can get in two final hours under the light of day, we're confident that we'll accomplish our mission," the General said. "I must stress the 'if'. We've neutralized a good percentage of their heavy guns, but their tanks remain a threat. We need one more solid sweep with our A-10's and Apache and Comanche gunships."

"And the Russian fleet?" Kathy asked.

"They're making poor time, but we expect them to have our ships in missile range by oh ten...excuse me, ten p.m. our time. In three more hours, we'll know whether we're in for it or not."

"You say they're making 'poor time'?"

"We're not sure if it's intentional or if they're fighting head winds and currents. We're checking the meteorological data now, and hoping to high heaven that it tells us that they're intentionally dragging their feet. That would be a positive sign."

Hope filled the woman president like a trade wind filling a mainsail. Perhaps she had gotten through to the Russian prexy.

The next three hours drug on as if time was standing still. The comings and goings in the Oval Office were many, with military attaches ferrying updates to the General every thirty minutes. Kathy now knew how John Kennedy must have felt some thirty years ago as he waited for the Cuban Missile Crisis to come to a head. As she moved around the office, from one conversation to the next, she wondered if the old grandfather clock in the corner had seemed thunderously loud to him too. Even with the tense voices of her advisors resonating through the room, she could hear the loud 'tick-tock' of the clock in the background, reminding her of the dwindling time separating them from the impending collision of the two fleets. When the clock finally chimed twelve, you could hear a pin drop. It was the only sound in the now silent room.

Nuclear war was unlikely, but there was always the possibility that human error or failing could occur. Nobody considered the Russian government stable these days, and the remote possibility of a nuclear holocaust hung like a guillotine over the heads of the worried American leaders. At twelve fifteen, a navy Admiral who had been running from one phone to the next approached the General and quietly presented him with the latest report. When Tarrenton turned to Kathy, the muscles in his jaw were bulging as though he were about to bite off his tongue.

"Admiral Hanover's reporting that the morning sorties went off without a hitch and reconnaissance flights and Seal ground observers are confirming that the enemy's offensive capabilities have been effectively neutralized. The mission is complete and, we believe, successful."

"Yes!" Andy cried out, clenching his fist. The rest of the room was filled with a spattering of sighs and a few more celebratory remarks, but their joy was tempered by the realization that the biggest hurdle was yet to come. The Russian fleet, mysteriously slow in reaching its destination, was finally slicing through the ice-cold waters of the Adriatic on a collision course with the American ships.

"Concerning the Russians, our task force's radars started picking up their signal fifteen minutes ago. They're continuing on course, but so far they've refrained from any offensive action."

"That's a good sign, General. Are we keeping our forces under wraps?" the President asked.

"Yes, ma'am. Our fighters are sitting on the Kitty Hawk's deck ready to launch, and our gun and missile crews are establishing locks on the approaching targets, but no action will be taken unless the other side fires first."

"So far, so good," Marva whispered to a perspiring Andy Mathers, who was standing next to her. The moment was so overwhelming that the Ivy Leaguer's discomfort at being near the president he had just kissed had dissipated. Unfortunately, the knot in his stomach remained in place and grew tighter and tighter with every tick of the clock.

Kathy's optimism was growing stronger as she listened to the General. And then her world came crashing down, like a house of cards in a hurricane.

"Madame President, there's something else. We air-dropped a SEAL team into the city, and I asked them to try and make contact with the relief group your husband is a part of."

"How did you know..." she stammered.

"I'm sorry," Andy interrupted, "but I informed the General this afternoon. I knew you wouldn't do it yourself."

"Ma'am, the team reached what's passing as a hospital over there a half an hour ago. I wanted you to know that they found your husband and he's fine."

"Thank God!" she sighed, grabbing Marva's arm for support.

"Madame President, I'm afraid there's more. Your husband asked the SEAL Team Commander to pass on a message. I'm very sorry to have to tell you this, but Dr. Canfield informed us that your son was killed in action outside of Sarajevo."

"No, oh no..." she moaned.

"Ma'am, I'm told he died saving the life of a civilian on the ground in an act of bravery. He gave his life in the very highest tradition of the United States Navy."

"Not Bill..."

"On behalf of the Navy, ma'am, I extend my sincerest condolences."

A mournful quiet came over the room, leaving the ticking of the old clock unchallenged, clicking away as its heavy brass weight swung from side to side. It was the only sound that penetrated the paralyzed Kathy's stupor, like a cruel messenger telling her Bill's time had run out.

CHAPTER FIFTEEN

Half way around the world, away from the personal tragedy gripping the White House, the crew of the Kitty Hawk continued to monitor the approaching Russian ships. The fleet's progress had been inexplicably slow, but the potent armada was now gliding into range as the final F-14's were returning to the mighty warship's deck. The Kitty Hawk's flight deck crews were scrambling feverishly to refuel and rearm the fighters in a frantic effort to ready them for a quick re-launch. A full complement of AIM-9 Sidewinder and AGM-84 Harpoon missiles were being latched to the undersides of the wings. If war was coming over the horizon, the men and women of the Kitty Hawk would be ready for it.

The ship's executive officer had to yell at the top of his lungs to be heard over the thunder of the jet turbines and the rest of the chaos on the carrier's deck. "Butch, the Winged Liberty squadron's been assigned the *Varyag*, the Kuznetsov class carrier anchoring their fleet. If the shit hits the fan, that's your target."

Butch Norton heard every word. More importantly, he understood the magnitude of what was about to take place. If both sides unleashed their formidable powers of destruction, there would be little left in the Adriatic when the battle was done but an Exxon Valdez-like oil slick.

"Yes sir, I'll brief my men," he hollered back, signaling his pilots to him with a wave of his arm.

"Good luck, Butch. You'll need it. Hell, we all will!"

Around them, pandemonium reigned. Norton barked out assignments to his young flyers as they huddled together in a corner of the carrier's deck. "We're gonna saddle up as soon as they refuel the planes. We've been assigned the carrier at the heart of the task force, and it's gonna be a bitch to get to. Odds are we'll be tied up by their fighters before we reach it." Their eyes filled with fear. "Stay with your wingman, hold onto your training. And whatever you do, stay cool!" Looking at their frightened faces, he knew if they launched, most of them would not be coming back. *Don't even have my best man,* he thought to himself. Lieutenant Canfield would not be with them this time.

On the bridge, the ship's Captain focused his binoculars on his potential adversaries. They were now in visual range, and slowing. He could see the *Varyag* maneuvering into the wind, as the Kitty Hawk itself had done, in order to enable its fighters to launch. *"Damn it! It's beginning,"* he thought. The thirty year naval veteran dropped the binoculars around his neck, and picked up the bridge's secured line to report to his superiors. Unbeknownst to him, communications had been re-routed directly to the Oval Office by order of the Chairman of the Joint Chiefs of Staff. It was

General Tarrenton himself who picked up the other end of the line when it rang.

"Tarrenton," he answered bluntly. He was standing not ten feet from the grief-stricken President. She sat on a striped couch with her closest confidante, swallowing a mild sedative Marva had given her.

"General Tarrenton, is that you?" the surprised captain asked.

"Yes, Bob. We've got you transferred directly to the Oval Office. I'm with the President now," the old soldier told his subordinate. "What's goin' on out there?" His grip on the phone was so tight, his knuckles were whitening.

Tarrenton could hear the strain in his old friend's voice. "We're just staring at each other, waiting to see who blinks first. They've thrown the *Varyag* into the wind, but so far nothing's left her deck."

"Are they still closing?" he asked. He tightened his grip on the phone a little bit more.

"All but the carrier, yes. They're coming at us slowly, maybe twenty knots. They should reach us in, oh, thirty minutes or so if they stay their present course and speed," the Captain estimated. "The good news is we've been within missile range for over forty-five minutes, and so far we're still here."

"Hang on a second, Bob." Tarrenton handed the phone to an aide to keep the line open, and stepped over to where Marva sat with the President. He did not expect the Commander in Chief to be in any condition to absorb his status report, but he had an obligation to deliver it.

"Excuse me, Madame President. The Russians have placed their carrier in a launch position and the rest of the fleet is continuing toward our ships. So far, no shots have been fired."

There was no reply or acknowledgement. "Madame President?" Tarrenton repeated.

"I'm sorry, General, what did you say?"

Tarrenton patiently repeated his report.

"Good, that's good," she replied half-heartedly.

"I recommend we scramble the planes immediately, ma'am. I can't have them sitting on the decks if this thing erupts."

"Sure, General," she said nodding. And then her eyes cleared, as though a switch had been flipped. "No! I mean, not yet. Not just yet."

"Madame President!" the Secretary of Defense objected.

"Give me one minute, gentlemen." Kathy gathered her strength and composure, and rose from the couch. It took Marva's help to steady her, but only a second for her to reach the red telephone. Blowing her nose and clearing her throat, she picked up the crimson receiver.

"Dimitri? Kathleen," she said succinctly. "We've completed our mission. We don't want a confrontation with you anymore than you do with us. As a show of good faith, I'm standing down our planes. Will you do the same?"

Dissent began immediately amongst those in the Oval Office. "Madame President, we can't place our men at such risk," Atkinson began.

"Please reconsider, Madame President," added the Secretary of State. "This is suicide!"

Martin Tarrenton stood alone in the background, stone-faced, one hand firmly wrapped around the phone to the Kitty Hawk's captain. He looked at Kathy from across the room. Her eye caught his, and in that instant he knew she was right. The General calmly placed his hand on Atkinson's shoulder. "No, Paul. Her instincts are right. We've gotta give 'em an excuse to de-escalate, an opportunity for Karpov to save face." He held up the phone in his hand. She nodded back.

Tarrenton put the receiver to his mouth. It was as dry as a summer day in Mojave. "Bob, we have a presidential order to stand down your planes. That's right, we want to send a signal that we'll offer no resistance, give 'em an out." There was a pause while the captain said his piece, then the General sat down the phone after a heartfelt, "Good luck." When he turned to Kathy, her eye was still on him, even as she continued her conversation with her Russian counterpart.

"By the way, I wanted to thank you for your expression of concern the other day regarding my son. I just learned that he was..." Her throat tightened up, and a sob crept into her speech. "...killed yesterday in Bosnia." There was a pause while the Russian president extended his sincerest condolences, and then the call ended.

Kathy turned to face the French doors opening onto the Rose Garden. She looked out at the fresh snow which had just begun to fall, laying a new and even blanket over the lawn. It was a perfect symbol for a new beginning. She wrapped her arms across her chest and began to cry, silently.

"What did he say?" Andy asked. He spoke for everyone in the room.

Kathy did not face them, her gaze remaining fixed on the falling snow. In a low, unsteady voice, she said, "He expressed his sorrow. Then he said he wouldn't allow my son's life to have been lost in vain."

They waited impatiently for some indication from the Kitty Hawk's captain that the Russians had altered their posture in the field. The General's hand remained in a firm, white grip on his phone, and Atkinson and the others repeatedly dabbed at the sweat on their brows. Not a shirt collar remained buttoned in the room.

Finally, the report came, and Tarrenton smiled in relief. "The *Varyag's* turning to port, out of launch position. The rest of the fleet's stopping dead in the water." The General let go of the phone. "I think we've done it, by George!"

Their sensitivity to the mother-president's loss tempered their celebration. Where there might have been whoops and hollers, enthusiastic hand shaking and back slapping followed instead. No one knew what to say, so they kept their respectful distance. It was Marva who eventually approached her as she stood alone.

"You did this, you know. Somehow you reached Karpov, in a way no one else could have," she said. "Had Burlington been here instead of you, we'd have been at war."

Kathy glanced at her from the corner of her reddened eye. Marva could see the tears glistening on her pale cheek. "It wasn't me, Mar. If anything, it was Bill. My son's gone, and I have this God-awful feeling his death was the price of peace, like some ancient offering to the gods."

"There aren't too many better causes to give your life for, are there? Than for peace..."

Kathy did not respond. It was too soon, and the thought brought no comfort.

"Mar, would you do me a favor and clear the room? And would you send for Chrissie, I need to break the news to her."

One by one, her advisors filed out through the doorway. Andy was the last to leave, offering his condolences awkwardly before closing the door behind him. "I'm so sorry, Kathy, so very sorry..."

Chrissie took the horrible news as might be expected. They spent the next two hours replaying the emotional scene from the night before, only with greater intensity, and for a different reason. *There was too much pain between these walls.*

* * * * * * * * * *

Early the next morning, at Kathy's direction, Andy visited Tom Gower. Today's color for tie and scarf was red. Blood red.

"Tom, the President wants you to let go of Farley," Andy said to the FBI chief. "She knows now he had nothing to do with the blackmail scheme."

Gower looked annoyed. "Can't do, Andy. The noose is around his neck, and I'm all dressed for the hanging," he said, fluffing up the scarf adorning his suit pocket. "Besides, if I let him off now, he'll be impossible to get later." His refusal reflected the independent power he had accrued and had become accustomed to exercising. "Look at it this way, my friend. The White House should consider this a preemptive strike. Farley's made threats against the President, and even though he wasn't responsible for the blackmail, it's just a matter of time before the sonofabitch gets around to hatching some other plot. Besides, deviants like Farley have no business in government."

The debate ended with finality when Gower's blonde bombshell of a secretary slinked in to tell them Stewart Farley's body had been discovered, crumpled over his office desk, a bullet lodged in his purplish-gray temple. His left hand still clutched the telephone receiver. The Smith and Wesson was in his right.

* * * * * * * * * *

Two days after the crisis ended, with Mark somewhere over the Atlantic on his way home with their son's body, Kathy received the news she wished had come several days before.

"We just got a call from Bethesda," Marva told her. "President Burlington just came out of his coma. He's still graded 'critical', but they're optimistic he'll recover fully. He's asking to see you." She sounded ambivalent, convinced his return would be a loss for the country, but believing in her heart it was the best thing for Kathy. She had held herself together since Bill's death, but in Marva's humble opinion, suppressing her pain was not what she needed right now. Kathy had made the greatest sacrifice anyone could for her country, now she deserved time to attend to her own needs.

"That's great news, Mar. Send for the car, and I'll go over there right now." And then as if to confirm her aide's feelings, she said, "I hope he's able to resume the office real soon. I need some time with my family."

When she reached Burlington's room at Bethesda, she was struck by how diminished the big man appeared. His tan had paled, his hulking frame seemed frail, his gray hair was matted to his head. Edith Burlington sat by his bedside, stroking his forehead, wearing a wrinkled blouse and an exhausted look of relief. When the President spoke, Kathy had to strain to hear him over the sounds of the medical equipment in the room.

"Thanks for comin'. Edith told me 'bout yer boy. Ah want ya ta know how sorry we both are."

"Thank you Mr. President." She smiled at his wife. "I'm glad to see you're doing better. We're all looking forward to your return."

"Specially you, I 'magine."

"Especially me."

"Look, Kathy, ah'm not much fer apologizing, but from everythin' ah've heard, ah owe ya one. A big one. Hell, a huge one." He coughed weakly a few times, before drinking some water from a cup his wife held for him. Weak, but annoyed by his circumstances, he tore the oxygen tubes from his nose. "Damned tubes! Cain't breathe through the damned things," he said. "As ah was sayin', ah owe ya an apology. Andy filled me in on how ya handled the Bosnian sit'ation and the Russians."

"Mr. President, you don't need to..."

"Hell ah don't! Ya'll handled things perfectly. Ah was wrong 'bout ya. Real wrong. I treated ya like dirt, hell ah was a real horse's ass, and ah'm truly sorry. Can ya forgive me?"

"Well, I uh... Certainly. Thank you."

"Now don't waste anymore of yer time on me, Madame President. Ya got work ta do back at the White House. 'Till ah get back, that is."

Kathy excused herself, shocked at the uncharacteristic treatment. It touched her nonetheless when she overheard the exchange from Burlington's room as she spoke with Andy in the hallway.

"Now Michael, that wasn't that hard now was it?" Edith Burlington said.

"Nope, mother. As usual, ya'll were right," Burlington replied. "Now, kin ah have that puddin' cup?"

* * * * * * * * * *

266

When Mark's plane landed at Dulles, the olive drab presidential helicopter was already on the tarmac to meet it. Kathy stood beside it, wearing black, looking much like another tragic White House occupant of thirty years before. When Mark limped from the airliner, he looked older to her, yet somehow stronger than when he had left. He saw her immediately, surrounded by the Secret Service contingent and military honor guard that had come to carry Bill's coffin from the plane. They made their way desperately for each other, seeking out the reassurance of their embrace.

"Oh, Mark!" She held him tighter than she ever had before. "God, I'm so glad you're all right. You are, aren't you?"

"I'm fine, physically anyway." She could tell he was as emotionally drained as she was, but there was a look of iron in his eyes. "God, it was awful over there, Kath."

"I know, honey, I know. I was so scared for you. I thought I was going to lose you both. I'm a wreck."

"Well, you're *my* wreck. I'm home now, and things are going to be different between us, I promise you," he said. "I love you more than anything in this world, more than life itself. I know that now and I know I always will." He held her tighter and kissed her hard on the lips.

Her heart leapt. "I love you too Mark. I can't tell you how much I needed to hear that. You and Chrissie mean more than anything to me. More than the White House."

They comforted each other on the runway, as the silver flag-draped coffin bearing their son's remains was unloaded gently from the baggage compartment of the large airliner by six red, white, and

267

blue-clad Marines. The broad shouldered soldiers lifted the casket up and into the rear of the waiting presidential helicopter.

"Mark, I've made arrangements for Bill to be buried at Arlington with full military honors, if that's all right with you," she said. "I thought about taking him back home to California, but I think he would have preferred this."

Mark took her gloved hand in his. "I'm sure he would have. By the way, there's someone back in Bosnia who wants to attend the funeral, but she won't be able to travel until Saturday. Can we hold the service 'till Sunday?"

She looked at him with a blank expression on her face. "I suppose. Who is it? Some dignitary?"

Mark grinned ever so slightly. "Nope. A close friend of Bill's. Someone I believe must have been very important to him."

"Who?" she asked.

"A girl."

Kathy stepped back. "How important?"

"Important enough," Mark measured his words, "...to give his life for."

CHAPTER SIXTEEN

The day of Bill's funeral, the sun was out above Arlington National Cemetery, casting a welcome warmth over the frozen ground. The sky was blue, the kind of blue that used to tug at the young flyer's heart, beckoning him to it. There was a light breeze in the air, enough to freshen, but not enough to chill. *'Flying weather', Bill used to call it,* Kathy recalled. And now he was a part of it, forever.

She wore a flattering black dress and hat, using the fortuitous sun as an excuse to hide her sunken eyes beneath a pair of sunglasses. There had been just too much damage for makeup to mitigate. Pinned to her bosom was a shiny gold pair of wings, Bill's aviator's wings. An identical pair was clipped to the jacket on the body in the flag-draped casket before her.

"I can't get over the size of the crowd," Mark whispered to her. "Bill would have been touched."

"Is touched," she answered, breathing life into her son's memory. "I'm sure he is." He took her hand in his, as though the act could bind the two of them into one. She held on tightly.

The cemetery was packed with a thousand people sharing in the Canfield family's grief. Well-dressed dignitaries representing over two hundred nations were in attendance, as were a substantial percentage of the members of Congress and the Cabinet. Edith Burlington was there too, standing by the family's side on behalf of her recovering husband. Politics prevented Dimitri Karpov from attending or dispatching a representative, but his moving, private phone call to the acting American President more than made up for it. At least in Kathy's heart, it did. Television cameras whirred from a half dozen vantage points on the tombstone-laden grounds, sending their pictures to not just the United States, but to the world. Millions felt a connection to the beautiful mother-president who had lost her son to the cause of peace.

"It's such a beautiful day, isn't it?" Kathy said to Mark, as though she were reaching for any straw she could find to help lessen her grief.

"Yes, baby. A beautiful day," he answered supportively.

"Ready, aim, fire!" Seven rifles aimed to the heavens fired in unison. Once, twice, thrice. Kathy and Mark winced with each volley given in Bill's honor. So did a tearful Marija, from her wheelchair by Mark's side. A second later, a squadron of F-14's thundered overhead, with one position in the formation symbolically vacant. Kathy bit her lower lip to keep it from trembling. Chrissie cried unabashedly. The military honor guard folded the flag with machine-like precision, its leader presenting the final triangle to the acting president, with the condolences of a nation.

"Madame President, on behalf of the United States of America, I extend my sincerest condolences for the loss of your son." The words sounded tritely ceremonial, but they spoke accurately for millions.

Kathy took the flag lovingly as though it were all she had left of him. "Thank you, captain. For my son, and for my family," she said bravely. She noticed the tall officer had a tear in his left eye, hiding in the shadows cast by the brim of his white cap. As he saluted her, it betrayed him and rolled down his face into the sunlight. She mouthed the words again: "Thank you."

At the conclusion of the service, Kathy lingered for an instant, running her palm across the pink marble headstone bearing her son's name. Its smooth surface felt cold to her touch, even though her fur-lined gloves. Its chill sliced straight to her bone. "Love you always, honey," she said, touching her fingers to her lips, then placing them back on the marble. "Always."

* * * * * * * * * *

At the rear of the huge crowd stood a solitary figure clothed in a navy blue stocking cap and a bulky winter cape capable of concealing most anything. As a Secret Service man eyed him, he turned and walked away cautiously. *Not today*, Miles O'Keefe told himself. *Too many people. Too much security. But she'll be back...*

* * * * * * * * * *

The family filled the trip back to the White House in the presidential limousine with stories about Bill, happy stories that kept him alive for Marija, enabling her to know him better, even if in absentia. When they arrived, they adjourned to the family quarters of the executive mansion to continue their

271

mourning and their tribute to their fallen hero. During it all, Mark and Kathy remained inseparable, as they had been since his return.

* * * * * * * *

Stealing quietly away from the family, Marva went to the Oval Office to "move some paper", as she put it. There she found it waiting on the President's desk. The child care bill - that six years of labor - had been overwhelmingly approved by a sympathetic, Farley-less Congress. It would be Kathleen Canfield's signature on the bottom line that placed it into law. "I'll be damned," she muttered. "She did it!" She grabbed the file to take it to Kathy as a day-ending pick-me-up. *As grandpa used to say, "Success is like a postage stamp. Just stick to one thing until you get there."*

* * * * * * * * *

When Mark and Kathy settled in that night in the green-walled Lincoln Bedroom, she knew it would be one of her last in the historic bed. Michael Burlington was continuing to recover and appeared ready to reclaim the powers of the presidency from *his* bed at the nearby Bethesda Hospital. As her lover held her in the warmth of his arms, she looked forward to returning to the canary yellow house in Georgetown, if only for a while. It was there they could be alone as a family to rediscover each other, to deal with their pain.

"I'm going to take some more days off from the practice, Kath," Mark said as he caressed her head. "I want to spend some time with you and Chrissie. And I want to finish that doll house Bill gave you. For him. For you."

It was the sweetest gesture, and it came when she needed it the most. "Mark, I think that would be wonderful. We can work on it together."

"I'll do the wiring and the construction."

"And I'll do what, pick out the wallpaper and furniture?"

He smiled. "Right. Woman's work," he joked.

She would always be grateful to him for the thoughtful gesture, and would remember it lovingly forever. Just before she fell asleep in the spacious bed, she thought she could feel not only his heartbeat, but his very soul, reaching out to touch hers. For all the pain Bill's death had caused, there was a part of her that had never felt so fulfilled, so loved. *The hole*, she thought. The one in her stomach that had followed her since childhood. *It's gone.*

"We'll be home in a few days, baby," Mark said to her as he kissed her goodnight. And then, in that instant, she understood. She *was* home. Home was wherever Mark was. It really always had been, and now she knew without a doubt. It always would be.

EPILOGUE

Washington D.C.
February, 1997

"C'mon, Madame *Vice* President, it's time to go!" Mark prodded. Kathy glided briskly down the winding staircase of the Vice President's mansion, fastening her earring as she went. Mark held her tan overcoat for her as she slipped into it. "You know, I always liked that word."

"Which one?" Kathy asked. She crinkled her nose and straightened his yellow paisley tie. "Vice, or madam?"

"Cute. Not touching that one. I plead the fifth." Mark looked up the long staircase and yelled for the last missing member of his family, "Christina! We're late, let's go!"

The teenager pranced down the staircase past them, flying out the door and nearly running over an off-guard Jack Cutter. "Whoa, young lady!" he said, "I know a moving target's harder to hit but slow it down or we won't be able to protect you!"

"Getting old, Cutty. Can't keep up anymore, eh?"

The agent looked as though he did not enjoy her jovial familiarity. He did.

The trip to Arlington National Cemetery was an uneventful one for the three car entourage. It was the family's first visit to Bill Canfield's grave since the funeral - the first of what they had vowed would be monthly visits. Somehow, the national press had uncovered and publicized the planned visit, to Cutter's concern and dismay. The agent took the seat in the front passenger seat of the Vice President's car, adjusting his earpiece as he turned to her. "Madame Vice President, we're going to take a longer route to Arlington. I don't want to make too much of the press leak, but every nutcase in the country knows you're going there today. I'd prefer to play it safe."

Kathy looked at her rugged guard dog. She trusted him, she trusted him with her life. "Whatever you think is best, Jack."

Cutter's instincts were correct. The entrance to Arlington was lined with a hundred expectant spectators, hoping to get a glimpse of his celebrity charge. A second Secret Service team, on loan at his request, covered the entrance. The five-man team looked like it had dressed from the same closet that morning: gray overcoats, navy blue suits, red ties, dark sunglasses. The 'cookie-cutter look', Chrissie called it. Cutter was pleased they were following procedure as the car passed through. Exacting in their efforts to screen the crowd, each person was being checked to determine their business and to pass them through a portable metal detector.

"Not getting paranoid are we, Jack?" Mark asked.

"Maybe, but I'd rather burn up a few tax dollars than lose someone in my protection. Besides, the President's safe at home, so we had a few teams to spare."

"A few?"

"This morning I placed one at the entrance and another near the grave site to cordon it off."

Kathy gave him a worried glance. This was as much protection as she had received when she hung her hat in the Oval Office. Her hand moved unconsciously toward the hair dangling in front of her ear.

Mark intercepted it, holding it gently. "You're a cautious guy, Jack," he said. "It's one of the qualities I like best about you." He looked at his wife, changing the subject. "By the way, I want to thank you, hon", he said as he straightened the pilot's wings still pinned to her coat. "You've kept your promise to spend more time with us."

She looked surprised he had harbored any doubts. "I gave you both my word, didn't I? Besides, since I got my old job back, it's been a lot easier. The Vice Presidency allows for free time...even with Burlington bringing me in from the cold, so to speak."

Mark's expression changed. "Damned. Did anybody remember the flowers? I left 'em on the table."

"Right here, Dad. They were wet and were staining the tabletop." Chrissie pulled a brown paper bag from under the limo seat, holding it up for him to see. "

"Mark Canfield! That table's government property. Heck, it might have belonged to Thomas Jefferson or Ben Franklin or someone," Kathy chided.

"Maybe it was Dick Nixon's, then I wouldn't feel so bad." She peered at him. "Sorry."

Exiting the limo some seventy-five yards from the grave, Kathy marveled at Arlington's peaceful beauty. She could hear a bird chirping from somewhere nearby, and the air felt clear and refreshing. It was a lot like the day Bill was buried four weeks ago, only there was no circus atmosphere, no cameras, no comparable crowd. Cutter's men had done their jobs well. Or so she thought.

* * * * * * * * * *

Fifty thousand bucks! Ten thousand now, forty when the job is done. I've arranged to have the money deposited directly to a Cayman Islands bank account in your name after her death hits the papers. My lawyer will have the bank account number. That's the deal, Farley had told Miles O'Keefe over the phone. *Look at revenge as, well, a little bonus.* O'Keefe shivered as he looked over his shoulder at the concrete casket casing next to him in the old mausoleum he had hidden away in the night before. *Glad I worked him up to a hundred. Ain't spending the night with a corpse for a penny less,* he thought to himself. He nervously checked the clip in his hunting rifle to make sure it was full, then fixed the makeshift silencer to the end of the blackened barrel. It was time. There was the Vice President's mini-motorcade, right in front of him, not a hundred yards from the mausoleum's wrought iron gate. He sighted his weapon. *Easy pickings,* he thought, as he shifted his weight from one sore, frozen elbow to the next.

* * * * * * * * * *

As Kathy made her way to the grave, she was oblivious to the threat. She was more concerned about her footing in the treacherous snow, and Mark had to help her just to get her there.   "Not the best place to wear high heels, Kath."

"Had my mind on other things this morning, I guess." She looked at the snow-covered grave and the expensive marble grave stone with Bill's name and picture on it. Dozens of floral arrangements, some fresh, others not so, lay in front of the headstone. "I can't believe how many flowers are here. Half the country must've stopped by to pay their respects."

Chrissie handed over the flowers she had brought with them. "Here mother, add these. They're the only ones that'd really mean anything to Bill, 'cause they're from us."

Kathy knelt down slowly, removing the single frozen bouquet that filled the brass flower vase at the base of the headstone. As she arranged the fresh yellow roses lovingly in the vase, she felt a gust of wind blow by. "We love you and miss you, honey," she said softly. She could feel his presence in the breeze.

* * * * * * * * * *

"Damn it!" O'Keefe muttered, just loud enough to create a weak echo within his concrete sniper's nest. *Damn it!* came the refrain. Jack Cutter was blocking his line of sight. The would-be assassin exhaled, drew a fresh, deep breath and returned the butt of the weapon to his right shoulder. "Sonofabitch!" His breath had fogged over the lens on the telescopic sight. *Sonofabitch!* said the echo. *A hundred grand*, he reminded himself. *Fuck the revenge, just gimme the money!*   One of the Secret

Service agents was coming his way. *Shit! Did he see my breath, a reflection from my sight?* He drew a bead on the clean-cut man with the gray overcoat and the sunglasses. *Can't see his eyes, can't tell if he sees me.* The agent came closer. He was so close, O'Keefe could see the writing on his Secret Service pin through his gun sight.

CLICK... THWACK!

The body dropped like a sandbag from the back of a truck, landing face first into the snow, a bullet square between the eyes. The nervous assassin pushed open the gate to his sanctuary carefully, and crept over to the body. Its glassy stare confirmed his marksmanship. O'Keefe grasped the back of the corpse's coat collar and drug it into the tomb, depositing it on the opposite side of the casket casing. Wiping the blood from his hand on the dead man's gray coat, he returned to his prone position and lifted the weapon back to the ready. Cutter no longer blocked his line of fire. The back of Kathleen Canfield's head filled his scope, a hundred thousand dollars filled his mind. *CLICK.* His finger hugged the trigger on the old bolt-action firearm, and placed the crosshairs on her gold hair clip.

* * * * * * * * * *

Jack Cutter scanned the horizon. One of his agents was not where he was supposed to be. *Something's not right.* He looked in the mausoleum's direction as another gust of wind came by, blowing the earpiece from his ear. A glint of sunlight reflected off the lens of the gun sight, catching his eye. He turned instinctively toward Kathy, recognizing the situation as clearly as though the assailant were standing next to him. "Get down!" he yelled, lurching to close the ten-foot gap between them. The breeze that had blown his earpiece free had also blown the fresh flowers over in the vase. As she stooped to fix them, Cutter could see a chunk of marble explode from the headstone in front of her. An instant later, the sound of the bullet ricocheting off the marble reached his ear.

"Get down!" he yelled again, throwing his body over hers even as Mark did the same.

The next minute was chaos. All Kathy saw was the bright yellows and reds of the agapanthus, daisies, and roses in her face as she lay sprawled over Bill's grave. She could hear yelling and screaming, and the firing of shots, rapid fire, from the compact automatic weapons the Secret Service carried. Sixty seconds later Miles O'Keefe lay dead, slumped over the steering wheel of his getaway car, covered in blood. Riddled with bullets, the late model sedan looked like the Bonnie and Clyde 'Death Car'. O'Keefe had underestimated his adversaries. And his luck.

"Are you all right?" Cutter asked after hearing the 'all clear' signal from his colleagues. He helped Mark lift her to her feet.

"I, I think so." She was understandably shaken and confused. "What happened?"

Mark answered for Cutter. "I think someone just took a shot at you."

She turned as ashen as the snow that covered her. "My God!"

"It's all right, we got him. Everything's all right. Let's get you back to the mansion, though, just to be safe," Cutter said.

As she walked back to the car, she felt the winter breeze blow by again. It caressed her face like a loving hand.

FROM THE AUTHOR

Dear Reader,

I hope you have enjoyed reading *Line of Succession – The Price of Power*. Writing this book was an investment of six months of my life, drafting, editing, and rewriting the story to its published form. Parts of it are built on my first career experience as a congressional aide, others on my visit to Croatia and surrounding areas during the Balkan conflict.

If you wouldn't mind taking a moment to write and *submit an honest review of the book on Amazon*, it would be very much appreciated. Positive or negative, as a writer, I would value your feedback. And of course, positive reviews will help ensure this book reaches a larger audience. Of course, you can join my Facebook page for updates on my writing as well at https://www.facebook.com/mvandor.

Best wishes, and thank you.

--

Michael Vandor

Made in the USA
Lexington, KY
18 August 2019